Oversoul Seven is:

MA-AH—a beautiful young black woman who lived in 35,000 B.C. She and her mate were primarily concerned with warmth and survival, until an inexplicable knowledge led her to a door in a mountainside—and to the Land of the Speakers. . . .

JOSEF—a seventeenth-century painter and lay-about. He was locked in a windowless room and threatened with starvation by his irate patron . . . and then he met an Old Man in his dreams. . . .

LYDIA—an aging twentieth-century poetess. She discovered that her poetry had really originated in an ancient civilization, and would reemerge in a future time. . . .

PROTEUS—who lived in the flying city of A.D. 2300, and longed for the earth he had never seen. After months of secret planning, he finally descended through the clouds and arrived at a system of tunnels and passageways that led to a ruin not recorded in the history books—the Dig of the Tellers. . . .

Books by Jane Roberts

The Coming of Seth
The Education of Oversoul Seven

Published by POCKET BOOKS

THE EDUCATION OF OVERSOUL SEVEN

by Jane Roberts

Illustrations by Robert F. Butts

PUBLISHED BY POCKET BOOKS NEW YORK

POCKET BOOKS, a Simon & Schuster division of
GULF & WESTERN CORPORATION
1230 Avenue of the Americas, New York, N.Y. 10020

Published by arrangement with Prentice-Hall, Inc.
Library of Congress Catalog Card Number: 73-446

ISBN: 0-671-83117-8

First Pocket Books printing December, 1976

10 9 8 7 6 5 4 3

Trademarks registered in the United States and other countries.

Printed in the U.S.A.

*Dedicated
to
The Speakers
In all "Times"
and to Those
Who
Recognize
the
Sumari Songs*

This Book
Is
Written
in
the Time of
Lydia

(Translated into
Vernacular English
Circa A.D. 1970s)

Contents

THE
EDUCATION
OF
OVERSOUL
SEVEN

Chapter One

Oversoul Seven's Examination and Josef's Dream

Oversoul Seven grimaced at Cyprus and began the examination. "Let's see," he said. "In Earth terms, using an analogy, I'm a man on Wednesday and Friday, a woman on Sunday and Thursday, and I have the rest of the time off for independent study.

"Actually, because of their time concepts this is somewhat more complicated," he said. "Each life is lived in a different, uh, area of time to which various designations are given." Cyprus smiled, and Seven continued. "As Lydia I'm in the twentieth century, as Josef in the seventeenth, as Ma-ah in 35,000 B.C., and as Proteus in the 23rd century, A.D. Then there's the further background in space, uh, different locations called countries. Then there's the ages of the personalities.

"I'm partial to Josef and Lydia, though I suppose I shouldn't be. Still, they show so much vitality and seem to enjoy themselves. Ma-ah cries a lot, and Proteus is always looking back to the good old days—"

Cyprus had been silent. Now she said, "You're wandering and not organizing your thoughts very well. Pretend that I know nothing about all this, and you're trying to explain it. You just told me that you had personalities in all those times, for example. So why should Proteus look back to the good old days?"

"Oh, I see. Sorry," Oversoul Seven said. "Proteus doesn't know that. He doesn't take anything for granted. He doesn't even take me for granted, or himself, for that matter. That is, he doesn't realize that he *is* a soul, much less that both of us are one. Certainly he doesn't know that other portions of us live in other times. I get lonely for him now and then, but there it is. In fact, sometimes I think we Oversouls aren't appreciated at all. We work and strive—"

Seven was suddenly struck by such a sense of desolation that he dematerialized his hallucinatory pencil. He brought it back as quickly as he could, but Cyprus shook her head at the lapse and said sharply, "Now, none of that. Dropping your hallucination loses you five points, you know. Suppose you were, say, Lydia on Earth, and she did something like that? Physical matter wouldn't be a dependable framework at all. One slip, that's all it takes! How would you like to be responsible for such a massive reaction? Then everyone would have to start over with a new . . . Oh, Seven, you just can't make errors like that. Pencils disappearing in mid-air!"

Oversoul Seven nodded, then suddenly, almost despite himself, he started to laugh. "Actually, Josef is almost on the edge of knowing. Once he forgot to materialize one of his painting brushes—he was in the throes of creativity—and bongo, the brush was just gone. Josef almost went out of his mind." Seven's eyes glowed with parental-like pride.

Cyprus said sternly, "None of your personalities are ready to understand that mind forms matter, and you know it. I hope you remedied the situation."

"I hallucinated the brush back at once," Oversoul Seven said. "But tell me, don't you find the affair even a little bit funny?"

2

"Not at all," Cyprus said, concealing a smile. "But now let's get back to your examination."

"Gladly," Oversoul Seven said. "But when I reach your position, I hope I retain my sense of humor."

Cyprus laughed. She laughed so hard that Seven got uncomfortable. Finally she said: "Your sense of humor includes only a small part of *my* sense of humor. There's so much you don't see. This examination of yours, for example—oh bless me—and having to maintain Earth-type conditions for it. Now *that's* funny. By the way, look around this room. There's something else that quite escapes you. Your visual is awful—"

Oversoul Seven looked around cautiously. He'd been secretly quite pleased with the environment he'd chosen and created. The classroom was authentic twentieth-century, like the one Lydia knew as a child. There were rows of desks, blackboards, windows, everything right down to stacks of paper—all individual new sheets—and an automatic pencil sharpener.

Then he blushed, all over his nice new cheeks and right up to the roots of the thick brown hair that sprang up from his forehead.

"Nice effect," Cyprus said, watching. "I meant to congratulate you on your form, very good fourteen-year-old male type, Caucasian, I believe. But for the other—"

"I found it, the error! There!" The wastepaper basket had been in the corner, complete with girth and thickness, exactly two feet high and as many around, but he'd forgotten to materialize it visually. Now he made it red, and with a flourish added scallops around the upper edge.

"But there's still another error," Cyprus said, looking nowhere in particular. Just at that moment a young man wearing a toga appeared. He looked around with a rather wild air, then shouted out at Seven: "Ah, there you are! I knew I'd find you again. Just the same, all this has to stop." He looked half mad, and yelled in tones of deepest outrage.

Cyprus raised her eyebrows at Oversoul Seven, who coughed several times and tried to look the other way.

"Well?" shouted the young man.

"How did you get here?" Seven asked. Then he whispered urgently to Cyprus. "That's Josef. He must be in a dreaming state, and sleeping on Earth."

"How did I get here? You tell me," Josef cried angrily.

3

"Next time I'm going to memorize the route. I see you in my dreams too often for comfort. Dreams aren't supposed to work that way." He broke off, frowning: "I am dreaming, aren't I? I must be. What a crazy place. What on Earth is that?" He was staring at the automatic pencil sharpener.

"Don't touch it! It's *not* on Earth. That's the point," Seven cried. But Josef was fascinated.

"It's authentic twentieth-century," Seven said, giving in. "Works by electricity."

Cyprus moaned. "I believe that Josef is your *seventeenth-century* personality," she said. "Electricity isn't utilized there."

Oversoul Seven blushed and dematerialized the pencil sharpener. "Just forget you saw it. Forget the whole thing," he said to Josef.

"Where did it go?" Josef stood staring.

"Listen, you aren't supposed to be here. Not here, of all places. I get demerits for this," Oversoul Seven said. "Go home. Go back to your body where you belong."

"What do you mean, go back to my body?" Josef demanded. He rose to his full stature and adjusted his toga with a dramatic gesture. "This is my dream, and nobody is going to put me out of it."

"Why are you wearing a toga?" Cyprus asked gently.

Josef looked down at himself with some amazement. "I don't know. I didn't realize that I had one on. I like to paint models in togas, though. You can do so much with the folds—" He broke off, angry again. "You aren't answering my questions at all. What's happening? How is it that I meet you in my dreams?" He paused and shook his head. "You look like a boy now, but most of the time you look like an old man. You can't fool me, though. You're the same one."

"I've told you before, but you never remember," Seven said. "I'm something like your mother and something like your father, but neither. We're closer than sister and brother, mother and daughter, or father and son. That's all I can tell you now. You have to learn some things for yourself. You *are* learning fast, but you wandered in where you shouldn't be. I know you had a reason, though: You never look for me unless you're in trouble."

Seven caught the rebuke in his own voice and added quickly: "That's all right. I understand. But what's bother-

4

ing you?" He looked around to see if Cyprus approved of the way he was handling the situation, but Cyprus had sympathetically dematerialized.

Josef never noticed. He said mournfully: "I'm twenty-four and I don't have any discipline. I can't keep myself at my easel two hours at a time, yet painting is what I want to do more than anything else in the world. If I don't learn some discipline, I'm afraid I'll lose what talent I have—and God knows how much that is, to begin with. On top of that I haven't felt any real inspiration for a year."

Seven shook his head. Before his eyes, Josef was turning into a big unhappy bear, his dark moustache transformed into fur, his eyes belligerent and sad at the same time, his toga changing into a blanket. Josef looked down at himself, hysterically. "I'm a circus bear; something for people to laugh at. Oh, what a dream. It's got to be a dream." Then the bear growled threateningly.

"Come on now," Seven said, and patted its head. "Turn back into yourself. In the dream state you take different forms as your feelings and thoughts change. You felt like a bear, so you look like one."

"Really?" Josef was himself again. Immediately he forgot what had happened. "If I don't do something, I'm going to ruin my life," he said.

"Oh, you can't do that," Oversoul Seven said. "You aren't aware of your real problem yet. It's one of my jobs to help you, so I'll get back to you shortly. In the meantime I'll do some little thing to tide you over."

As he spoke, Oversoul Seven created in his mind an excellent art studio, made to Josef's personal requirements. On the easel was a painting of the precise farmhouse in which Josef was staying on earth. The painting was signed in the corner: Josef Landsdatter, 1615. "Now I've made this dream for you," Seven said. "Look at the painting well. You'll begin work on it tomorrow. You'll be so filled with inspiration that you'll paint all day." He transmitted the dream to Josef telepathically, then said: "When you get all you want out of the dream, then wake up in your bedroom."

Josef nodded and dutifully disappeared.

"What did you think of him?" Seven asked.

Cyprus laughed richly, then returned visually. "Well, I see the similarity between the two of you," she said.

"Stop joking. He has a serious problem."

5

"That's something else about you, Seven," Cyprus said. "Your sense of humor doesn't extend to yourself or your personalities. By the time you reach Oversoul Eight stage, you'll know better. You *did* handle the situation well, however."

"I worry about Josef," Seven said. "He's so impetuous."

"As *you* are," Cyprus said. "Remember, your various personalities, while independent, also reflect qualities of your own. You can't create without giving of yourself.

"Now technically you *do* get three demerits," she said. "You should have been aware of Josef's approach and waylaid him. But rules are also flexible, and his achievement is noteworthy, regardless of the circumstances. So I'll note that in your files.

"The schoolroom environment was also well done, though I'm waiting for you to discover your one other error. Your appearance as the fourteen-year-old male was symbolically valid. You've demonstrated that you have an excellent understanding of Earth's conventions. Let's dispense with them now, though, and get down to the more serious aspects of your examination."

As Cyprus spoke, the room disappeared, and the trees outside the windows. Last to go was the wastepaper basket with the scalloped edges. A lovely touch, Seven thought, feeling a bit of dismay as it vanished. . . .

Now Oversoul Seven and Cyprus were two brilliant points of consciousness, without form. Oversoul Seven felt himself expand mentally, psychically. He breathed a symbolic sigh of relief. He and Cyprus communicated telepathically through the use of mental images that changed with each alteration of meaning, and were instantly perceived and understood. In Earth terms, it boiled down to this conversation:

"Creating yourself physically certainly is demanding," Seven said. "But even now, when I'm not Earth-oriented, I can appreciate Josef and all the rest, and feel the splendid growth of their vitality."

"I know how you want to handle this part of the examination," Cyprus said. "But remember, you can't contact any of your people. If they contact *you*, that's all right. But you can't correct any of their errors. I want to see how they're progressing, so this part of the exam involves you only as a bystander. Knowing how impetuous you are, let me emphasize that point. Later, of course, how well you

6

communicate with your personalities will be an important factor."

All at once Oversoul Seven felt apprehensive. He heard the voice before Cyprus did, because it was directed to him.

"Tweety! Tweety!"

"That's a human voice," Cyprus said. "How can that be? No humans should be able to reach us here."

"Maybe it's a mistake," Seven said weakly. But already it was too late.

"Is it time yet?" asked the voice.

"Go back where you came from," Seven said desperately. "No it's not time yet, and for all I know it may never be."

"But I'm all ready," said the voice.

"No you aren't. That's just the trouble," Seven said. "If you were, you'd have better sense. This is my superior, by the way."

"Oh, Tweety!" cried the voice, desolate.

"*Tweety?*" Cyprus asked.

"Uh. We're old friends. It's Daga. Whenever Daga's a female she calls me Tweety. Right now she's a female and helping me with my independent study. At least we think she's female. When *I* am, I call her Tweety." In confusion, Seven took on the fourteen-year-old form again. "Earth language doesn't have any words for what we really are, no, uh, pronouns for beings that are male and female at once, so it makes explanations difficult."

"We aren't ready to go into your independent study yet," Cyprus said. "But I must admit that I'm curious. And I must note that you seem to have some difficulty in keeping track of your various projects."

"See?" Oversoul Seven said. "Daga, please go away."

"If you insist," the voice said. "But I've got my birth date planned, and—"

"Go away!" Seven cried, in consternation.

Cyprus pretended not to hear. She said: "I presume that you'll have a good explanation for this later on. Now if you don't mind, let's get down to the *scheduled* phases of your examination."

Oversoul Seven tried not to be nervous. "All right," he said. "Let's look in on Lydia. I certainly hope that she's having a good day. First, there's a few things I'd like to explain about her. She—"

"Sorry. From now on I must see for myself," Cyprus said.

Seven sighed. He thought of Lydia, lovingly brought her image into his awareness until it filled him, taking precedence over all the other memories of his many selves. Together he and Cyprus blinked off and on, rode piggyback on a million molecules, and emerged.

Chapter Two

Part One of the Examination
A Quick Peek at Lydia,
Proteus, Ma-ah, and Josef

THE PRESENT (MORE OR LESS)

Lydia felt nervous, as if someone was watching her, beside Lawrence. It was a thunderstormy morning, eleven o'clock, with great dashes of rain pounding against the windows. She was seventy-three, and angrier than usual about it on dark days.

Lawrence sat on the blue couch. "Well, what do you say? I do wish you'd quit prowling around and give me some kind of an answer," he said.

She frowned and put down her rye and ginger. "My kids won't like it much, not that it makes any difference. God, *they're* hitting fifty, and Anna in particular is pretty pompous. But I just might do it, Larry. The aged poetess on her last binge! I like college-age people, too. They haven't got into the establishment yet and we're out of it, thank heaven. My kids would okay the idea of a tour, of course. But you and me traveling around the country together in a trailer, unmarried—well, you know how conventional they are. But they can hardly call you a dirty old man, since I'm older than you are! So to hell with it. I'll go."

He was so excited that he almost dropped his pipe. "We'll fill the camper with books and food and liquor—"

"And two of my cats. Tuckie and Greenacre have to go, and Mr. George, my goldfish."

He groaned. "The two cats, *and* Mr. George."

She wanted to cry but she wouldn't. Defiance rose up so that she thrust her head backward in an old gesture that had been startlingly dramatic when she was young. "I'll make out papers before we leave, giving the house to my children. I don't imagine really that we'll be coming back."

"We will. Goddammit, we will." He stood up, but knowing how she was, he didn't put his arms around her. He only said, again, "We'll both come back."

"Oh, to hell with it. If you say we will, we will. After all, what difference does it make? Forget it. You know, I meant to tell you—not to change the subject—that those dreams of mine are getting nuttier all the time. Last night none of them made sense. Yet right now, talking to you, it almost seems as if they did, if only I could remember them."

Lawrence said: "When you talk like that, then I'm sure that we've known each other before—before we met, I mean. You are, after all, what? Fifteen years older than I am? But in some odd manner it always seems to me that you're younger."

"My dear love," she said flippantly. "In the world's eyes we make one hell of a funny pair. The thing is, no one ever thinks they'll really grow old. It always comes as a surprise, and the world sort of hates you for it. Growing old, gracefully or not, just isn't the polite or tasteful thing to do. And you can't blame the young either, because when we were young we felt the same way. Too bad, because in one way I feel freer than I ever did before—"

"You look ten years younger than you are," he said.

"Don't be trite. Telling a woman that she looks sixty-three instead of seventy-three isn't likely to win her favor.

You'd be smarter to say nothing. For some reason that I've never understood, growing old is considered bad enough for a man, but an unforgivable crime for a woman. But best I don't get on *that* subject."

She took another sip of her drink. "It's true, I suppose, in good light and if I bothered to wear makeup, I could look near your age—maybe. But as it is I look like a scrawny boy grown suddenly old, with white hair and gaunt face and quite incredulous about how it all happened. As I am, of course. Yet what I am, I am. I can't see dying my hair, for example. In a way it's pretty damn lucky to be seventy-three years old, and get white, to begin with."

He was silent. Then he said: "If the doctors *are* right, and my heart does go suddenly—"

"Then I'll follow our plan," she said. "For that matter, I don't know how long *I'll* hold out. I'm quite aware that the first stages of my . . . condition have already come upon me. My memory should be all right, generally, for a while, though. But you can never tell. If not, then *you* follow our plan. When I can't recite my own poetry right, then I suppose I'll know that something's wrong."

And suddenly it seemed really funny, beautifully hilarious to each of them. He said, "We'll beat their hospitals, their rest homes and final asylums." Exuberance flashed through his thin nervous frame.

She laughed with him, then stopped. "My electric pencil sharpener," she said. "I just remembered. I dreamed of my old eighth-grade classroom. Only my electric pencil sharpener was in it, which is ridiculous, of course. They didn't have them then. Now I wonder what that means?"

"A bleedthrough from one dream state to another," Oversoul Seven said to Cyprus. They were suspended in two green leaves that rustled in the wind outside the windows.

"You heard what she said about the pencil sharpener? That was the error you missed," Cyprus said, and Seven grinned.

"Wait," Lydia said. "I was a man in the dream, fairly young. Funny, how some of it comes back."

Lawrence frowned suddenly. "Never question the dream messages of the gods," he said dramatically. "You might find out what they mean."

"Now don't say things like that," she cried. "It makes

11

me nervous. And look at those leaves outside. How alive they seem, how . . . watchful. God, I wish the damned storm would stop."

"The sound of rain on a trailer roof will be different," Lawrence said.

She smiled over at him. He'd just closed his leather shop for good. He'd upholstered the whole camper-trailer, and half of her books had leather covers that he'd made for her. She almost gasped: how could they be so in love and so old? "In my dream, someone was taking an examination," she said. "I was thinking of my books, and just remembered."

"I was, dear Lydia. We both are!" Oversoul Seven was all ready to transmit the words to Lydia when Cyprus said gently, "No prompting, remember."

The leaves were really tossing in all that wind. Oversoul Seven filled himself with the uniqueness of it, because Cyprus was saying: "All right, we have to leave now. The first part of the examination allows for a quick viewing only."

And the scene changed. . . .

TWENTY-THIRD CENTURY A.D.

Proteus secretly yearned to be a girl: they were so much freer to express themselves. Instead he was stuck at home in the living nodule with his father, and only innocuous hobbies to content him. He also yearned for the sight of something naturally green, growing, real. In fact, this desire had grown so strong that he determined to do something about it.

He said eagerly: "Surely we could take some small space and devote it to a natural miniature farm. Say the whole thing only took up one living nodule. It would be self-sufficient. Someone ought to be able to give us permission—"

Mithias, his father, frowned: "Life grows. *That* kind of life grows, anyhow. There's no stopping it. It's wild. We've spent two centuries developing an artificial environment that we could handle. If you gave *that* kind of life freedom, people would have children all the time. You'd be dead at sixty or seventy. Our way of life is balanced. But I can't expect you to really understand that at sixteen."

He paused and said with a grunt, "When we had our

12

'natural' environment, the women were kept busy having children. Men had the positions of power. Otherwise, I can't think of anything good about those days. They were filled with sickness, wars, social diseases—"

"You're right as usual," Proteus said. But he was still sick of being cooped up inside with his father all day.

Mithias was watching his son's face. "Now don't start brooding," he said. "We're due for a rain at noon. Why don't you go outside and watch? It always lifts your spirits."

"I might," Proteus said. He was shy, diffident, but strangely arrogant too. The suggestion sounded too much like an order, so he just stood there.

"It's almost noon now," Mithias said, irritably.

So Proteus scowled and went through the door of their spacious nodule. He stood on the small plastic sidewalk, and looked up at the plastic trees. Down there beneath him, where the real Earth was, who knew what was going on? Really? No one, he thought. Except for the scientific expeditions, no one went there any more. But then he stopped thinking as the rain began. Usually it excited him. Now he felt more depressed. It would rain politely for fifteen minutes. The water would run down the plastic drains and be saved and purified, and then fall tomorrow for fifteen minutes someplace else.

When he was small he had a schedule of all the rainfalls. He knew exactly where and when it would rain. His own nodule area held fifteen subites, with over a million people, and he'd run over the plastic sidewalks, frantic with excitement, keeping up with the rain.

He squinted up. Three clouds passed. They always did, at rain-time. If you didn't know that the artificial sky stopped one-eighth of a mile up, or if you tried to forget it, like he used to, then you could imagine that the rain was real, and the clouds. They were real *enough*, he thought. Only they were man-made and regulated. He scowled, then grinned. Imagine seeing four clouds one day, or even two, how *that* would shake everyone up! But the rain fell from the sky of the floating city, and there would never be one cloud more or less. He almost wanted to cry but he didn't, remembering his age.

What would a real flood be like, he wondered, or a windstorm? For a minute his eyes almost closed under the impact of sheer emotional excitement: he'd seen microfilms of ancient natural disasters in which the power of nature was unleashed, and now he imagined great brown curls of floodwater emerging from real rivers, torrents of rain that fell with great force, winds that whipped a world apart.

Yet Earth had survived. It was still down there. And down there great climatic changes still existed; heat and cold, as they *were,* despite their convenience or inconvenience to man. To be pitted against that—Proteus held his breath, almost whoosy with the thought of it—to exist *in* the context of nature! What excitement it must have generated. Just a real rainstorm, coming from nowhere—appearing out of . . . itself, out of nature, sinking down into real ground filled with dirt and bugs and roots!

His eyes stung. The polite rain was done. It was all sham. The plastic trees didn't need nourishment. They didn't grow. Psychologists thought that the Earth-type environment helped man feel secure. Proteus knew this, but now he stared angrily at the meticulous street and went back inside.

Mithias was waiting for him. "There's no way that you could set up natural life conditions inside a subite, son," he said. "You know that. Don't torment yourself. You'd have to go to Earth."

"Well, people *do* go there," Proteus said. His face flushed. He lowered his eyes.

"But they don't live there—"

"A few do! Microfilms mention them. Historians go down; scientists. They have to make repairs on their equipment sometime."

"So what?" his father said. "There's no future on Earth. The whole place is drained dry, useless, stripped of anything worthwhile. It's just a husk." He paused and said more gently: "And Proteus, you *are* a boy, not a girl. It's true that your opportunities aren't as extensive as they might be, but there are plenty of places for you to fit into, here. Even if there were opportunities on Earth, and there aren't, then they'd go to women."

Proteus looked out the window. The sidewalk was already dry. The suction equipment had absorbed all the water so that none was wasted. He turned so that his father couldn't see his face. "Everything's the same all the time," he said, dully. "Don't you ever think about how fantastic it

14

must have been? Just people with all colors of skin. That alone. Now we're all homogenized."

At this Mithias laughed. "What's wrong with everyone having olive skin?" he asked. "You're just arguing for the sake of it now. There's all kinds of variations if you want to look for them, from yellow-olive to brown-olive to—"

"Olive-olive," Proteus said. "You just don't understand at all. Centuries ago there were black men and white men and yellow men—"

"And they all fought with each other," Mithias said, wearily. "Now there's one less thing to fight about. The races merged. What's so wrong about that? Will you stop trying to pick an argument with me, and find something constructive to do?"

Proteus nodded, but he realized suddenly that he was finished arguing. His father wanted him to do something constructive, and he would. Somehow he'd get to Earth. Somehow he'd recreate an ancient farm there. Instead of dreaming and being frustrated, he'd act. Someday he'd stand on real ground, while real rain fell, and then this would seem like the dream.

"You're going to have trouble with that one," Cyprus said to Oversoul Seven. They were conversing in the further reaches of the room's plastic dome.

"Well, he's not one of my favorites," Seven said. "He's so gloomy half the time."

Cyprus waited. Then she said, "There's a connection that you seem to have missed. Shall I point it out to you?"

"No, give me another chance," Seven said. "I don't need any more demerits, not even one." He reviewed the entire scene, including the thoughts he'd received telepathically from Proteus. Then he blushed. "Of course, the farm! Proteus wants to set up a farm on Earth. It's just possible that he had a dream last night about a farm or a picture of one—"

"Exactly," Cyprus said.

"Well, Proteus has had that idea for some time," Seven said. "But if he did participate in Josef's dream, he'd use it in his own way, of course. You know, in a way he acts older than Lydia. He broods so."

Cyprus smiled. "Do you know why?"

"No."

"I'm sure you'll discover the reason for yourself. It's

15

not up to me to tell you. But now suppose we look in on your Ma-ah."

Oversoul Seven was delighted to change the subject.

35,000 B.C.

The wolf cubs sped across the cliffs in the moonlight. Ma-ah crouched in the shadows, waiting. She was hungry, but then she usually was, her belly pushed in almost to her backbone. She ran across the cliffs when the wolf cubs vanished, and scurried to the clearing where they'd been forced to leave the kill they'd found. She'd frightened the cubs off by throwing rocks. Rampa came over from the other side of the cliff. He'd used bow and arrows. The two of them found little: only a dead hare. But they ate it at once, ravenously.

The hides they wore protected them somewhat against the wind and they crouched, unspeaking, while the ice cracked along the cliffs almost in sequence, and the air rushed in and out of the rock crevices.

Cyprus said to Oversoul Seven: "I didn't know you were that adventurous."

Oversoul Seven shrugged with just a hint of smugness. Then he said: "Proteus should experience this, if he wants to know what the real Earth is like. He'd probably plead for some artificial pretty rain that stops on time."

Cyprus smiled but said nothing.

Ma-ah and Rampa finished eating. They ran down into a nearby cave, pulling in out of the cold; satisfied. The damp smell of the hides rose to their nostrils. Their bellies felt warm from the food. A sense of peace descended upon them. They fell asleep. Their satisfaction was transmitted to Cyprus and Seven, who also felt the cold wind that rushed past the cave entrance.

"I could make the wind die down just a bit, couldn't I?" Seven asked. Cyprus nodded.

"Oh! oh!" Seven said. The change in the wind had alerted Ma-ah even in her sleep. In a moment her spirit body came out of the cave. She saw them.

"Oh, it's you, old man," she said.

"She's very good," Seven said to Cyprus. "But she always sees me as an old man."

'Why not? You always *are* an old man when I see you,"

16

Ma-ah said. "Are you going to help me keep watch to-night?"

"Not tonight," he said, adding to Cyprus, "Uh, I help her watch sometimes when she's tired, so the wolves don't find the cave."

"You know that you're out of your physical body?" Cyprus asked.

"Of course," Ma-ah said scornfully. "If I didn't go out in the spirit at night, who'd watch over my body while it slept? Only I don't like to get too far away from my body. Rampa hardly ever comes awake when he's asleep. Whose spirit are you?"

"I'll tell you sometime," Cyprus said. Then she and Seven disappeared.

"Ma-ah *always* sees me as an old man," Seven sighed. "Come to think of it, she sees me as black because she's black. Josef sees me in lots of different ways, but he likes to see me as an old man, too. It gives him confidence in me, for some silly reason. But Proteus never sees me at all."

"So?" Cyprus said.

"Well, none of them see me as I *am*, male and female, ageless, beyond any image. Even Lydia. I mean, she doesn't let herself believe in her soul at all, at least not on an intellectual level."

"Now who's brooding?" Cyprus said. "You sound as downhearted as Proteus."

"Proteus! He'll probably never see me if he keeps on the way he's going," Seven said. "But you've already met Josef, so I presume that this part of the examination is over."

"I'd like to see him when he's awake in his time, if you don't mind," Cyprus said dryly. . . .

1615

Just as Oversoul Seven and Cyprus arrived at Josef's, there was a tremendous pounding at his door. Josef Landsdatter moaned, bounded out of bed, ran his fingers through his bushy hair, and almost sobbed. He'd never felt so cornered in his life.

"Coming. Yes. Yes," he shouted. He hoped that he sounded enraged, impatient, anything but scared. He grabbed a paintbrush, dipped it into a jar of varnish, held

17

it between his teeth, and threw open the door. "I'm working. Working. Can't you see? I'm busy. But come in, if you must."

Elgren Hosentauf reminded himself that his wife was watching from the first-floor landing, so he strode through the door briskly. It was after all his house, his extra room. The place was a mess of rumpled clothing, tossed bedding, paint jars, and canvases in various stages of completion. "Ah, were you sleeping or painting? My wife swears that you were still in bed."

"What does it look like? Do you think I sleep with my paintbrush in my mouth?" Joseph pushed the brush toward Hosentauf's nose so that the smell of fresh varnish made the older man's eyes water and his nose run. "You distrust me," Josef said, now that he had the advantage. "You've always distrusted me. How can I work under such conditions?"

Hosentauf stepped back. "All right. But my wife tells me that you eat more than ten farmhands put together, and I won't be taken advantage of. We've yet to see a glimmer of our painting. You've been here six weeks now, eating our good food, using our nice room. The painter my cousin had did his portrait in two weeks and was gone."

"And the painting probably won't last much longer than that," Josef retorted, getting into it. "A good artist needs time." He pointed dramatically to the draped easel. "Your portrait is covered, I've told you. It makes me nervous to show a painting before it's done. And it took me a good two weeks to get started as it is; your wife put me in such a mood that I couldn't think, much less paint."

"Shush." Hosentauf's light blue eyes lowered. Some of the belligerence drained from his face. He'd been shaking his finger at Josef. Now he fussed with his shirt instead, and looked almost pleadingly up into Josef's stormy face. "My wife is impatient to see the painting. Women, they cannot wait."

"Ah, don't I know," Josef said, as if they shared a dark mysterious secret. "But very soon now I'll unveil the portrait." He threw his arms out dramatically, smiled grandly. "You will see your family immortalized through the ages. *The Hosentauf Family.* The portrait will go down through the generations, from father to son—"

"He's a lazy clout, and you should put him out in the

18

snow like the cur he is," yelled Avona Hosentauf from the stairs.

Flinching, her husband closed the door.

"Ahh, very well," shouted Josef. "I'll burn my painting rather than give it to the likes of that one. None of you deserves fine art. You're worse than shopkeepers." He rummaged through the room, picking up his belongings. Then he stopped in front of the covered easel.

"You will never be completed, never," he moaned. "Some silly woman prevents it. Ah well, if they resent the few morsels of food I eat, the use of this tiny room in exchange for a masterpiece—"

Hosentauf was an unimaginative man, at least generally speaking. It didn't occur to him at this point that anyone could fake such anguish. "Now, now," he said hurriedly. "I'll talk things over with my wife. I'll see what she says." He backed out of the room and closed the door.

Cyprus and Oversoul Seven were now two flakes of snow on the windowsill. Embarrassed, Seven said, "Josef's very excitable." Just then, Josef threw the cover off the easel, displaying not a half-completed painting at all, but the empty canvas beneath.

"And quite deceitful," Cyprus said.

"No, no, I'm sure he doesn't mean to be," Seven answered uneasily, because obviously it wasn't going to be one of Josef's better days.

Josef stared at the canvas hatefully. "Blank. All blank," he muttered. "Bah!" Completely disgusted, he planked down on the bed. Hosentauf wouldn't be back, he knew, but his wife would, with her eldest son. They'd boot him out. There'd be no more hedging or excuses. He'd be back on the plains on his skis, with his supplies on his back, cold and hungry, until he could find another farmer willing to give him bed and board for a painting. And worst, he just couldn't make himself paint anything at all.

This time his torment was quite real. He threw the sticky varnish-covered brush across the room and wondered what to do.

"Your dream," Oversoul Seven said. "Cyprus, can't I remind him? The painting I gave him in the dream! He's forgotten all about it."

"No, you cannot," she said. "No prompting in this part of the examination. You know that. Twenty-five demerits in case you have any ideas."

19

"Examination or not, I mean, he *is* in trouble," Seven said.

"Oh, somebody help me," Josef moaned.

"How many demerits?" Seven asked.

"Twenty-five, and you have several already," she reminded him.

"And you still won't tell me what happens if I fail? Or pass?"

She said gently, "That's part of the examination, too. You have to find that out."

"Oh, dear God, I'll never lie or cheat again if you'll just help me now," Josef prayed.

"Your dream!" Seven transmitted the words directly into Josef's mind. "The painting in the dream!"

The instant transformation in Josef was extraordinary. Suddenly he shouted, leapt up from the bed, threw his arms around himself, and danced about the room.

Oversoul Seven almost burst with excitement himself.

Cyprus made a determined effort not to show any expression at all, and to guard her thoughts.

"Get to it," Seven signaled Josef.

Now, standing before the easel, Josef grinned from ear to ear. In his mind's eye, as clearly as he'd ever seen anything in his life, he saw an oil painting of the Hosentauf farm in the summer, the fields rich, the sturdy house surrounded by tulips. The greens glowed with vitality. It was in the middle of the season, with only sneaky touches of brown hinting at the overripeness that would be its own undoing. Even the grays beneath the yellows and whites of the house suggested that the farmhouse, while secure, would not triumph over time. Yet somehow the overall effect was still one of vitality, as if the entire scene would endure even while it was so physically vulnerable. He'd never seen a painting so clearly in his mind before.

The canvas was coated, all ready to work, and as the thoughts went flying through his mind, Josef's hands were busily mixing the colors for his palette, combining the dry pigments with linseed oil. He felt swift, sure, godlike, with this sudden unexpected rush of inspiration. Singing, almost shouting, he began to paint.

Partaking of Josef's experience, Oversoul Seven forgot everything else. Once when Josef picked the wrong color, Seven called, "No, no, you'll spoil it. You want earth

20

tones there." Another time he cried, "No, you dunce, this is only the underpainting."

Cyprus waited, never interfering. Only once she spoke. "This part of the examination is only supposed to involve a brief viewing," she said, making her tone as neutral as possible.

"Yes, yes, I'll be with you shortly," Seven muttered. Then, "No, no, transparent color there. Not opaque," he called to Josef.

Five hours of Earth time passed. There was a knock at the door. "Go away. I'm working," Josef shouted.

The door flew open. Mrs. Hosentauf and her eldest son, Jonathan, came pounding into the room. "Ahhh, now maybe we'll get a look at the painting that isn't there. I want to see underneath that cover. I don't believe a word you say—" Mrs. Hosentauf shouted. Then she and her son both stopped, speechless.

"Now you see. Go, go leave me alone," Josef muttered. Nothing mattered but the painting.

"It's of my lovely house," Mrs. Hosentauf said. "It's beautiful."

"An inspiration," Jonathan said. "Man to man, let me apologize."

"Apologize then, and let me work. Can't you see I'm busy? I'm not finished. I've barely begun—"

"And you've started the portrait too?" Jonathan asked hastily.

"Yes, yes, yes," Josef cried automatically.

"Liar," Seven shouted, to Josef's mind. "You promised not to lie or cheat again."

A sudden pang of guilt just made Josef angry. He wanted to get on with his painting. "You'll have your portrait in good time," he said. "Can't a man have peace to work?"

Mrs. Hosentauf and her son moved toward the door, almost deferentially.

Josef yelled after them, triumphantly: "The house was meant as a bonus to repay you for your great kindness."

"Oh, Josef," Seven sighed.

Cyprus said, "You realize what you've done, of course: become so involved in Josef's difficulties that you've forgotten everything. Even the examination."

Seven came back to himself with dismay. "But I have to wait till he finishes the underpainting, now that I've

21

started," he said. "Then Josef can do the rest himself well enough."

"I'll speak to you when you're finished, then," Cyprus said. For a moment Seven wondered why he couldn't pick up more of Cyprus's thoughts, but already she was gone. Seven stayed there while Josef continued to paint, his brush like a perfect extension of the picture in his mind.

Chapter Three

Ma-ah's Trek:
The Earthization
of Oversoul Seven
Part Two of the Examination

Oversoul Seven and Cyprus were
two points of light.

"I chose Lydia's study for our discussion for several reasons," Cyprus said. "For one thing, the next part of your examination will definitely be Earth-oriented, and in ways that you may not suspect—"

"Suspect?" Oversoul Seven said. "I don't like the implications of that word. Are you sure you're using the language properly?"

"Yes, I am, and I used the word purposely, to give you a clue as to what might happen," she said. "For another thing, we have to take Earth forms, invisible of course, and I want you to relate to the environment the way humans do. For example, let's get off the windowsill and move properly into the room. We'll sit in one of those chairs there."

"Now tell me precisely where and when we are," Cyprus said. She materialized, to Seven at least, as a young woman of mature years, or as a mature woman of young years. Either way it seemed to fit. Yet if you kept looking at her, she became a young man of mature years or a mature man of young years. She laughed: "It's according to which part of my personality you focus on. I'm not as Earth-oriented as you, and I just can't get all of myself into an exclusively male or female form. No one ever does, of course. At my level it's just more apparent.

"But what form do *you* want to adopt?" she asked. "You'll have to use it for all of our discussions, so make up your mind. For one thing, I want to see how good you are, remembering details."

Seven's point of light wiggled indecisively. "I hadn't counted on a test of form," he said. "But since details are important, I'll pick something with as few of them as possible. What about a glowing round orange ball?"

"No," she sighed. "A human form."

Seven grinned and adopted the fourteen-year-old guise he'd used in the first part of the examination. "Now to answer your questions," he said briskly. "This is a day in April in the year 1975, in the northeastern part of the United States, which is a country, and it's four o'clock—"

"Oh, I see," Cyprus said. "Four o'clock is in the United States, then—"

"Not exactly—well, yes and no—" Seven said. "It's four o'clock here in the study, but that doesn't mean that four o'clock *is* here—"

"If you can't explain when we are, and how *when* fits into *where,* no wonder you have trouble keeping track of your personalities," Cyprus said. "But never mind. I have something quite serious to discuss with you. I'm giving you a multiple-choice section next, so listen carefully."

Seven frowned, but Cyprus continued. "The second part of the examination was dependent upon your performance in the first part," she said, "though as you know, all of it is really taking place at once. But several things have become apparent. I feel as if I know Lydia and Josef much

24

better than I do Proteus. And Ma-ah I know hardly at all—"

"Hmm," Seven said. He sat docilely enough in his best fourteen-year-old male form, but he was beginning to feel a flash of irritation.

"Could it be that you didn't tune into Proteus and Ma-ah as well as you did the others?" Cyprus said. "You couldn't get away from Ma-ah fast enough, it seemed to me."

"It's just *them*," Seven answered, rather put out now. "Proteus is gloomy a good deal of the time. Ma-ah sees me as an old man, *always*, I told you that, and she always wants me to do something boring, like keeping watch over the cave. Well, she's quite demanding."

"I'm afraid that you've been a very distant oversoul to both of them," Cyprus said severely. "That's one of the issues we hope to take care of in this examination. You have to learn to relate to your personalities better. And why do you think Ma-ah sees you as an old man? Never mind, don't answer me now. And she doesn't see you as a *jolly* old man either, which would be something quite different. No, Seven, those qualities you see in Ma-ah and Proteus are your own, too, a fact that you conveniently forget. And you don't come to grips with them at all."

"But *I'm not* gloomy," Oversoul Seven cried, "or demanding either."

"You can only endow your personalities with your own attributes. They're born from your own joy and vitality and creativity, but they also have your characteristics. You're their raw material, so to speak—"

"I don't like that phrase much either," Seven said. "I like to think of myself as their . . . creator, or of them as my creations."

"Just as I thought," Cyprus said. "Oh, Seven, I don't know how you'll ever reach Oversoul Eight stage."

"You're leading up to something," Seven said. "And you tricked me into making my last statement—"

"You tricked yourself into that," she said. "But the fact is that you don't relate well to Proteus and Ma-ah at all. And worse, you're playing favorites. As a result, both of them are missing something important that only you can give them. They're each missing a part of their soul—"

Seven was so upset that his image blurred around the edges.

"Watch your form," Cyprus corrected. "There you go

25

again. Details are important, too. I don't mean to be overly severe, but suppose something like that happened to Ma-ah? Or Josef?"

"Josef would get out of it somehow," Seven said.

"But Ma-ah wouldn't?"

"You're just trying to confuse me," Seven wailed.

"This must be your low point," Cyprus said dryly. "Oversouls don't cry—"

"I'm not crying. I'm wailing. There's a difference," Seven said. "Anyway, why not?" he added defiantly.

"Because when they're using all their abilities, then they see more clearly; and they know that there are no obstacles, only those you believe in. But never mind, here's Part Two of your examination. It's an in-depth Life Composition."

Oversoul Seven regained his composure.

"You have a choice between Ma-ah and Proteus," Cyprus said. "But you must focus your attention on one of them and identify as best you can with whichever one you choose."

"It sounds easy enough," Oversoul Seven said. "But I have a feeling that there's something you aren't telling me."

"That you'll have to find out for yourself," she said. "Which one do you choose?"

"Well, I suppose I should do Ma-ah because I related to her poorest of all," Seven said. "All right, I choose Ma-ah."

"Remember, you must try to identify with her as well as you can," Cyprus said, "And with that portion of you from which she came. Good luck, dear Seven."

"Cyprus, wait. I've a lot of questions!"

"Oh, it's you again, old man," Ma-ah said.

Oversoul Seven just frowned. Cyprus was gone. Lydia's study was gone, and instead Ma-ah stood in her spirit body outside of her everlasting cave.

"Why do you always see me as an old man?" he asked.

"If you're not one, why do you look like one?" she retorted.

"I *don't* look like one, that's the point," he said.

She shrugged. "I don't care if you do or don't, but at least you could be pleasant."

"I'm trying to be," he said, irritably. "And I'm apt to be around for some time, so I wish . . . oh, never mind." This is a great start, he said to himself.

But Ma-ah had already gone back into her body. She

didn't have the greatest disposition in the world, Seven thought, looking about. The cold wind swept scraps of dry weed past his face, and the cliffs were white with frost. Seven sighed: she didn't have the greatest environment in the world, either. The cliffs rose straight up in the air, making dry curious noises as if the rocks were coughing.

Seven was impervious to the weather, but he found the view fascinating and he entertained himself by dematerializing from the valley, appearing on a cliff peak, and looking down at where he'd just been. Then, guiltily, he remembered his instructions: "Identify as best you can with Ma-ah," Cyprus had said. Clearly, he thought, she had something else in mind. Uneasily he went into Ma-ah's cave.

She lay asleep on a few hides, bundled in another that was used as cloak and cover. Her brown straight hair was matted, all emphasis gone from her dark face, making her look vulnerable and more like twelve than the twenty Earth years she had to her credit. Seven sighed again: Cyprus was right, he had maintained too great a distance. Unaccountably he felt suddenly drawn to Ma-ah as he never had before. At the same time, a curious lassitude possessed him.

He saw Ma-ah's mate, Rampa, sleeping beside her, but then without warning he felt Rampa's breath coming in warm waves at his own face, astoundingly close. His viewpoint changed too. Rampa was now beside *him;* beside . . . Ma-ah. He was feeling Rampa's breath *from* Ma-ah's body . . . Because he was *in* Ma-ah's body!

How odd settling down into a real body was! Ma-ah wasn't aware of him, of course. Since he was Ma-ah and Ma-ah was himself, there was no conflict. Yet so far she only knew herself as Ma-ah, and him as the old man when she was out of her body. Seven was confused. He tried to get his thoughts in order. In one way, then, he thought, he was getting to know himself better by getting to know her.

Still, Seven's consciousness wriggled uneasily. To be confined to one body for all practical purposes—it wouldn't be like changing forms whenever you wanted to, as he did. To have the responsibility for keeping the same body going all the while! The details involved really threw him for a loop when he thought of it. Of course, *his* energy helped maintain her body to begin with—his was the spark, so

27

to speak, from which her body grew, from which her spirit had come, but . . .

He stopped that line of thought, aware of the strangest ambiguity. Being in a real body was so intimate; he could feel his consciousness nestling in all the atoms and molecules. He was aware of their million separate yet combined consciousnesses; so tumultuous, like the infinite buzzing of innumerable bees, warm, too close, throbbing. For a moment he felt frightened, confined.

On the other hand he was transfixed, attracted to the body experience as to a magnet. He'd never allowed himself to enter the complete physical experience of one of his personalities before. For one thing, he'd never been invited, but suddenly it occurred to him that far more than that was involved. All Oversouls were individual, and related to their personalities in their own fashion. He *was* adventurous, and he'd set himself and his personalities some great challenges; but the truth was, he didn't want to get *too* involved. Worse, he was beginning to suspect that his personalities were setting *him* some challenges too.

Like right now. This full alliance with flesh and blood was startling; pleasant and unpleasant, and it was growing more unpleasant each minute. He felt . . . clotted, thickened, caught in a rich, dizzy gestalt of interaction. That was enough of that!

Seven roused himself. But nothing happened. His consciousness was intact, whole, itself, yet it was somehow dispersed throughout Ma-ah's body, stuck in the cells and wiggly organs, locked in labyrinthine tangled chambers of bone and blood.

The body's left shoulder was cold. *That's* what cold was. He knew the meaning of the word, but the feeling of draft, of empty wind blowing on exposed flesh, this was something new. Seven felt the tiny hairs on the arm raise, arch, stiffen. They stood up so taut and straight that it seemed they'd pull right out of the flesh. Ma-ah turned over suddenly in her sleep, shoving the shoulder beneath her. The hairs instantly softened.

Seven groaned. Ma-ah's eyes were closed, and he didn't seem able to manufacture any vision of his own, or do anything for that matter, but experience reality through her body. "Cyprus, this is too much," he called mentally, but there was no answer. He shivered, or Ma-ah did. He wanted to turn the wind down as he'd done before, but now he was imprisoned in Ma-ah and at the wind's mercy as she'd been (and *was*)! "You could at least turn the wind down," he moaned to Cyprus, but again there was no response.

His first day was incredible. He experienced morning, noon, and night in sequence, through the body's senses as Ma-ah did. No more mixing and matching of times and seasons. He saw the world from her viewpoint. That is, he saw only what she saw, though he could interpret events in his own way. He'd never felt so limited. He couldn't get out of Ma-ah's day, no matter how he tried.

By late afternoon it was already growing dark. Again the wind began rising. A low moon appeared on the horizon. Ma-ah and Rampa finished eating some particularly bitter roots that they'd gathered during the day. The remainder they strapped about their waists with a rope made of tough weeds. Looking through Ma-ah's eyes, Seven realized that they were too far away from the cave to make it back by nightfall, and the cliffs here rose straight and smooth-faced, offering no chance of shelter. The body was very cold. The hides rubbed against the skin with irritating regularity, and the hide moccasins were badly worn. The feet, Seven realized, were losing all feeling.

So far the body sensations had taken all of Seven's attention. He'd never handled such a barrage of constantly applied stimuli without being able to shut it off at will. He heard what Ma-ah said to Rampa, but he was so engrossed in the tongue's feelings and the sensations involved in speech—the rush of air through the throat—that he ignored the conversation itself.

Didn't she know the feet were near-frozen? Didn't she know that the body needed help?

Then, as if in answer to his questions, Ma-ah's emotions avalanched upon his consciousness, only they snuffed *his* out. He could feel his own awareness disappear beneath sudden fear, anger—the words and feelings instantly translated. "It's Rampa's fault. I shouldn't have listened to him. I knew we went too far. My feet! and *he's* limping."

The emotions immediately transformed the body. The shoulders slumped, the mouth drooped. The blood was called to too many places at once. The belly swelled; gas collected. Seven felt himself crushed, threatened to extinction. ("Scared silly," Cyprus would say, later.)

29

But he roused himself, pulled himself up from the maze of Ma-ahness. He knew something important. What was it? Desperately he tried to make a small point of silence, a framework to hold him above all that tumult. He knew what to do and where to go, if only he could make himself remember. The confusion of body noises, activity, and emotions was still there. But Seven hung his consciousness above it all somewhere, like a spider in the rafters of a high ceiling, and brooded.

Ma-ah trudged on. Seven distinguished her voice now from the other jungles of vowels, syllables, gurgles, and body sounds, keeping track of what activity was happening inside her, and what originated from without. Rampa's voice, coming from the outside, definitely affected the inside of Ma-ah's body, though. Whenever Rampa spoke, a variety of mixed responses were aroused in Ma-ah's consciousness, and each of these had instant physical repercussions. Her emotions rose and fell in such staggered rhythm that for a moment Seven confused it with the rise and fall the thighs made in walking.

But he managed to cling to the precarious nest of silence he'd made, and he concentrated as hard as he could. Unfamiliar webs of energy grew from his alertness. He could feel them. They went stretching out into the night, searching. Finally they pointed clearly to the southeast. But why? What did they mean? Seven only knew that he must follow them.

Their body fell down. Again, without knowing how he did it, Seven picked the body up and started it walking once more. All the while, he kept concentrating. What was it he knew and had forgotten?

The webs of light moved again. They converged on one particular cliff not too far away. And suddenly the rock became transparent to Seven. Within it he glimpsed light, distance, and activity. Seven grappled with the problem. He knew he had to get Rampa and Ma-ah over to that cliff.

He tried to signal her mentally. "Ma-ah, Ma-ah. This way." Nothing. She kept trudging along, half-crying with frustration and cold. Seven's own sense of futility was almost more than he could bear; he was afraid he'd fall back into the tumult of her body and emotions again. Fighting for control, he felt his separate consciousness slipping, and as he lost his hard-won isolation, he was Ma-ah.

30

"Oh, we've got to get to that cliff," she thought frantically. She signaled Rampa. She'd been acting so strangely all day that Rampa nodded half out of sheer exhaustion, and half in surprise that she seemed so sure of herself. Ma-ah clenched her teeth in determination. At the same time, she wondered why the cliff was so important, and how she knew that they must reach it.

Both of them just slumped against the rock when they got there. Ma-ah cried with exasperation. Whatever she'd had in mind, the cliff was smooth, unbroken. Her disappointment smothered her. She was too tired to go on. Her thoughts grew hazy. And Seven found his own consciousness once more suspended somewhere within Ma-ah, but apart. He experimented cautiously, stood the body up, opened its eyes, and felt the cliff walls with its hands. For this, in his predicament anyhow, he needed the hands' sensitivity.

But Ma-ah's fingers found the spot that Seven was seeking, and the door that he'd somehow known was there opened. Seven pulled the body in. He couldn't work Rampa's body from the inside, and Rampa didn't seem able to work it much himself. Worse, Seven knew that the door would close automatically in only a few seconds. And his own energy was fluctuating. One instant everything was brilliantly clear. The next, his awareness dimmed.

Seven cried out, "Rampa!" but the words came out of Ma-ah's lips, in her voice. Rampa raised his head and half rose, dragging himself over to her. As soon as he was inside, the door closed.

From that higher point of awareness Seven thought smugly, "I should get an A on *that* part of the examination." Then, confused, he wondered what he meant.

Chapter Four

The Descent of Proteus

Proteus had been aware of his emotional pull toward the Earth for as long as he could remember. It was shared by practically no one. None of his school friends showed the slightest interest. During the long afternoons when they sat in their separate living areas for television classes, and when they chatted back and forth via video during discussion periods, Earth was hardly ever mentioned.

They did talk about going outside when school was over and the sets turned off, but none of them seemed to realize that outside wasn't really outside. Of course, the plastic trees were replicas of real ones, and the shade they provided was real enough. But the steadily illuminated inner sky beneath the dome was never that bright; shade wasn't needed that badly. It was just for effect. No birds flew through the branches either, and no matter how well cared for the trees were, they always looked artificial to him. It seemed sometimes as if he knew better, that in some forgotten past he'd known real trees and would never be satisfied with fake ones. Which was impossible, of course.

The floating cities were held in place by atomically powered motors that automatically compensated for any drift relative to particular designated points on Earth. No one alive remembered the time when people lived on Earth in any numbers. And there had never been real trees in the domed city complexes. But despite this, he dreamed frequently of Earth as it used to be. He felt angry on its behalf. They'd simply abandoned it, given it up. He began devouring the microfilms that were available from the vast video library. Often he sat up late at night, secretly, watching the films until morning.

His excitement grew with his knowledge. There were various outposts on Earth: archeological sites and diggings, several scientific installations, and, he suspected, a few back-to-nature communities that somehow eluded satellite surveillance. He couldn't be sure of this, he told himself for the hundredth time, but it was a possibility.

He began to gather supplies weeks in advance of his plan. His mother had an administrative position, coming home only a few weekends in a six-month period. So hiding his intent from her was no problem. Maintaining secrecy in the face of his father's almost constant presence was something else again. Mithias was a group father, though, keeping track of some thirty boys and girls on closed-circuit television, overseeing their studies and scheduled activities. Seeing his father so engaged always made Proteus angry: Why couldn't classes be held in one big school nodule as they had in ages past?

This afternoon, though, every thought but one fled from Proteus's concern. Each Tuesday he and his friend, Grek, went hiking, an activity favored by almost everyone, to ensure sufficient muscular and motor development. This Tuesday would be different though, from any other. Proteus thought that Grek would sense his excitement the minute they met, no matter how he tried to hide it. But Grek just walked beside him, talking as usual about everyday events.

Everything Proteus did or said himself seemed unnatural and suspicious to him. He kept throwing sideways glances

33

at Grek, sure that he'd somehow given himself away, but Grek obviously saw nothing different about the day or about Proteus. They'd taken their lunch as usual. Out of sheer nervousness, Proteus suggested that they see which of the two of them could eat the quickest.

So they went down the plastic streets, whooping and laughing, popping the lunch pills (L.P.'s) in their mouths as fast as possible. They each had two protein-basics (P.B.'s), two carbohydrate-simples (C.S.'s), and an amino acid supplement (A.A.S.). Proteus let Grek win, because he felt guilty about hiding his plans from him, and he was feeling guiltier each minute.

The game had been foolish, too, he thought. It would be the last time he'd gobble his L.P.'s so nonchalantly, so sure of a constant supply. Had he stashed away enough of them? He was sure that he had. Still . . .

"You sure are quiet," Grek said.

"Oh, it's the same old thing," Proteus said. "Walking down these streets depresses me, though I know it shouldn't. And I keep wishing boys were given the same training that girls are, taken into the heart of business and politics at a young age, so they can see how the world works. If we were girls we'd be studying seriously at our age, not just passively watching our fathers manage the living nodules or learning unimportant, mundane skills—" Actually, Proteus was surprised at the normal sound of dissatisfaction in his voice, because he was only talking for something to say. But he wasn't concerned with problems like that any more. Not him.

A few boys went by on aero-skis. A man sat out on the porch of a nodule, his face expressionless as they passed. "See?" Proteus said. "He looks as artificial as the trees. Well, not really. My father knows him. He's got as much responsibility as any man around here, but it just isn't enough. He manages rain regulation, but it's all computerized anyway—"

"Oh, don't start on that stuff again," Grek said. "My father says you'll end up in real trouble. You're so damn dissatisfied all the time."

This sent Proteus into a laughing fit. "If you only knew—" he said. "I mean, how funny that is! What kind of trouble can you get into around here?"

"I don't know," Grek said, uneasily.

"That's it. None," Proteus went on. His talk was sup-

34

posed to keep Grek occupied while he went over his own last-minute plans. As the time approached for him to make his move, he was getting more and more nervous. Soon Grek would suggest that they return. As usual they'd be expected home before supper, and they'd been walking about two hours. It was near 6 P.M. Would he miss his father? Grek? Wasn't there something he could say to Grek without giving the whole thing away? Something that Grek could remember afterward?

"Grek . . . we're friends, aren't we? Look, I like you a lot—"

Grek stopped and stared at him. "What did you need to say that for? Sure we're friends—"

"I don't know." Proteus felt like laughing, like crying. He felt secretive, yet like shouting his secret aloud where everyone could hear it. He caught himself—he needed the two-hour headstart. He had to get to the ramp that he'd staked out. He said, nonchalantly, "Let's go back a different way."

He paused and looked around as if trying to make up his mind which way to take. Actually, he was taking a long last look at the neighborhood in which he'd lived as long as he remembered. The living nodules stretched as far as he could see. Each complex was a duplication of ancient Earth conditions, as perfect as Art and Science could make it. Each city was done in the decor of a particular Earth period. This one was nineteenth-century America. He lived in the Ohio block.

"We always go home the way we came," Grek said.

"I know, but the lunch race gave me an idea. Let's each take a different route to my nodule and see who gets there first. I'll go a block to the left and you go a block to the right. It's just an idea. If you don't want to—" Proteus broke off. He knew Grek would agree. Any kind of challenge was always fun.

"All right. Ready, set, go!" Grek shouted. He turned around without looking back, and began to run as fast as he could to the right. Shocked, Proteus just stood there for a moment. He hadn't realized that Grek would take off so quickly or that there wouldn't be time to make some gesture, some veiled good-by. Grek disappeared around the corner. Proteus began to run himself, going faster and faster now, stopping only when he had to catch his breath.

The slightly springy material of the sidewalk gave just a

35

trifle with each step, so that he felt an added sense of acceleration, as if he were running so quickly that he could just take off above the treetops. His feet were strangely cold, although the air was maintained at a constant 73.2, and his heart was pounding when he finally came out onto the five-acre area of artificial trees and fields that surrounded the city complex.

Benches were neatly placed around the landscape, each with one bush beside it and a potful of simulated flowers. Now at suppertime the area was vacant. Some of the flowers were growing brittle. Scientists were working on a new material that might actually reproduce itself, or at least repair itself, maintaining a more natural look. Proteus wondered if he'd ever come back, and if he did, whether or not the new plastic "life" would replace the old.

A week ago he'd carefully cut out a whole chunk of "grass" and placed his survival kit and supplies beneath. Now he retrieved them hurriedly. It would be dark at seven, when the day lights automatically lowered to minimum illumination. A panicky feeling flickered behind his forehead. Ignoring it, he inflated his aero-skis, put his survival kit over his back, and glided through the quiet air. The skis worked by reacting against the air beneath them. His were a boy's set, allowing only an elevation of six feet; but they could go fast enough.

He was too much in a rush now to enjoy sky-skiing as he usually did, but his love of the sport paid off. He was an expert at riding the soft eddies of regulated air that rose and fell. And the skis could go almost thirty miles an hour. The light began to dim to early twilight. It would last for forty-five minutes. He wasn't nearly as obvious as he would have been in maximum daylight, and if anyone saw him he'd just look like any boy, sky-skiing—if you didn't happen to notice his direction. Because now he was heading away from the complex.

In another half-hour he was at his destination. He floated down, deflated the skis, and tied them around his waist just as the inner sky turned to night light. The ramp entrance had taken him months to discover. Now it was only ten minutes away. No one came to this area except maintenance crews. Here, no effort had been made to decorate; a series of gray sprawling plastoid buildings stood silently. He reached the ramp entrance. None of them were guarded; no one but the women crews used them to begin with.

Proteus stood, uncertain. Soon Grek would wonder what had happened to him. His father would be worried. Should he go back while he could? Was he doing the right thing? His eyes stung. Boys rarely even competed in the examination for Historical Training, since it was a woman's field—his father said they rewrote history—but he'd tried and flunked. If they'd taken him, he probably never would have decided to strike out on his own; to discover Earth on his own. He would have been content with records.

Remembering, his resolve came back with a warm rush. The grating was beneath him. He pulled it up easily—it was made for women's lighter hands—and closed it from inside. Quickly he began to descend the dimly lighted ladderlike stairs.

His steps echoed through the aluminum tunnel. His scalp prickled and his ears rang. Suppose, just suppose, that he couldn't get out at the lower end, and someone locked the upper entrance? "You're just acting like a scared kid," he told himself scornfully. He knew that the ramps only extended a few hundred feet, yet it seemed that the steps would never end.

There were other ramps, but many were used to transport scientific supplies and he didn't know their schedules. That's why he'd chosen a utility ramp, because they were visited only several times a year for inspection purposes. But now it occurred to him that if anything happened and he couldn't get out, it would be a long time until he was found. Not that he didn't have enough supplies, he told himself quickly, because he did. He was just nervous because he couldn't have known ahead of time how he'd feel.

The descent *was* oddly distasteful. He felt like one of the archaic-looking insects he'd seen in microfilms, creeping inside the huge ramp that descended from the underside of the city. Maybe it was just the knowledge that each step took him nearer the ramp's end that bothered him, he thought.

Twice he stopped to rest, gripping the thin railing with both hands and slipping his survival pack down on the stairs. At the same time he kept thinking of his father, who must know of his disappearance by now—he was probably questioning Grek at this very moment.

37

To show himself that he didn't really care, he started to run down the stairs, the echo of his steps growing even louder. Then the steps ended. A small door read: "Outlets—Surface." It opened automatically at his touch and closed behind him. A narrow hall lined with machinery ended with a second door.

Proteus gulped. If he was right, he should be in one of the infrequently used atomic-powered skylevators on the underside of the floating city, with nothing between him and Earth but seven miles of empty space! He looked around at the small globular room in which he stood. He'd made it—the dials on the wall console told him he was in a skylevator. But suppose he couldn't run it?

Suddenly a whirring noise began; an odd droning. Proteus held his breath. His entrance must have activated the mechanism. Even now his weight and dimensions were probably being fed into the minicomputers in charge of descent. A red light flashed on. At the same time, three signs glowed into life: AUTOMATIC DROP, PAUSE FOR INSTRUCTIONS, and HOLD ON WAIT.

The room itself began to vibrate softly. Proteus gulped again, pressed the button marked AUTOMATIC DROP, and closed his eyes as tightly as he could. His stomach lurched. His head snapped back. The skylevator dropped out of its nest beneath the city, and began its descent.

Proteus's eyes flew open. Inside, the lights dimmed. A dial flashed: 35,000 ft. The sight of it almost made him sick as he realized that plans were one thing, and their realization was something quite different. Here he was, 35,000 feet up in space, alone, falling steadily away from the only world he knew. One side of the skylevator was a transparent window. He looked out, hardly believing what he saw.

Bright emptiness stretched all around him, an endless blue sky through which he was descending. Then he looked down—in terror—for below there were mountains of black-gray clouds, heavy and threatening, like an ever-moving uneven floor upon which the skylevator must surely crash. Despairingly he looked up, to see the dark undersides of the city disappearing as he plunged further down. Could he make the skylevator reverse itself in mid-air? He eyed the dials. No, he thought, even with the little he knew, he was sure that reversal was impossible.

Now the dial read: 30,000 ft. He looked down again,

astonished, for as he approached the clouds, holes appeared in them as if by magic. He'd never seen clouds before—not natural ones—only the three tamed ones that went past with each fifteen-minute rain, but he knew about them academically. No film or account could begin to describe what they were really like, though, and involuntarily he shouted out with wonder as the skylevator dropped through one of the cloud-holes. He gasped—the clouds gave way, as if on purpose. The clouds *knew*. They're alive, he thought, like sky creatures. It seemed to him that they were rushing from all over the open sky, to watch.

Proteus stood, hands pressed against the window, transfixed. There were layers and layers of clouds. Again he thought of sky creatures, grazing. What did they think as they watched him plunge past? Then, suddenly, they thinned out, moved away, *rushed* away as if frightened. Once more he cried out involuntarily as the curve of the Earth appeared, with the sun at one rim, splashing the most incredible rays of light that he'd ever seen or imagined. He'd seen microfilms of sunsets but they never even hinted at this shimmering vitality.

He eyed the dial quickly and looked out again, fascinated. 20,000 feet. The ground—the *surface* of Earth suddenly emerged. Giant patches of color were visible, some dark, almost blue-black—real shadows cast by the real sun!—some so brilliant that he could hardly look at them. His excitement grew as the skylevator dropped further down. The mountains were like gigantic teeth rising out of an open mouth. He was going to land in a perfectly flat area, the floor of the "mouth." He held his breath as the skylevator fell into the shadows, below the horizon, and the ground came rushing up.

Motion stopped. The skylevator landed. The door—impossibly—opened. A light blinked on: WAITING FOR INSTRUCTIONS. Two dials shone, one saying, KEEP ON HOLD, and the other, AUTOMATIC RETURN. Proteus bit his lips. If only he dared set the control on HOLD, just in case. How good to know he could get back, if he wanted to. Once the skylevator was gone, his connections with home were broken. But no, the skylevator mustn't be missed. His hand trembled, but he pushed the RETURN button. Then he ran out as fast as he could, afraid that the vehicle might take off while he was still inside. He rushed out onto the small ramp, down the steps, and took his first step upon the ground.

As he stood there, the skylevator shuddered and four small rockets fired, sending their hungry flames outward. The skylevator lifted, wobbled slightly, and then slowly and surely began its steady rise. He felt as if he were losing—everything. "Good-by," he shouted. Then, resolutely, he turned away.

At first glance, the scene before him was terrifying. Instinctively Proteus looked up, but no plastic dome covered the real harsh sky. Now that it was all above him, on *top* of him, not around him, it made him uneasy. The late sunset blazed across the rocky plains that reached into the distance where they were finally ringed by high hills. The sun's brilliance hurt his eyes, but more than this, he was unprepared for the spectacular reaches of open space in which he suddenly felt very small and vulnerable. He shivered. He'd never felt so unprotected in his life.

He looked again, this time in the opposite direction. The gobular skylevator was rising, growing smaller and dearer each minute, looking now like a balloon. Soon he wouldn't be able to see it at all. Proteus watched, thinking of the floating city complex to which it would return. He sighed, realizing how snugly he had been held within that plastic bauble. Now he almost yearned for the skylevator's sheltering walls.

Already his skin prickled. The air was wild here, not controlled and even. Surprisingly soft, still it pushed against his face, thrust itself all around him, pushed him, though gently. It felt alive. But then so did the ground, which seemed to be a litter of sand granules and stones and small weeds. He was so surprised to be walking on an uneven surface that once he stopped dead still, almost afraid to go on. He wobbled when he walked. The stones hurt his feet, and he realized that in no time at all his shoes would be a complete loss. The sun fell a few notches in the sky.

How many other human beings were on the Earth? Suddenly he felt brave, heroic, caught up in a rush of exaltation. Once his mother had taken him on a business trip to the Moon with her, but the Moon was civilized and quite mundane in the domed areas. Earth was different. It was primitive, real. In a strange manner, he felt that he'd come home.

40

His aero-skis would save his shoes and feet until he got used to walking on the surface. He inflated them, and took off, whizzing just above the rocks and stones. But at once he was in trouble. Too late he realized that the skis had been developed for the comparatively even air currents inside the complexes. It was impossible to glide smoothly in this bumpy, undisciplined air.

Trying to navigate, he looked down beneath him. So this was Section 7! The entire Earth's surface was designated by symbols now, though archeologists and historians could rattle off the old names with ease. Still, he wished he knew the name for his landing place. It seemed sad not to know.

He searched his mind, but all he could remember was the name Cyprus, which referred to an island, he thought, not a large body of land. Still a name was a name, and better than none. His skis wobbled in a sudden eddy of air, but already he could tell that he was beginning to handle himself in the new air currents. He glided almost easily over a good-sized air-hill, and yelled down at the land, "I name you Cyprus."

Just then he realized that the sun's rays were disappearing. While he didn't need a sheltered spot to put up his small living nodule, the thought of staying out in the open area frightened him. Hopefully he eyed the hills—if only he could reach them before night came—the real night—without the city's gentle illumination. He tried not to think of the ancient Earth night as he'd read of it in old records. For the first time he wondered how far the hills were in actual miles from—well, from Cyprus.

Chapter Five

Oversoul Seven's Mini-Vacation

Oversoul Seven kept making platforms to hold himself above the well of Ma-ah's experience, only to topple down into it again. His apartness from her was slipping, and in those moments of his own lucidity he thought that this wasn't fair at all. Cyprus was going too far. This part of the examination was too difficult for his stage of development. He'd fail miserably, if he didn't end up losing himself in Ma-ah completely, if that was possible.

The only time he managed to reassert himself was when he was called on consciously or unconsciously by one of his other personalities, or when Ma-ah needed him in some direct manner. For example, he was lost within Ma-ah, or thought he was, when suddenly he was aware of Proteus's descent to Earth. Quick, clear images came to him as Proteus landed. Once he saw the entire landscape from the tip of one of Proteus's skis. What on Earth was *he* up to? Seven wondered irritably.

And what was happening to Josef and Lydia while he was trapped (what else could you call it?) inside Ma-ah's body? Ma-ah, it seemed, needed his help at every turn. When he *was* Ma-ah, losing his independence, then he felt her own fear and insecurity, unmitigated, without the benefit of his own superior knowledge. And her fear threatened to devour him. He had to get *her* above it, he realized suddenly. Only her release would free them both.

Actually, she was pretty aggressive and independent on her own, except when her fear made her forget everything she knew. As it had yesterday—was it yesterday?—when they'd been found. The men who captured them were different in appearance from any people that Ma-ah or Rampa had ever seen, and it was this that frightened them so completely.

Ma-ah cried out as they were led down the hall beneath torches that were set in the wall niches. She and Rampa were terrified of fire, Seven discovered. Both of them cowered at the fire itself, and at the dark shadows that leaped up the rocky gray walls. Their captors—or rescuers? —were approximately nine feet tall, as Lydia would have measured them, to Ma-ah's five-foot-three and Rampa's five-eight. Besides this, the men wore robes dyed with brilliant colors, and obviously not made of hides.

Seven knew that he had some information concerning these people, but Ma-ah's emotions kept blocking out his own awareness. In the cave now, Ma-ah stared at the wall. She and Rampa were chattering, wondering whether or when they would be freed. They'd just finished eating the last of the roots they'd gathered and tied about their waists.

A torch burned high above them. The top of the room was open in the center. The two of them were less frightened now. They'd been left alone for hours. The cave's door refused to budge, but otherwise they were not restrained in any way. Oversoul Seven let his own consciousness climb up again wearily. He peered through Ma-ah's eyes, but as he did so, images appeared on the cave wall. They were apparent to him, but not to Ma-ah, who paid no attention. Briefly he thought that this was strange, since they were, after all, *her* eyes he was looking through. The pictures were milky and opaque at first, then they turned clear, soft, vivid. To Seven, but not to Ma-ah, the wall disappeared as if it did not exist.

Mentally, to no one in particular, Lydia had just called for help. The trailer wall was blurring before her eyes, and she knew what that meant. It was one of those trailer-camper trucks. Lawrence was driving. She'd been reading at the small table that was hinged to the half-wall behind the driver's seat. One slim bony hand still rested on the book. Now it trembled suddenly, without warning.

Another . . . petit stroke. Quickly she leaned back while she still could, anchoring herself so that she wouldn't fall off the chair. And she wouldn't call Lawrence. She'd determined not to. Let him drive on, unknowing. The edges of her vision were blurring faster now. Something within her was giving way. She braced herself for the confusion, maybe for unconsciousness. . . .

Would Lawrence have the guts to give her the pills? You promised, she thought wildly. I won't die senile . . . in a home, locked up. Her eyes flew to the small high cabinet where the pills were kept. If she didn't come out of it . . . right . . . if her mind was . . . gone . . . if she couldn't keep up, Lawrence knew what to do. Looking at the cabinet was the last thing she remembered.

As usual when she came out of "it" she didn't know what had happened. Lawrence was still driving, and listening to the radio. Then she hadn't called out, or he hadn't heard if she had. The book was still beside her. She felt dizzy, that was all. She . . . but who was she? Panic splashed over the frightened surfaces of her mind. How could she forget? How could the body forget its name? The body's name? Did the body have a name? Oh Lord. She closed her eyes, feeling as if tiny islands of knowledge were crumbling away, falling into endless oceans of oblivion.

So quickly that he hardly realized what he was doing, Oversoul Seven leapt from Ma-ah to Lydia's body. With all-knowing finesse he quickened her blood, thinned it, gave orders to the body consciousness to increase circulation, filled in with the commands necessary. "Count, Lydia. Remember. Remember. Count," he directed.

She suddenly recalled a trick that sometimes worked.

44

Quickly she found the name for the first number, one. She saw it in her mind and concentrated on it visually. Then two. Then three, continuing in order until finally the panic cleared and her own name, Lydia, floated back to her between fifteen and sixteen.

Oversoul Seven returned, again without knowing how he did so, to Ma-ah. He thought triumphantly: he wasn't trapped inside Ma-ah for good, then. He'd left, if only momentarily. Still, his distance from his personalities *was* vanishing. He must have agreed. No experience was ever thrust upon a soul—or a personality, for that matter. But when had he agreed? And what else had he agreed to? Seven felt petulant. Already Ma-ah was getting restless again. What was *she* so upset for? Lydia could have lost her life right then—and he knew she wasn't ready. The thought intrigued him. If she wasn't ready, she wouldn't lose it, of course.

Actually, Lydia was thinking the same thing. Here she was. The attack was over. She was alive, and as far as she could tell, she was still sane enough. She forced herself to concentrate on Lawrence, and away from herself. How close he was, yet how far away! She watched the back of his head . . . like a big bleached walnut, she thought, the brown-white hair so alive, bristly; the cords on the back of his neck so responsive. Oh, the ease with which his neck shifted as he watched the road!

"You're awfully quiet back there," Lawrence called cheerfully.

"Am I?" Her first spoken words after the attack were so bright, her voice so crystal clear and lovely, and sane and normal, that she wanted to shout out with joy. Oh God, how great life . . . consciousness . . . was! "It's such a great day. A shame to read and not pay attention," she said. "So I've been looking out the window."

"We'll stop soon, for supper," he said.

"Mmm." She opened her pocketbook and looked into the compact mirror. Her face was . . . intact. How old. The eyes, flecked with orange, looked clear, alert, knowing, sardonic as usual. The face wasn't even terribly wrinkled for seventy-three—she was too thin to get wrinkled, she supposed; the mouth small, drawn down at the corners now though; the thick white bubble of hair still vigorous. Yet what happened in those . . . what? Three minutes?

45

Not enough blood to the brain, as the doctor described it. And unnoticed the small cells die, one by one, blinking off. Taking memory and desire with them. What events had disappeared that she would no longer recall? What fine discriminations necessary to ordinary life had vanished? How many did you have to lose before it showed? Pity the poor body, the poor mind, so thoughtlessly losing its precious cargo.

"Shit!" she snapped to herself. That kind of thinking was worse than, well, maybe even a stroke itself. It bled the will dry. Live in the moment. She looked out, filling her mind with the view. It was autumn. Why had fall always made her feel exhilarated? Yet it did.

They passed brown-gray lawns and others that were deep in orange fallen leaves, and soon they were driving through a small town. There were all the houses, she thought; and each was secret and mysterious, containing within dimensions of human experience that could never be put into words. Would words finally desert her too? They would, she supposed. Yet here she was, seventy-three, traveling through these towns and villages in this today.

Suddenly she laughed. All at once it seemed that the houses and trees were all artificial in some way she couldn't put her finger on; that the leaves would somehow be . . . recycled and used again. And no one would know the difference except maybe a very few; children, perhaps. Yet a great nostalgia filled her at the same time, as if the whole town had already gone beyond recall, or as if she had left it in some way she couldn't understand.

Simultaneously a sheer rush of love for the real physical world filled her. This was a real Earth, after all. And she was still in it, still rational and alive in it. She felt exultant. "These lovely Ohio towns," she said. . . .

"It's Proteus's memory of the Ohio block and its artificial foliage that just struck Lydia, in bleedthrough fashion. And it's Proteus's fresh astonishment with the natural Earth that's reviving her spirits right now," Cyprus said to Oversoul Seven. "Proteus, in the twenty-third century, is erecting his living nodule at the same time that Lydia and Lawrence hook up their small tent to the camper—in the twentieth century. Do you understand? There are points of association brought into activity—"

Seven blinked. This conversation with Cyprus had obviously been going on for some time, and he had only now become aware of it. "Of course. It's obvious," he said, desperately trying to cover up.

"But you so often overlook the details," Cyprus said. "When you help one personality, you help all the others. Unconsciously, each feels the effects. For that matter, each personality helps the other, and when you're in contact with one, you're also in communication with each of them—"

"But who helps *me?*" Seven asked petulantly. "I've been pelted around like a volleyball—"

"A most apt Earth description," Cyprus said, smiling. "But what makes you think you haven't been helped?"

"How long have we been talking like this?" Seven asked, ignoring the question.

"In whose terms?"

"In *any* terms," Seven said. "You're just dancing rings around me. And you think it's funny. Ma-ah and Lydia are in real trouble; and maybe Proteus, who knows? And I get stuck inside Ma-ah, just trapped there except for now— and only let out when somebody needs me. It's not at all fair, examination or not."

"You make your own reality," Cyprus reminded him, gently. "We all do. Each consciousness does. So, dear Seven, try to remember what you've forgotten. Or better still, just take it for granted that you really know what you're doing, and go on from there."

"Take what for granted?" Seven asked. "There you go again."

"Your ... predicament."

"Ma-ah's in a predicament. And Lydia, and Proteus. I'm not, except for this ridiculous examination."

Cyprus could no longer contain her amusement. She sighed. "Oh, Seven, you'll have to go back to Ma-ah for a while. Outside of your present context of operations, I'm sure you'll agree with me. You still don't understand."

"But I want to know what's happening to Josef," Seven objected. "And I don't want to go back inside Ma-ah. You have no idea how terribly confining that is, and I keep getting lost in her till I think I'll never get out. Couldn't we take a break? A recess? And look in on Josef?" Oversoul

Seven had adopted the fourteen-year-old image again. He found it most effective in dealing with Cyprus.

She smiled and said, "All right. But remember, this is to be a very brief vacation. Think of Josef's painting."

The landscape of the farm and grounds was on the easel. Josef was in the process of applying a series of transparent glazes to it. Bianka, the eighteen-year-old Hosentauf daughter, sat on the messed bed, watching. (As he saw her, Seven moaned.) Josef was obviously showing off, standing with strong thighs apart, leaning backward, staring at the painting with his heavy brows lowered dramatically—and very conscious of Bianka's admiring glances.

"You better get out of here," he said. "If anyone catches you in my room, I'll really be thrown out on my ear—or ass."

She blushed, stood up, and wiggled over to him, teasingly. She still hadn't retied her bodice so that, looking down, Josef saw her bare breasts. She grinned, shamelessly, he thought; flipped one breast out of the bodice at him, and ran, laughing, about the room.

"They'll hear you. Hush. Shut up—" he yelled.

"They aren't home yet and you know it. Worried?" She giggled breathlessly, her brown eyes alight with excitement.

"Well, your youngest brother is. You can't bribe him to leave us alone forever. What if he tells?"

"La la, that's your concern," she laughed. "I'll just lie about the whole thing."

"Well, so will I! So will I!" he shouted. He never knew how to handle her when she got in this kind of mood, and she knew it. "Ah, the hell with it!" he yelled, hopelessly. He grabbed her, threw her on the bed, and grinned while she ripped his clothes off. Again.

Seven was very quiet. He and Cyprus had merged with the landscape painting, peering through it, out into the room. "Well, he's certainly having a good time," Seven said finally.

"I thought that's why you liked him so much, because he *did* enjoy himself," Cyprus answered.

"Well . . . he *is*, isn't he? There's something in all of this that I don't like," Seven said doubtfully. In the meantime he and Cyprus discreetly blocked out the scene so as not to invade Josef's privacy in such a personal moment. They

48

simply stayed in the landscape, while putting a mental shield between themselves and the room.

When Seven peeked back out, the girl was gone. A disheveled Josef sat unhappily on the bed, muttering to himself. He'd lost most of the good daylight painting hours, and now he was so disgusted with himself that he didn't feel like working. And if he didn't work, he'd just feel worse. More, as he eyed the painting, he had the uneasy suspicion that something was wrong. For one thing the glazes didn't look nearly as clear and glowing as they could. There was a suggestion of murkiness creeping into the color. He went over to the easel and stood glowering at the painting.

Three days ago, the painting had looked great to him. This morning it had looked great. Now he had projected all of his dissatisfaction with himself into the landscape. Flaws he hadn't noticed earlier became readily apparent. Had he grayed his colors down too much? Had he put on the top glaze before the one beneath was dry? Or was the problem in the dry pigment itself as he mixed it with the oil?

He almost snarled. The thing was ruined. Ruined beyond repair. His great inspiration, the best in his life—and he'd messed it up. To hell with it; he'd never be a good painter. To hell with Bianka and her damned family and the three lousy meals a day they gave him. He even had to eat with the farmhands.

It was Bianka's fault for tempting him to begin with, keeping his mind from his work. In a rage he shouted and kicked the bedside chair across the room. Then, to Oversoul Seven's utter disbelief, he grabbed the landscape and sent it flying to the floor with sudden fury.

At first Seven thought that the landscape had come to life in some mysterious fashion. What he saw before him *was* a landscape, but different, a three-dimensional one that stretched all around him. He looked around, trying to get his bearings.

Cyprus and Josef were gone. He was Ma-ah again. She stood gripping Rampa's hand. Before them were acres of green trees and flowering bushes, such as they'd never seen before. The entire area was ringed by immense sheer cliffs, obviously impossible to climb. They were in a secret valley. A group of robed people stood in a circle on a small

49

grassy knoll, and Ma-ah and Rampa were being led toward them.

Seven felt himself falling headlong into Ma-ah's experience again. Yet oddly enough, descending into the body almost seemed like coming home.

Chapter Six

Josef's Second Dream

Josef felt alone, as if his soul had left him, or as if part of his soul had been in the painting that he'd just destroyed. He hadn't the heart to look at it again. One glimpse of the smeared topcoating of glaze had been enough. In portions, the paint had been gouged out right down to the bare canvas.

Memory of the painting's initial, almost blinding inspiration rose up to mock him. He hadn't lived up to it, of course. The one great inspiration of his life, and he'd ruined it in a fit of anger. Or had it been flawed beyond repair even before he destroyed it? Had he known all along that he'd never be able to paint the masterpiece that he saw so vividly in his mind?

Josef didn't like to examine his feelings. He just liked to

give in to them, or paint them. Self-examination made him nervous. Yet these thoughts kept returning as he grappled with quite unpleasant practical considerations. He had to get out of there as quickly as possible. Jonathan would give him the beating of his life, and with the painting gone, he had nothing to bargain with. He could fight Jonathan if he had to—they were about the same size—but Jonathan would be self-righteous about it, furious, and he'd just be out to protect himself.

So it had come to this! Grumbling, he gathered his gear together, the dry pigments, jars of oil and varnish, brushes, three rolled canvases. Feeling sorrier for himself each minute, he stacked the stuff by the door and looked out the window at the snowy plains and low hills. There were occasional farmhouses where he could stop. If it was only summer, he thought, when he could do sketches at town festivals, flatter the ladies in the marketplace—*then* there was no trouble finding a place to stay. But it was winter, and he'd spoiled his nest.

He flopped down on the bed, eyeing the bundle of belongings. Now he saw it all differently. He hadn't been kicked out yet. Why should he put himself out in the middle of winter? Maybe he could save himself. Maybe he could think up a good enough story. Maybe . . . Briefly the face of Avona Hosentauf came into his mind—she was particularly taken with the damned painting—her face when she saw it would be a study in rage.

But it was all too much. Josef fell into an exhausted sleep, tossing fitfully, expecting the Hosentauf force to be upon him at any moment. When he awakened it was past midnight, and the house was still. Hardly believing his good fortune, he got up quietly and opened the window. The Hosentaufs must have returned late and gone to bed, he thought. Holding his breath, grinning at his own craftiness, Josef threw his gear out the window, well into the snow. He didn't dare use the stairs—they creaked. Instead he went to the other window and cautiously dropped down the few feet to the shed roof.

It was below zero, but now the cold air was exciting and added to his sudden mood of exuberance. As he leaped to the ground, he thought of Hosentauf's impotent rage when they found him gone, the painting ruined. With good luck they'd never discover his escape until morning, giving him at least a good head start. And why should they follow him? They'd just yell and sputter instead. They knew he had no way of paying them back for his room and board, even if they did take all the trouble to track him down.

He attached his skis, threw his knapsack over his shoulders and started off. At first it was pleasant in all that quiet night snow, but he'd forgotten how heavy his gear was; and after being inside all winter, the unaccustomed cold began to annoy him, then to upset him, until finally it was all he could think about. He wasn't that good a skier, either. He felt bulkier than usual—which he was. He'd worn all his clothes—three sweaters, two pair of pants, and two sets of underwear—and now his body itched and sweated inside, while his face felt frozen to the bone. But it was worth it, he thought, trying to regain his earlier cheerfulness. The end of an era. Saved again.

They caught up with him near morning He'd stopped to rest in the early dawn, when he saw the horse-driven sleigh approaching, and heard the stupid ringing of the little bells, and felt that awful hard lump in the pit of his stomach. They'd be on him in no time. There was no place to hide, and they'd seen him already. He could tell by the vicious intent set to Jonathan's head and shoulders as he drove the sled. There was no mistaking that obstinate outline.

The Fates were after him, chasing him in the figures of Elgren and Jonathan, and the other two who sat behind —probably Elgren's brothers, Josef thought. To his own surprise he just felt transfixed, unable to move, or do anything but watch their approach. The sleigh drew ever closer. its gray outlines taking on definite shape, the red color getting brighter and brighter, more and more real. He felt as if the whole thing—sled. horses. and riders— rode from some nightmare place in his own mind, out here to pursue him On the other hand, it seemed that they'd always chased him, the pursuit would never let up, and the moment would never end.

Why did they bother? he wondered, with a mild astonishment that didn't even begin to touch his panic. Revenge? Why else? But already the stocky figure of Jonathan leapt into life, and jumped from the sled with his father right after, followed by the two others from the back seat. All at once they were at him. They had ropes which they threw about his body, pinning down his arms.

"AaaaaHhhhh," Jonathan kept shouting. "You brigand! Thief! Aaahhh—More rope. Tie him up good—"

The sight of the rope made Josef really crazy. He suddenly began kicking, yelling, biting. They threw him down and took his skis off and tossed him in the back of the sled. Elgren's brothers, both big, usually good-hearted men, were laughing now. They thought it was one big joke. Between them, all trussed-up, Josef glared. Jonathan was swearing steadily from the front seat, and his father, Elgren, kept grunting, "Yes, yes."

During the entire trip they amused themselves by pretending to consider the most gory of revenges, all the while assuring him that he needn't worry: his fate was already settled with a punishment most fitted to his crime. Josef pretended not to hear a word.

What did they really have in store for him? Josef closed his eyes and tried not to think about it. Did they know about him and Bianka? he wondered desperately. The suspense made him dizzier than the sled's motion, which unaccountably had now begun to bother him.

Finally the trip was over. Shouting triumphantly, they dragged him off the sled, up the steps, and into the kitchen where Bianka and her mother and the two smaller boys stood—pointing, giggling, in a great mood. They whisked him through, pushed him upstairs, and threw him in his room. Jonathan shoved him over to the bed.

"We've decided what to do with you, famous artist," Jonathan said. His round head bobbed. He wet his lips. His gray eyes sparkled. He put his hands on his stocky hips. "Haven't we, everybody?"

"Yes," came the shouts from outside the door where the rest of the family gathered, peeking in, from the top of the stairs.

"We are putting you in jail. It's too much trouble to take you to town and swear warrants. Good farmers like us can't take all that time. So this room is your jail—"

Nods and shouts all around. Josef squirmed underneath the ropes, and glowered.

"You're going to do us a painting, as you promised. And you don't get fed unless you do. Every day one of us will come up with some food, and if you aren't working on a painting that takes our fancy, well then you'll just get lighter and lighter and thinner and thinner."

Bianka poked her mother and laughed.

Elgren stepped to the front. "It's only fair. A bargain is a bargain. You don't leave this room, no matter how long

54

it takes, until we get a decent painting. My wife, here, wants a painting of the farmhouse, just like it was. She had her heart set on it, and that's what she's going to get."

"I can't just copy one painting over," Josef yelled. "You can never get one painting just like another—"

"You better learn how, then," Avona said, coming forward, shaking her apron in his face. "Thought you got away with it, didn't you? You never had any intention of finishing that painting, and if poor Bianka hadn't felt ill last night and couldn't sleep, she never would have been up so late and looked out to see your tracks reaching out there in the snow—"

Bianka lowered her eyes. Josef could have killed her.

"And we're boarding up the windows to make it more like a real jail," Jonathan said. "Then you'll work harder to get out of here. When you've given us a picture we like for all the good food you ate, then we'll let you go your way."

"You just can't keep me a prisoner that way," Josef managed to say. "Why, it's . . . it's immoral. I won't be able to paint, all locked up. And I need light to begin with. You can't board up the windows." At first he was just relieved—he was alive, after all. But loneliness and isolation would be unbearable, he realized. They picked the one thing most likely to drive him out of his mind.

He'd escape somehow, he told himself, as he stared up at their flushed, triumphant faces.

But that afternoon, they boarded up the windows. There was no food that entire day or night, and he couldn't paint. They left lanterns, but he just sat there in the gloomy darkness without lighting them. He couldn't sleep. Finally he just paced the room . . . angrier and angrier . . . and banged on the door in the middle of the night. He'd drive them crazy with his noise at least. But no one paid the slightest attention.

He wore himself out, slamming his body against the door, shouting, throwing furniture. Disgusted, he realized that nothing would work. "They mean what they said," he said aloud, wonderingly. He hadn't really believed them. But a bargain *was* a bargain to Elgren and Jonathan. It was as simple as that. If he showed signs of real starvation, they'd probably just send the women to relatives so that his condition didn't weaken their resolve.

Prickles of panicky sweat broke out on his face, trickling

into his moustache. He didn't even know if he could produce a decent painting now to begin with. Being forced to work would just make things worse. If he couldn't make *himself* work, how could anything else? He glowered at the boarded windows. Hosentauf really meant to lock him up for good, to starve him if necessary. He could hardly believe it, he thought again. He'd never hurt anyone in his life. To begin with, how had they taken him so seriously?

His thoughts wavered. Once he felt his teeth crunch down into an apple. With great gusto he bit into the crisp skin. It split with a popping sound. Cursing, he sat up and looked about the room which now had an ominous waiting air that made him pull the blankets up to his chin.

In the morning, Jonathan and Elgren came up together. They glanced about. "No work, no food," Jonathan said.

"The atmosphere isn't exactly inspiring," Josef yelled from the bed, but the two marched out without another word, locking the door behind them. "I'll die of starvation before I lift a brush to do a painting for you," Josef shouted. No one answered. There was no one to talk with. He drank the water they were big-hearted enough to leave in the pitcher, but he was getting dizzy from lack of food.

The next day he just lay on the bed, brooding, and watching the few shafts of light that fell through the crevices in the boarded windows. A twilight cast filled the room. He felt lethargic. He'd almost convinced himself that Bianka would certainly sneak up with some food for him, when he began to doze.

The next thing he knew, he was dreaming. Then the dream itself shuddered, split open. The air shimmered. He was staring at his double, who looked down at him, moustache bristling, eyes warm and oddly understanding. "What are you doing here?" Josef said. "You're another me? I'm dreaming again. One of me gets in enough trouble. I certainly don't need two—"

"I thought your own image would be reassuring," Oversoul Seven said.

"Reassuring! That's how little you know—" Josef shouted. He turned his head to the wall.

"All right. All right," Oversoul Seven said, hurt. He changed into the image of a wise old man. "Is this better? Turn around so you can see me," he said.

"Thank heaven. Now you're somebody I can trust," Josef

said. "Where have you been? I haven't seen you in my dreams at all lately."

"I've been very busy," Seven said. "For that matter, I probably shouldn't even be here. But I always relate to you. More and more, you remind me of myself. Except that you get in such trouble all the time; and it's always needless. You could so easily avoid it. This time you've really done it. The Hosentaufs won't let you out, either, unless you produce. You've roused their sense of virtue. They're going to teach you a lesson, even if you die of starvation—"

"Am I dreaming?"

"Yes and no. You're sleeping. I'm really here, if that's what you mean. But I'm not staying."

"You can't just go away and leave me," Josef pleaded. "I haven't had anyone to talk to for days. I'll go crazy, if I haven't already. You've got to help me."

"I gave you the idea for that painting. And what did you do? Ruin it. You must like trouble," Seven said, fading out.

"You can't go. I won't have it," Josef cried. "If you *have* to go, take me with you."

In utter astonishment at the suggestion, Seven rematerialized. He debated. "It's not sensible. It's not at all wise," he said. "You aren't even resourceful like Ma-ah or Proteus or Lydia. And I can't trust a word you say, because you change your mind all the time—"

"You'll take me?" Josef asked.

"I'll take you," Seven said, sighing. "Only because something in me always worries about you, though. But you've got to do what I say, and you probably won't remember much when you wake up. If you were awake in *your* terms, then you wouldn't have asked the question."

"What question?" Josef asked.

"Never mind. Look around the room and tell me what you see."

Josef shrugged. "A chair, easel, windows, and a funny yellow monkey—"

"The monkey isn't really there. You're hallucinating it," Seven said. "Make it go away or you'll just get all confused."

"Make it go away?" Josef asked.

"Do you have a monkey in your room ordinarily?" Seven asked, as if he were speaking to a slow learner.

"No."

"Then it shouldn't be here now. It's a dream element. Tell it to disappear or I'm going on without you."

"Go away," Josef said to the monkey, and it just disappeared. Josef stared. A sense of power made him smile brightly. "What about you?" he said. "Suppose I make you go away?"

"Then what will you do?" Seven asked.

"I see what you mean. What's next?"

"Well," Seven said. "I'm not too happy at the thought of dragging you along, but there's someone I have to look in on before I go back—Proteus. Never mind. Just follow me and don't look back at the bed. Here, we'll do it the easy way. Take my hand."

As soon as Josef did, the two of them began to rise in the air. Josef's consciousness blinked out for a moment as Seven thought it probably would. Unconscious, Josef was much more reasonable and easier to handle.

Cyprus watched Seven as he toted Josef along, but she just smiled to herself and made no attempt to contact him. His technique, she decided, was anything but unobtrusive.

Chapter Seven

The Further Descent of
Proteus and
the Rest of Josef's Dream

Proteus's small living nodule floated so gently when he went camping at home, that you simply forgot that it rested on air. Now it was only a few feet up from the ground, the collapsible steps reaching down to the rocky earth. But here the air currents pushed it every which way, and when Proteus looked out through the small transparent window-holes, earth's opaque darkness stretched out as far as he could see.

He sat on an air pillow, eating his late meal, all he allotted himself, a minimum diet of supper pills washed down by water. He'd been under the impression that on the real Earth it rained often and abundantly, providing natural water that didn't even need to be recycled. He knew it didn't rain-on-time as it did at home, but he'd been sure it rained every day or so. For that reason he hadn't carried much water with him, and now he thought of his plastoid sack, hanging open outside, from his nodule. If it rained, he'd hear it filling, and try to make sure that it didn't spill.

Sitting alone with all that dark space around made him uneasy, not afraid, he told himself—there was a difference. Actually, he missed the gentle dim illumination that passed for night in the floating city, even though his camping nodule lighted itself up automatically when the sun went down. Besides this, he was becoming worried about the nodule itself. It was drifting some, and he tried not to think what might happen if a really strong Earth wind began to blow. Could it rip the nodule to bits? It wasn't made to stand free air currents.

But what if it drifted? Unless he got tangled up in trees, what could happen? Still, it might be wise to take another look around, he thought—unhappily. The skylevator ride hadn't frightened him in the same way that going outside did now. For one thing, he trusted the skylevator, but the nodule floor wobbled when he stood up, opened the door, and went out to the tiny platform. The steps were flying out horizontally in the air, and the breeze seemed determined to pull his hair out by the roots; he still found unsteady air scary, and his eyes stung. You could fall and break a leg, he thought, holding on.

With his motion, the nodule flipped. Proteus fell off, sprawling on the ground. Desperately he sprang to his feet, trying to catch the waving steps. They eluded him, as if on purpose, he thought, until finally he jumped higher than he ever had in his life, grabbed the lowest step, and just hung on. His weight pulled the nodule down low enough so that he could climb aboard. Half-crying, out of breath, sick with relief, he went inside and drew the steps in after him, where they disappeared beneath the couch in storage position.

The wind, which actually had been a slight breeze, grew stronger. Bumpily the illuminated nodule drifted through the air, with Proteus inside, looking out, afraid that he'd run into an area of trees or shrubs that could damage the nodule beyond repair.

He'd taken to talking to the nodule in the last few hours. Now he said, "We can make it. Don't you worry." As he was chattering, his eyes fell on the small TV unit, but there would be no stations here, he told himself—for the tenth time. Still . . . He turned the set on and just sat there, staring at the glowing empty screen, until finally he fell into an uneasy sleep.

The next thing he knew, he was wide awake. The time-dial showed that he'd slept for several hours. But something had awakened him. What was it? It took him several moments before he realized that a pattern was trying to form on the TV screen. Quickly he leaned forward, but the pattern wouldn't stabilize. Instead there was static. His excitement grew, and suddenly the static turned into words.

"Turn off your illumination at once. Then leave your nodule," the voice said. The patterns jumped, but no images formed.

"What? Are you talking to me? Who are you?" Proteus shouted.

"Repeat. Proteus. Turn off your illumination. Then leave your nodule. Search parties are out looking for you. We can't take the chance of using this channel any longer. If you receive this message, follow our directions. Wait for us. We're friends. You have nothing to be worried about."

"How do you know who I am? Who are you? Where are the search parties?" But the screen turned opaque. Proteus tried the other channels, but they were dead. For a moment he thought he'd imagined the whole thing. Who was out there? What did they want? Should he do what they said? The bumpy air was rushing all around the nodule. Any second now it could crash to the ground; ruined. He'd collapse it because of *that;* to save it, he thought. Then find a hiding place and see what happened. He couldn't turn the illumination off anyhow as long as the nodule was inflated; the lighting was automatic.

He looked out again, this time searching for what he'd hoped to avoid earlier—an area of trees—only with a clearing to settle down in. It was a good hour before the nodule drifted close to any brush at all. Even then Proteus hesitated. He was under surveillance! He couldn't get over it. He'd seen no signs of anyone, and he certainly hadn't seen any Earth copters, such as a search party from home might use here.

The brush was coming closer. Quickly he grabbed his survival kit and pressed the nodule-collapse lever. Holding his breath, he came outside on the platform again, down the wobbly steps to the ground. The nodule shuddered, wrinkled, and collapsed beside him, a small white plastoid bag the size of a valise.

He yanked his belongings out of the clearing and ducked into the shrubbery. There were short stubby trees, brambles, and vines. Proteus ran as fast as he could, his head down, his camp shoes automatically shooting out their small circles of light from the toes, illuminating the ground beneath his feet. They were a present from his mother—a luxury—hardly a necessity at the camps he attended with their gently lighted grounds. But here—he paused, best not to think of his parents, he thought. Not now.

His feet hurt already. The shoes would wear out quickly on this uneven surface. But he felt excited. At least things were happening, and he was on his own. He was scared, he finally admitted, but even that was exhilarating. He felt very hunted but very free. Then a new worry bothered him. Suppose the people who contacted him were really from home and trying to trick him?

Still, Proteus thought, they'd be more apt to send out women on the search, and the voice he'd heard had been masculine. He looked up through the thicket at the black sky and thought that despite everything, he wouldn't be caught and sent home. He never felt so . . . like himself before.

Suddenly Proteus stopped, his shoe-lights illuminating the beginning of a hill, or a drop of some kind. Cautiously he inched forward, then stopped again, staring. He was on the high brim of a strange round hill. Within were dark, curious shapes, like buildings, that were situated a good thirty feet down. Actually, he was on the edge of a circular valley he saw. Quickly he found a more inclined area and began to make his way down.

There were no hills in the floating city. He wasn't used to climbing. Several times he fell. When he was halfway down, he stopped, staring through the darkness. As he did, streaks of light ribboned through the clouds—his first sight of dawn. He looked up, marveling at the way dawn happened (all by itself, not by prearranged signals, as at home). He knew all the scientific reasons, but again the phenomenon at first sight was amazing. The sky shivered. Clumps of cloud turned from gray-black to gray to . . . puffs of perfect muted colors which themselves began to change the moment they appeared.

For a moment, until he looked back down, he'd forgotten the scene below. Now in the growing light, the buildings sprang clearly upward from the litter; ruins of such an extent that Proteus stepped back involuntarily. And what ruins! There were portions of sprawling walls, high pillars such as he'd seen in some video tapes, and piles of rubble. A few tall white towers still stood, half-covered now with vines and foliage.

Delighted, forgetting everything else, Proteus ran down the hill as fast as he could go. The rocky ground hurt his feet. Brambles caught his clothes. He hardly noticed. Twice he dropped his survival kit, picked it up automatically, and ran on. What kind of people had lived there and when? The area was being worked; some machinery stood silently nearby.

Then off to the side he saw buildings, ruins in better shape than elsewhere, that looked inhabited. Rough material hung at the windows. Perhaps laborers or archeologists stayed there. Cautiously, Proteus stopped, then set out in the opposite direction, walking as quietly as he could.

It didn't take him long to come to the largest rock platform in the middle of the dig. As soon as he approached, a small dog ran suddenly out from behind a broken statue of a man. Proteus knew it was a dog though he'd only seen them in zoos, so he ran after it. The dog never barked, though it might, Proteus thought suddenly, and awaken whoever might be sleeping at the dig. Instead . . . could he be mistaken? . . . No, the dog was trying to lead him somewhere. It kept wagging its stubby tail, and running to him, then back to the statue.

Finally Proteus followed. A round hole was visible beside the statue, and the dog ran down a flight of stairs beneath. Proteus couldn't tell how deep the hole was, for the stairs turned, but already the dog had disappeared.

An open invitation? A trained dog? Did it belong to the man who'd contacted him on TV? Was it a trap? Proteus's arguments with himself were only academic, and he knew it. Already he had taken his first step down. A trapdoor within the Earth, on the other side of the surface—he'd never really expected to see any such thing. After traveling down in the skylevator *to* the ground, what an opportunity now to descend ever further, inside it!

But where had the dog gone? When Proteus went down perhaps ten of the stone steps, a noise attracted his attention just as the light suddenly changed. Whipping around,

63

he was just in time to see the hole close above him, and a round arc of blackness shut out the morning sky. It was only then that he realized that the steps were dimly lighted. Simultaneously he wondered if the statue above had changed position and stood now solidly atop the hole.

Again his excitement conquered his fear—almost. Only now and then his scalp prickled and the blood pounded alarmingly loud in his ears. For one thing, he'd never smelled such odors before, a mixture of minerals and moisture and thickly packed dirt, long untouched—a musty yet evocative pungency that kept reminding him that he was actually on the other side of the Earth's surface.

The passageway turned. Again Proteus wondered where the dog was. Insects dashed out of the dimness into the circle of light cast by his camping shoes. Proteus recoiled, but they scurried away. Here and there large stones littered the steps, holes in the rocky wall showing where they had fallen; and often the walls were slimy with moisture.

Finally the steps ended after another turn. There, silently, sat the dog, tail wagging, eyes friendly. Was it mute? Proteus wondered. To the right was a door. It opened easily. Proteus found himself in a large room without windows dimly lighted from the ceiling. The entire area was filled with long tables loaded with tools, stone busts, and piles of debris.

It *was* an archeological site, then. Proteus hadn't realized that such work was carried on this far underground. Maybe they'd let him stay and learn while he worked? But then another idea came to him. The dog had crossed the floor and was waiting for him at another door at the far end of the room. It was all too pat, Proteus thought. Suppose there was a reward out for him, and the archeologists were going to turn him over to his parents or a search party?

He couldn't even imagine seeing his mother, but the thought of seeing his father surprised him. He felt a pang of loneliness, an unexpected rush of tenderness that he instantly tried to hide from himself. He adapted a jaunty stance and opened the door. The dog ran into the small room on the other side, and he followed. A creaky funny old elevator! Instantly the door closed, the tiny room moved downward, with bumps and squeaks as if it hadn't been used for centuries. It stopped. The dog began to bark impatiently, as if it had just been given voice. The door opened and the dog ran straight out into the arms of a man who stood not three feet away.

"Good job, Winter," the man said, picking the dog up. The man had brown hair, thick brown brows, a humped nose, and wore loose flowing overalls and a long-sleeved shirt or blouse. But it was his manner that caught Proteus's attention at once. He'd never met a man with such presence, with such an easy yet assured air of friendly command.

"My name is Window," the man said. "And you're Proteus. You've caused us quite a bit of concern, though you didn't know it, of course. You could have ruined everything."

"*I* could have? Ruined what? You're an archeologist, aren't you? Are you the man who sent me the message? Are there really search parties out for me?" Proteus had so many questions that he didn't know where to start. At the same time he noted the long stone tables at one end of the bare room, the clay tablets lined up on raised wooden platforms, and the murals, in various stages of completion. that lined the walls. "A man named Window. I never knew of anyone with a name like that," he said. "And isn't Winter a funny name for a dog?"

"We have names that have meaning to us. I'm Window because I can see through things sometimes," the man said. "And we found the dog in the wintertime. You're in the Dig of the Tellers, but there'll be plenty of time to explain. Right now you're a danger to all of us, drawing search parties in this direction. Usually the Floaters leave us alone."

"The Floaters?" Proteus said.

"Your people." Window said, with a sardonic grunt. "Now come along with me. I hope you like what you see, because you're going to be around here for some time."

Proteus looked around uneasily now. "You mean, I'm a prisoner?" he asked.

Window shrugged and smiled. "Definitions are funny things. I wouldn't define your position here as that of a prisoner, no. But for your own good as well as ours, I believe that you'll voluntarily agree to limit your experience to the Dig of the Tellers for a while."

Oversoul Seven and Josef had watched Proteus ever since he awakened from sleep and heard the Teller's voice on the television set. Now they stood, invisible, in one corner of the room. Josef said, enraged. "What's going on? What are they going to do with that boy? Why don't you do something? You *can*, can't you? If you didn't help him when he fell out of his strange bubble, I don't suppose you'll do anything now, though." He paused and shivered. "And that foul tunnel or whatever it was—"

"Can't you be quiet?" Oversoul Seven said. "You've done nothing but yell since we started. I knew I shouldn't have taken you along."

"Yell? Being dragged through the air by the hair of my head almost! I've never had a dream in my life like this before. I suppose it's because I'm half-starved—"

"In a way it is," Seven said. "It clears the mind."

"Clears the mind? You call this clearing the mind?" Josef yelled. "Who's that? That soldier or whoever it is?"

Seven looked to where Josef was pointing. "He's just another hallucination of yours. Why do you keep doing that? I told you: if he disappears, you'll know he's not real—at least not to anyone else. If he stays put, then he's a part of physical reality or mass hallucination. Can't you keep that straight?"

While they were talking, Proteus and Window left the room. "They're going," Josef said. "Aren't you going to follow them?"

"Proteus never even knows when I'm around," Seven said. "But I can't stay here any longer. I think he'll be all right. I'm sure he will. He's so resourceful—"

"What's wrong with that?" Josef said. "It didn't sound like a compliment."

"You're not supposed to question *me* like that," Seven said. "Don't try to switch roles with me. Come on, I'm taking you back."

"But that boy!" Josef said. "At the mercy of God knows what—"

"That's your trouble. You always exaggerate," Seven said. He sighed, touched Josef on the arm, and thought of Josef's bedroom. This time Josef only felt a flash of air, a whoosh of sound, and then a strange scrambled-up sensation. The next thing he knew he was lying above the bed, looking down at his own body or all he could see of it, bundled in a hump beneath the blankets.

"Is that me?" he said. "I've been out all over everywhere without my body?" The realization terrified him. He froze.

"Turn around," Oversoul Seven said. "Your head's at your feet. You've got to line up with your body."

"I can't. I don't know how to. Suppose I don't get back in?"

"Getting back in is easiest of all," Seven said. "You just have to want to. And I suggest that you give some thought to solving some of your other problems. In fact, what you've seen tonight should help you considerably. But this time it's up to you. I've given you the ingredients for something, but you have to use them. Now get back inside your body. Just drop in—"

"Drop in?" Josef asked.

Seven sighed and gave Josef a slight nudge that lined him up with his physical body. "Go *ahead*."

Josef stared at him distrustfully, but he dutifully tried to do what Seven suggested. A funny falling sensation rushed through him. In panic his eyes flew open. He was in bed. The room was perfectly normal, except for a toy-man soldier who stood in the corner.

"You forgot to dismiss your hallucination," Seven called helpfully. He himself disappeared.

"Go away," Josef yelled, and the soldier vanished before his eyes. He sat up, shaking and sweating, and lit the lantern. What a nightmare, he thought. Tomorrow he was going to start a painting for the Hosentaufs, no matter what it was. The lack of food was driving him out of his mind.

Suddenly he jumped to his feet, fully alert. Scenes from his "dream" rushed into consciousness. He saw those old ruins rising up from the gray dawn. What an idea for a painting, he thought. Already the experience with Seven was disappearing, first into a dream, then into the memory of a dream, then into the feeling that he'd had a dream that he'd forgotten. Only a clear image of the ruins remained. Josef lit another lantern and began a quick preliminary sketch of the circular hill and ruins at the Dig of the Tellers. As the charcoal lines outlined the scene, he had the weirdest feeling that the place was somehow familiar, as if he'd been there once and forgotten.

Chapter Eight

Proteus in the Dig of the Tellers and Story's Tale

Window stood watching the sky as the dusk settled down, filling the wide earthen cup that held the ruins. His head was thrust upward, his long humped nose pointing at the suspiciously empty air above. The search party had not returned as they said they would. For hours he'd waited for their copter's shocking emergence in the usually silent sky. Floaters were leary of Earth night. It was odd that he hadn't heard from them earlier. Window thought back: they had no reason to doubt his word when he told them he hadn't seen the boy, and promised to contact them if he did.

He opened his inner senses as fully as possible, but he could perceive no strangers in the immediate area, on the Earth surface, beneath it, or above. No alien thoughts nibbled at the far reaches of his mind; no unfamiliar shapes rose out of the darkness of his inner concentration. He smiled to himself—either Window wasn't open, or the area was safe for the night. Still, he didn't like it. He sat down, fingering a piece of broken pottery. A picture of the woman who made it so many centuries ago flashed into his mind. It was of early twentieth-century origin, fashioned apparently for show rather than use. Irritably Window dismissed the images, not wanting to be distracted. No skylevator had descended or risen that day, so his scouts told him. Then where was the search party?

All they needed was a lost search party, he thought, wearily. That would bring more Floaters down to investigate. Such a situation could be more of a calamity than any they'd ever faced. He looked up. The sky was darkening. Window became aware of a familiar inner sense of motion . . . activity approaching . . . still some distance away. He closed his eyes. The inner darkness vibrated, trembled, broke, and a miniature image in full color formed—the searchers' copter.

Mentally Window enlarged the picture, then his consciousness entered it. There were the same three women he'd spoken to yesterday. He picked up their thoughts and conversation at once, so he really couldn't differentiate between what was said or only mentally decided upon. He grinned: they weren't going to return, that much was clear. With typical Floaters' arrogance, they didn't think that he and his men could possibly find the boy if they hadn't.

He laughed suddenly, discovering deeper reasons beneath their consciousness. They'd stayed on Earth later than they'd planned in a last attempt to find Proteus, and they felt uneasy about landing at the dig at night with men around who weren't under their thumb. Besides, they were convinced that the skylevator simply malfunctioned the day Proteus disappeared, releasing itself and leaving evidence of the unauthorized trip on its log—a coincidence that led them to a futile Earth search.

Again their prejudice came into play: they should have known that a boy wouldn't be daring enough to attempt such a journey. Now they were convinced that he was hiding someplace in the floating city, where they should have concentrated their efforts all along.

It was odd, Window thought, but their prejudice against men did annoy him, even though he understood its roots.

But prejudice itself, the sensed feel of it, had a bitter shape to the inner senses. It felt like a prickly bush, whose needles jabbed against his own soft acquiescence to all forms of life. Enough. There was no need to wait the actual appearance of the copter in the sky. It would not stop. They'd already notified the floating city hours ago, and a skylevator would be picking up the search party, copter and all.

He kicked at some debris, went inside one of the small shacks ostensibly used for the dig, pressed a portion of the woodwork, and crossed to the center of the floor. At once a trapdoor opened. He went down the few stairs to the elevator which dropped him quickly and directly to the inner dig, where Proteus would be waiting.

Proteus heard him coming and leapt to his feet. He was full of questions.

"Well," Window said. "Your search party is leaving. They've decided that you're not on Earth because a boy couldn't be bold enough to pull such a stunt alone; and being men, we couldn't find you if they didn't." Window smiled dryly. "They're wrong on several points. We have men and women here, and the ruins above—the dig—is just camouflage. We live beneath, as you know, obviously."

"How many of you are there?" Proteus asked. "How do you get away with it?" He was refreshed after a good night's sleep. All he could think of now was the fact that people were actually living beneath the Earth, unknown to the people above it.

"I can't tell you everything at once," Window said, smiling. "We're supposed to be part of a minor archeological society, with our own funds. We report to our own mother group, in the floating city. Archeology is considered a harmless male activity, no longer taken seriously since the main population left Earth. So no one bothers us."

"I guess I don't understand," Proteus said. "Do men rule things here?"

Window shook his head. "Each sex has tried to rule the other, throughout history. In a way, the results were more disastrous when men had the upper hand. They became so alienated from themselves as simple individuals that they could only relate through sex-directed activities. But the women are doing a poor job, too, as you should know, with your background. They tried to retaliate and turn the tables until they took on many of the unfavorable traits

70

they thought were male. I'll explain more about it later, but I can honestly say that we relate here as individuals. Each person is respected for his or her uniqueness. Even names have individual meanings, and aren't sexually based."

"But how many of there are you?" Proteus asked again. "When will you show me around? Why are you called Tellers?"

"As for our name, it's like this," Window said. "In ages past, archeologists used the term *tell* to refer to the artificial mounds that cover the remains of past ruins. Finally they called themselves Tellers." He shrugged and smiled. "As for some of your other questions, I'm afraid the answers will have to wait for a while. Maybe before too long, you'll learn the rest."

"Maybe?" Proteus said.

"Maybe," Window repeated. "Many of our ways will be directly counter to those you've been brought up with. We have to decide just how much you can assimilate and accept. We may have to keep you on the outer edges, so to speak. I hope not—"

"But what could be so strange to me?" Proteus asked. He was tired of sitting around; he wanted to explore the place. "I think you're hedging," he said, looking away.

"You do, huh?" Window said. "I am, in a way. But there's someone I want you to meet—" He pressed a button, and a doorway slid open.

Proteus was already gearing himself. Something in Window's tone told him that some type of a test was involved. If he failed it, what could they do? What would it mean? Before he had time to think any more about it, a girl entered. She was a little older than he, slender, dressed like Window in flowing overalls and overblouse.

"This is Story," Window said.

As she came forward, smiling, suddenly her eyes darkened. She took a step backward, shivered slightly, and turned to Window as if for support.

"What is it?" Window asked.

"I don't know yet." Her voice was so soft that Proteus had to strain to listen. She said, "I just feel . . . that he's a bigger threat than we realized, but in an entirely different way than we thought. I don't know why. The story's only just beginning to come—"

"Could you be wrong?" Window asked.

71

"Of course," she said, irritably. "All of my stories have to be deciphered. Maybe I'm reading it wrong. Some are true now. but not later. Or later, but not now—"

"What are you staring at me like that for? And what are you talking about?" Proteus asked, hurt. "We've just met. What do you mean, about stories?" He frowned at Window unhappily, and wouldn't look at the girl's face.

"She's called Story because often stories come to her that are true. They've actually happened or will happen."

"But that's just superstition," Proteus said. "I don't want to hurt your feelings, but—"

"You don't, huh?" Window interrupted, smiling.

"Well. if he doesn't understand anything at all, then what's the point?" Story cried, exasperated.

"Never mind, tell your story," Window said. "I'm sure that Proteus will be polite enough to listen anyway."

Proteus shrugged airily, half-intimidated. half-curious. He tried to ignore the goosepimples that thickened up on the insides of his arms. After all, he thought, what could the girl possibly say? Why did he feel that she could ruin everything?

"I can only tell the story as it comes to me," she said. "I just trust it, whether or not it seems to make sense right away. So don't be angry if it sounds strange—"

"I'm not angry," Proteus said, too loud. He blushed.

She kept her eyes open, but looked way over to one side. "Well. first I see an old man and woman. She's . . . giddy and maybe ready to die. Or maybe he is. They're in some kind of vehicle that was used on Earth centuries ago. . . . Something is about to happen. Or maybe it just *has*. She seems to be talking to some man who's dead and his body is nearby. The two of them are connected with Proteus."

Proteus stared at her, transfixed yet scandalized. What nonsense. he thought, wondering how Window could take Story so seriously.

"Then there's another man," she said. "Older than Proteus, but still young. He's imprisoned in a room all alone. And there's a painting of an ancient farmhouse, with trees all around."

Proteus started and leaned forward. He'd dreamed of such a painting or one like it. The trees had fired his imagination and made him even more determined to go to the Earth's surface.

"What is it, Proteus?" Window asked.

"Nothing," Proteus lowered his eyes uneasily. He wasn't lying, he told himself. It was just coincidence.

Story's eyes never changed direction. She kept staring over to the right without turning her head until Proteus was tempted to turn himself, to see what she was looking at.

"Anyhow, I don't like this particular man too much," she said, "the one locked in the room. He's terribly self-indulgent. And I see a young black woman too. She's connected with us, with the Tellers, in some odd fashion. And—" Story broke off for a moment, her face so grave that Proteus didn't interrupt as he wanted to. Despite himself, he felt frightened . . . or anticipatory. He couldn't tell which.

"She has something to do with archeology too," Story went on. "Or with ruins or a god or spirit of some kind. I see her standing by pyramids. But the threat to us comes through her!" Story looked at Window now, almost appealingly. "That's all I have so far," she said. "Does any of it make sense to you, Proteus?"

He shook his head. "To me least of all. I think that it's, well, just a story. If you want to believe that stuff, that's up to you, but it made no sense at all to me. If it did, I'd tell you."

"If you get anything more, Story, make sure you tell me," Window said. "And Proteus too."

"But if Proteus doesn't understand, and I don't know that he ever will—"

"Wait, now," Window said. "Proteus, listen to me for a moment. When the women took over, they tried to emphasize physical agility, strength, boldness, logic—all the qualities that men insisted were prerogatives of the male in the past. They minimized some other excellent characteristics, because they erroneously considered them beneath their new status, and a threat to it. They tried to ignore the intuitive understanding with which they were basically gifted, for example. So there are many quite normal human abilities that you're probably prejudiced against, because of your background—"

"But I'm very open-minded," Proteus objected.

"What about seeing into the future or into the past? Or reading minds? Just before the massive takeover by the women, scientists were realizing that such things were quite possible. The world was at a point of new discovery—"

"But all that represents the superstitions that the women were able to wipe out," Proteus said. "Granted, they've made a lot of errors, and I was anything but happy as a Floater, as you call it, but the women *are* logical. I'm open-minded about . . . well, real things."

"He's going to be quite impossible," Story said, coldly, to Window. She tried not to sound angry, but she felt quite upset and personally insulted. "No one ever doubted my stories before," she said. "What they mean isn't always apparent at once, but everyone always took it for granted that a meaning was there. The stories *do* stand for something real. My name's Story because my stories began when I was a child. We pick our names when we're seven, with our parents' help, and confirm them at fourteen. So you're saying that my name doesn't mean anything. You're trying to deny my whole existence—"

Her outburst so surprised Proteus that he didn't know what to say. Hopefully he looked to Window, who unaccountably looked the other way, so Proteus was forced to come to his own defense.

"That's not what I meant," he said. "I'm not saying that your name is wrong, or you're wrong. Well, the story you told didn't make sense to me, but it was a story of sorts. So you *do* tell stories, and your name is right. I just don't think that the story really had anything to do with me." In utter confusion, with his face reddening, he said, "That's all I can say."

"And not one thing made sense to you?" she asked, persistent.

Proteus shook his head. Then he said, "One small thing sounded familiar, but that was just coincidence or something. You mentioned a painting that sounded like one I've dreamed of several times; not that I remember many of my dreams, because I don't. That one stuck in my mind because it made me want to come to the Earth's surface even more than I did already."

Proteus hadn't realized that Story had been so tense, with her shoulders all raised up until he finished speaking and she suddenly smiled. Her shoulders relaxed, and a flush of warmth transformed her face.

"But that isn't anything," he said quickly. He turned to Window, but Window was smiling at Story.

"Why should such a small thing make you feel better?"

Proteus asked, genuinely surprised. "Nothing else made any sense to me at all."

Window said, "The dream may have had something to do with your coming here—"

"But I already intended to."

Window turned and placed his hands on Story's shoulders. "You should have learned something from this," he said. "You have to trust your own abilities, and not doubt them because someone else does. If we do carry out our present plans, you'll have to hold your own sense of integrity in the face of skepticism just like Proteus's."

Then, turning to Proteus, Window said, "You'll be good for her. She isn't used to anyone doubting her word. You'll end up teaching each other." To Story he added, soberly, "If you get more on the implied threat, let me know." Then, gently, "Distortion could account for it; you could unconsciously consider Proteus a threat to begin with, particularly if you doubt your own abilities in any way. I'll see what I can get, too, though, using my own methods."

"What do you mean?" Proteus asked, shocked. "You don't do the same thing?"

"Window *sees*," Story said.

"Sees what? I *see*," Proteus said to her.

"Enough for now," Window said. "Proteus, we've given you and ourselves enough to think of for one day."

"But, if you really think I'm a threat to you in some way, how come you're taking me in?"

"Threats are often challenges," Window said simply.

Proteus tried to stall for time. He could tell that the interview would be ended in a minute. Had the meeting with Story involved some kind of test? And had he failed it? Should he have pretended to go along with what she said? "Are you going to show me around?" he asked, uneasily. "Now I feel as if you won't, or as if you've put me on probation. And you still didn't tell me how many people are here—"

Window stood stood up. "I think we'll show you the dig by stages, Proteus. We'll begin in the morning. And I'll find something meaningful for you to do while you're here, but some of your questions will have to wait."

Proteus nodded, but he felt very alone and increasingly dissatisfied. A girl named Story whose stories were supposed to be true, though they sounded like nonsense; and a man called Window who could see! See what? And they were only going to show him what they wanted him to know. Already he decided that one way or another, sixteen years old or not, he was going to discover whatever it was they were hiding.

Chapter Nine

Cyprus and Oversoul Seven
Beginning Part Three
of the Examination

Oversoul Seven was the fourteen-year-old male again, and Cyprus was talking to him. "You seem to have been neglecting Lydia," she commented.

Oversoul Seven concentrated as hard as he could, bringing his consciousness entirely into focus. They were in Lydia's study. Autumn leaves fell past the windows so fast that Seven blinked. Then, enlarging his visual he saw that the room was a flurry of activity. Three men were banging drawers open, and throwing their contents on the blue rug. "You could have picked a quieter place," Seven said. "What's going on here? And is this another of those conversations that have been going on without my conscious knowledge? They always confuse me."

"Lydia's family has sold the house," Cyprus said. "She

deeded it to them, so that they could do what they wanted with their inheritance without waiting for her to die—"

"Couldn't you put that more delicately?" Seven asked, grumpily.

"That's how Lydia put it, as you'd know if you'd been keeping good track of her," Cyprus said.

"But I have," Seven protested. "She had another stroke. It practically catapulted me out of Ma-ah, and I helped her, Lydia, that is; in fact, until then I couldn't get out of Ma-ah." Seven said, suddenly remembering, "You told me to identify with Ma-ah as completely as I could, and I agreed. But I didn't realize how completely I *could* identify with her, or I might not have agreed so readily." He shivered. "All that body around all the time," he said.

"*They* have their bodies around them all of the time," Cyprus pointed out. She kept changing almost imperceptibly from a beautiful woman of indeterminate age to a handsome man of indeterminate age. Every once in a while there was a moment when the two images merged, blended, achieved oneness and stability.

"You seem to be having some trouble with your own physical form," Seven said. "If that was me, acting like that, you'd give me three demerits."

"I know more of myself than you do of yourself," she said. "So it's much more difficult, in fact, almost impossible, to create a physical image to express my known reality. But I've told you that before."

"You certainly have good answers," Seven said. The two of them were sitting nicely on the couch. Suddenly Seven sprang up: "Look at that," he shouted. "That lughead just dumped the entire contents of Lydia's shell collection on the floor! That's no way to do," he yelled at the mover. And in a flash the shells flew back into the drawer.

"Seven, stop that," Cyprus said urgently.

The mover turned around, and stared at the drawer. "I could have sworn that I dumped all that stuff out," he said, turning toward the other mover.

"Put it back," Cyprus ordered. "Now."

The shells went from the drawer, singly, to the floor while the mover's back was turned. When he looked back, the drawer was empty. "Why, I did," he yelled. "I mean . . . I could swear—"

"That's how rumors get started about places being haunted," Cyprus said.

"Well, they're Lydia's favorite shells," Seven muttered. "I don't like meeting here like this anyhow. Can't we go someplace else?"

"All right. Think of a cloud," Cyprus said. She and Seven left immediately. At the last moment, Seven dematerialized one perfectly shaped shell to save for Lydia. He and Cyprus emerged on a cloud just within the borders of Earth's atmosphere.

"I want to give you a quick review before I tell you about the next part of your examination," Cyprus said. "First of all, though, what did you learn so far?"

"Well," Seven said, frowning. "I have trouble staying with Ma-ah exclusively. At first I couldn't get away from her. Now I get called willy-nilly from one personality to the other as they get into trouble, and it seems like something comes up constantly for me to deal with. Then, I lose my sense of perspective—"

He went on. "Proteus still doesn't believe in anything but the good old days. Lydia doesn't recognize me, and I've always liked her," he said petulantly. "Josef knows me, more or less, but he just gets in needless trouble. Ma-ah, well, I like her much better now. But I have the feeling that you're holding out on me again."

"I'm holding out on you?" Cyprus said, smiling. "How about that shell?"

Seven just shimmered around the edges. "Oh, *that*," he said. "Well, I peeked into Lydia's future and there's one place where she could really use it; I mean, where the shell could help her."

"That's what I thought." Cyprus sighed. "Now what's illogical about that statement?"

"But there's a difference between ideal circumstances and practical action," Seven exploded.

Cyprus looked as stern as Seven had ever seen her. He said, "All right. I know I'm supposed to experience time as they do, day by day, and I have. I've only snitched a few glimpses into the future—"

"Into what?" Cyprus said.

"Into . . . uh, the *probable* future," Seven amended quickly.

"Your personalities have free will just as you do," Cyprus said. "You must never forget that. You looked into one of the probable futures as they exist for Lydia; and at

79

any point she can alter circumstances and choose one probable future over another. Do you understand?"

Seven nodded, properly chastised.

"Now let me expain this more clearly," Cyprus said. "You're Proteus, Lydia, Ma-ah and Josef in all of their probable presents, pasts and futures; and yet they are themselves, and also more than the selves they know themselves to be. And you, of course, are more than the Oversoul Seven you presently identify with. As you help them and instruct them when you can, others who *you* may not recognize help and instruct you—"

"And I'm a part of them?" Oversoul Seven asked.

"Precisely," Cyprus said. "But here let me show you how it works, using images as a method of instruction." And before Seven's eyes, a wide endless flat surface stretched as far as he could see in all directions. Looking down, he saw all the centuries man had known and was knowing and would know laid out like countries all at once. He couldn't see everything though, simply because there seemed to be no end to the glittering surface.

Cyprus said, "Now watch as closely as you can."

"I *am* watching closely," Oversoul Seven said emphatically.

This time, the endless flat surface became the top part of an infinite circle, so that while the scene itself filled up all space, Seven could only see a portion of the circle itself. And from each century, other spirals constantly arose.

"I'm getting dizzy," Seven complained.

"Seven, pay attention to your lesson," Cyprus demanded. "Now all of that is just one Moment-Point; one 'point' wherein creativity knows itself. So in Earth terms, probable presents are born in each 'moment.' The one that is physically materialized is the only one that your personalities accept as real. But you'll learn how to keep track of all of them." She paused and added, "theoretically."

"But in all of that, how can I know myself?" Seven asked—reasonably enough, he thought.

"You *do* know yourself though, don't you? You certainly know enough to ask questions," Cyprus said. "Your knowledge of yourself is self-evident." (So is your lack of it, she thought, smiling figuratively.)

"I got that!" Seven shouted.

"Oh well, you *are* improving then," Cyprus said.

"You wanted me to get it. You were testing me all

along," Seven said, suddenly understanding. "It takes the edge off my triumph."

"You may not know all of yourself, but that's a process of self-discovery, of becoming," Cyprus said. "The more you discover of yourself, the more you are—"

"I can hardly handle the parts of me I know already," Seven said sadly. "But can't you show me more of the images?"

"You just aren't ready, Seven," Cyprus said. "And you have to learn through direct experience. There really isn't any other way. Now, for the next part of your examination—"

A jet passed by. Cyprus and Seven dropped down on top of it and rode along, occasionally looking down at the Earth. "You have to get through to Proteus and Lydia," Cyprus said, without pausing. "And you have to get all of your personalities together in some way, so they can better benefit from each other's separate experiences."

"How on Earth am I going to do that?" Seven asked.

"How *can* you do it, on Earth?" she asked, smiling. Then she added, "But Seven, you must become more involved in the activities of your personalities. But then, I know that you will."

"I don't like the way you said that," Seven answered, worried. "And there's one thing I want to know. How long has this conversation between us been going on? Before I came in on it, I mean?"

She just looked at him. For a brief instant the handsome man of indeterminate age and the beautiful woman of indeterminate age materialized again and merged, stabilized, focused until it was so vivid and brilliant that Seven could hardly bear it.

"Don't you know? Don't you know?" The musical voice seemed to come from everywhere, from inside Oversoul Seven, and outside him, from the clouds and the jet. The words seemed to echo through time as he knew it and didn't know it, until he felt that Lydia and Proteus and Josef and Ma-ah were all singing, and asking the question all at once.

The phenomenon vanished so quickly and completely that Seven almost lost the balance of his consciousness. "What was that?" he gasped. "What happened?"

"Every once in a while you ask a really important question," Cyprus said. "Or rather, the question that you ac-

81

tually ask has a really important one hidden inside of it. Then you get an answer."

"But now I've forgotten what the question was, much less what was hidden inside it," Seven cried. "And I don't know what the answer meant."

"Dear Seven," Cyprus said, with some compassion, "you *do* understand. A part of you does. But before you go back, I want to give you one hint. You make your own reality, and your personalities make their own realities too."

"But I know that," Seven said, disappointed. "I thought you were going to give me a big hint—"

"I have," she said. "And I suggest that you begin with Lydia this time. Remember: you make your own reality."

Seven mused about it: you make your own reality . . . and instantly he lost track of the constant conversation. As Cyprus knew he would.

Chapter Ten

Lydia and Lawrence:
A Trip Is Interrupted

"How's Mr. George?" Lawrence yelled. "Okay," Lydia called. Usually she kept Mr. George, the goldfish, in a bowl on the trailer bookcase, propped up with books so that the bowl wouldn't fall off. Every once in a while she went to check on him to see that the water didn't slosh out with the bumps in the road. Now she was driving. Lawrence was reading in back, and Mr. George was in the front seat beside her. Greenacre, the Angora cat, lay curled around the bowl.

Lydia drove on at a good pace, chain-smoking, listening to the radio, and occasionally talking at Mr. George or Greenacre. She had sunglasses on, and a visor set on her cropped white hair, and she was wearing a leather peace sign suspended on a strap around her neck—a gift from

Lawrence. She felt jaunty, wearing it. When any black people went by in a car, or young people with their flowing hair, she grinned and made the peace sign.

Still, blacks resented liberals these days, she thought, "do-gooders." So maybe she should stop the practice, as far as they were concerned. After all, if *they* didn't like it, what was the point? A car passed by, with a black couple in front. Lydia gave the peace sign. The man smiled and returned the gesture. Lovely man, Lydia thought. Now I can go on doing it.

"Aren't you ever going to quit reading?" she called back to Lawrence. No response. Well, he probably dozed off, she thought, let him sleep. "Wouldn't you say, Greenacre?" No response there either, not even the flicker of an ear. She changed the radio station.

A half-hour went by. An Indiana dusk was beginning to fall. She wondered if they'd make it to the University of Iowa in time for her lecture and poetry reading. "We should stop for supper soon," she called, keeping her eyes on the road. Then, "Greenacre, go wake Lawrence and tell him it's almost time to eat." Greenacre opened one eye. "Lawrence," she called again. She switched off the radio. There were no sounds from the rear—no snoring or heavy breathing (or gasps, in case he'd had a heart attack). Silly, of course he hadn't. He was years younger than she; doctor or no, his heart would last for years.

"Lawrence!" Be calm, she told herself. "Shall we put up at the next road park? Supper isn't exactly gourmet food —hotdogs, rolls, salad—" Even as she went on speaking normally, she was pulling up at the side of the road. It was a four-lane highway, but traffic was light.

The trailer seemed filled to the ceiling with silence, stuffed with it like cotton. She felt as if it was packed in her mouth. "Get up, Lawrence. It's time for supper," she said. Her words sounded all woolly. She went back to him, her face rigidly smiling and found him just sitting there, eyes open, mouth open; quite dead. In her mind she heard him say, "How's Mr. George?" How long ago was that? He must have . . . right after that, while she was giving the peace sign and calling back to him.

She looked at him intently and tried to take his pulse. There was none. She breathed into his mouth as hard as she could trying to fill him with air, so much that he'd float

84

up to life like a balloon, but it was like trying to fill up a tire with a hole in it, or— She broke off.

"We were positive I'd go first," she said. "Because of my age. And you'd have to be the one to decide what to do when my mind went. . . ." She tried to keep a conversational tone, not to panic. For one thing, they'd promised each other not to cry.

A few cars passed. She felt as if Lawrence was still alive, but obviously not in that body. How had it let him escape? She eyed it, accusingly, became angry at it. A chuckle started up in her throat and she caught herself. A sign of panic, she thought, to be avoided at all costs. Lawrence was dead and his body was dead. She didn't believe in an afterlife.

She paused, staring at Lawrence's body, trying to be very matter of fact. She must be detached to avoid panic, to protect her own sanity, and be as normal as possible. What would she do if everything was all right? The answer came. She got milk, bread, and jam from the midget refrigerator, sat down across from Lawrence's body and began to eat, careful not to spill any crumbs upon the floor. Careful about everything. He was sitting upright. People passing by in their cars saw an elderly man and woman facing each other in a camper-trailer, with a lamp warmly shining behind yellow transparent window curtains.

Finishing her milk and jelly sandwich, Lydia put the stuff away and fed the cats.

Plans, she thought. If her mind was failing her, and she was sure it was, then she had to be crafty; and careful. They'd promised each other no funerals and no flowers, no calling of relatives until everything was over; none of the rituals or nauseating rites reserved for the dying, dead, and aged.

"Lydia."

She sprang around, certain that someone had called her name. Involuntarily she said, "Lawrence?"

"Am I dead?" he asked. But where were the words coming from, inside her head or outside?

"Of course you are, don't be cruel. You know my mind does funny things sometimes," she said. "I'm not hearing a thing. I'm making it all up."

"Your mind can't make me up. I'm over here," Lawrence said.

"Lawrence, I don't believe in spirits—"

"But neither do I," he said. "Is my heart beating?"

"No!" she shouted. "You don't have any pulse at all. Now stop it. Where is your voice coming from?"

"Why, from me, I suppose. I'm over by the couch. At least I think I am. I had a heart attack—"

"I know you did," she cried, exasperated. "Now be quiet and let me think." Silence. She had to return to normalcy, wait until this period of . . . irrationality passed. The open eyes of Lawrence's body gave her the shivers but she couldn't bring herself to close them, so she put a book in his lap and started to clean out the refrigerator. They'd been on the road just long enough to collect unused leftovers. But she got confused and started to throw away good food. Once, unaccountably, she forgot how to open the crisper door underneath, and had to stop to remember.

"Lydia, why the hell are you cleaning out the refrigerator at a time like this?" Lawrence asked.

"Now stop it," she shouted, thoroughly distracted.

"You aren't crazy. I'm here," he announced forcibly. "You don't believe in spirits generally, but you believe in me, and *I'm* here; it's got something to do with that, why you can hear me."

"But Lawrence, the dead don't talk, so I must be mad."

"What would you rather believe?" he asked; and suddenly she didn't care if she was crazy or not, or what was happening. For all she knew, maybe she was just having a nightmare. "All *right*," she said, aloud. "What's next on the agenda?" The sweetness of madness, she thought, the freedom. She'd just go along. What else could she do? Lawrence was there; somehow he was going to help her figure out what to do with his body. She just couldn't cart it around forever. It would be a terrible nuisance.

He wanted her to just leave it somewhere, where it was peaceful and quiet and could just rot away by itself. She started the trailer up again, after putting Mr. George back on the bookcase. She *felt*, anyway, that Lawrence was beside her on the seat.

"The readers never got a chance to know you at all," she said suddenly.

"What readers? What are you talking about?" Lawrence said.

"I don't know. It just slipped into my mind," she said. "But what are we going to do now?"

"Just leave my body somewhere. There's no law against

86

it that I know. Maybe local health laws. But after all, what could they do to you?"

"Well, it's more or less what we planned in case one of us died. At least you didn't change your ideas," she said. "If you're here, and I can't see you," she added, nervously.

"Well, I must be dead, I mean, really dead, and too stupid to know it," he answered. "If I was really dead, though, how could I be talking? You know—'ashes to ashes and dust to dust'—"

"Don't joke about something like that," she snapped. "Honestly."

"I'm just staying around to help," he said.

"A big help you are," Oversoul Seven said. He'd been around for the entire episode, but Lydia, as usual, wasn't aware of his presence.

"I thought someone else was here, but I wasn't sure," Lawrence said. "I don't see anyone though."

"That's because you don't know how to really *see* yet, or you're afraid to—"

"Well, look here, am I dead or not?" Lawrence asked. "Lydia and I are quite confused about it all. And who are you?"

"Yours was one of the easiest, most proficient transitions I've ever seen," Seven said. "You're to be congratulated. Most people make much more fuss about it. Of course, you weren't in pain for any long period or anything. Still, it was very good. You won't be around long, though. Someone will probably come for you. I'm a . . . friend of Lydia's."

"Really? I thought I knew all her friends," Lawrence said.

"Who are you talking to, for heaven's sake?" Lydia asked.

"Don't you hear him, too?"

"No, I don't hear anyone but you, and I shouldn't be hearing *you*. There!" she got that stiff smile on her face and turned the radio on, loud, to drown out his voice. But Lawrence said, "There's a state park, Lydia. Drive in there."

She felt as if she was in some kind of trance, and did as she was directed. She had to pay fifty cents and pass two guards who smiled and said what a great day it was. And Lydia thought, if she *was* in a trance, or dreaming, how come everything was so vivid?

"I don't know if this is altogether a good idea," Oversoul Seven said.

"A man has a right to do what he wants with his own body when he's finished with it," Lawrence said. Lydia frowned: Lawrence didn't sound crazy, or at least no crazier than usual. "There. That way. Turn left," he said.

She drove past rows of tents and campfires and children playing in the fields, now dark with dusk. A crowd was singing "Someone's in the kitchen with Dinah," and the air was full of the smell of hotdogs, steak, and onions. Lydia had given up all attempts to understand what was happening. Somebody—Lawrence?—was telling her what to do anyway, which was just as well, she thought, because she was incapable of making any decisions on her own.

"Further on," Lawrence directed.

The road became more isolated. Giant fir trees rose into the twilight darkness. They came to a park area of even green grass, dotted with benches. It was empty. "Here, Lydia, pull up," Lawrence said. "I haven't much time, darling. I can tell. Hurry."

She pulled the trailer up as close as she could to the nearest bench.

"Oh, the next one," Lawrence said. "The view is so much nicer."

She parked and went into the back of the camper. Lawrence's body was still there, with the book in its lap. "Well, that's that, then. I can't move it alone," she said.

"Just push it off the chair," Lawrence said.

"I can't!" She stood there, staring. "I've got to have a cigarette," she thought. She went outside, lit up, and looked out at the park and the woods and the benches and breathed the cool night air. Then, sure that she'd cleared her mind, she went back inside. It was all a dream: Lawrence wasn't dead, and he'd be in his body where he was supposed to be.

She went back inside. The body was still there. How bad was her mind? She had no way of knowing. All right, then! She yanked Lawrence's body down, dragged it the length of the trailer, down the steps, and over to the bench. Katydids were calling. She got a stone in one of her platform shoes, and had to take it off. It was much more difficult to tug the body *up*, but she did, until it sat nicely on the green bench, looking out across the fields to the woods.

"Admirable," Lawrence said. Then, to Seven, "Will you

stay around to help her out? She's going to need help, you know. I hear someone calling me, and I have the feeling—" With that, Lawrence disappeared and Seven couldn't see him any longer. Lydia never had.

She got back in the camper, stared out at Lawrence's old-man body, and wanted to cry, but she couldn't. She started up the motor, left the state park, and just kept on driving. The road seemed real. Nothing else. At the same time, some inner, usually quiet part of her was alert, and talking mentally. This part was usually masked by her conscious thoughts, but there were great holes in her usual consciousness, through which these inner reasonings came. She was retreating, and had been for some time: that much was clear. The trip cross-country was to help her shake loose from her normal surroundings, for they held her . . . kept her oriented.

She was finished with orientation. She didn't want to relate any more. Lawrence hadn't wanted to reach sixty either (a milepost that hadn't bothered her a bit), and he hadn't. But she didn't want to go quickly, suddenly, like that. She'd go slowly, step by step, mental slip by mental slip, she thought; retreat easily, so imperceptibly that she, herself, could forget what she was doing. Like mental sleeping pills.

Lydia was only half-aware of these thoughts, even now. The picture of Lawrence's body on its bench kept coming into her mind. She blocked it out and kept driving. In the morning she fed Greenacre and Tuckie and Mr. George, and ate breakfast at the side of the road.

Seven kept trying to talk to her, but she didn't hear him; she didn't believe in spirits, except in Lawrence's, and it seemed to have deserted her.

They finally caught up with her three days later, when Lawrence's body had been traced. The police were very understanding. Lydia's children came for her. She explained what had happened and they all pretended that the events were quite normal, so she saw that they didn't believe a word that she said; and she didn't much care. She eyed her offspring with great detachment. They seemed too . . . solid, unimaginative . . . limited.

For a week her daughter, Anna, took her. She left with the cats and Mr. George, carrying his bowl in her arms, while Anna was out at bridge. They found her within a few hours. Roger, her son, had her next. But she looked around the suburban home and garden, and the whole environment seemed too pat, unreal; no longer where she belonged. It seemed quite clear; she didn't belong anyplace. Her interest in the world was fading. Vaguely she wondered that she'd ever taken it seriously at all.

They were giving her tranquilizers because every once in a while she kept talking about how Lawrence picked out the bench she'd left his body on, even though he'd been dead for hours. She thought it mystifying herself.

One night she didn't take the tranquilizers, and sneaked out after everyone was asleep. It was early autumn. The orange leaves were all dull and soft and falling everywhere. She ran—agile for her age, she thought—through all the backyards, ducking under clotheslines, avoiding garbage cans, sprinting past lighted windows showing glimpses of glowing television sets.

A great exhilaration filled her. Her nightgown flapped at her ankles as she ran. She lost her slippers, and luxuriated in the wet grass against her bare feet. They'd raise hell if they found her. Dimly she wondered when and why she'd stopped doing things like this. When she was a child? From the distance she heard alarmed voices—probably Roger and his wife calling—but she ran on and on.

For a while she almost felt as if someone was running with her, or keeping up to her in some funny way, and once she would have fallen over an old tree stump, but a voice in her head said, "Look out," or at least she thought that it did. She wasn't aware of Oversoul Seven though. Actually, he kept calling her name, but this inner voice merged with the shouts of Lydia's son and daughter-in-law, and in any case Seven kept feeling himself being pulled further and further away from Lydia, till he could hardly sense her at all. Instead, another scene was coming into reality for him. The backyards vanished, and shining mosaics took the place of the grass.

Chapter Eleven

Ma-ah in the Land of the Speakers

Ma-ah had never seen mosaics before. She stared at the courtyard's spectacular floor, gazed in marvel at the brilliant blue, green, and purple tiles that glittered in the afternoon sunshine. The multitudinous patterns almost made her dizzy. There were strange wiggly lines, odd shapes, circles and squares, all flowing one into the other.

At one point, one shimmering blue fish-shaped flat stone fitted into a shining green one, of a bird. But it was almost impossible to find the dividing line, so that before her eyes the fish turned into the bird. And the same with all the other patterns. The various representations were so fluid and bright that she hesitated to walk on them. Sumpter went ahead, without looking down at all though, so she followed docilely enough. Long shadows lay clearly over

91

the tiles, cast by the towering sheer cliffs that surrounded the courtyard.

"Sumtoa," Sumpter said, waiting for her. She was growing used to him; he'd been her steady companion for the two days that she'd been separated from Rampa. "Sumtoa," he said again.

She didn't have the slightest idea what the word itself meant, but his meaning was obvious from his gesture. He pointed at the cliff wall nearest them. She turned to look, and leapt back, startled. An image of a man was etched in the rock so cleverly that she thought him real for a moment; one arm close enough to brush her own. Like Sumpter, he was giant-sized, dressed in a violet-colored robe, and like all the people she'd seen here he had very light brown skin and blue eyes, flecked with orange.

"Sum-to-a," he said, more slowly this time.

She shook her head, saying in her own language, "I don't understand."

He pointed again. Once more she turned to look. The entire cliff wall was painted with figures and drawings. Now she wondered how she could have missed them before. So craftily were these executed that it looked as if real people blended with the rocks, emerging from the crevices.

"Crom a taum," Sumpter said, smiling.

Ma-ah shrugged, almost angrily. What did he want her to do? And where was Rampa? Every time she asked, Sumpter answered with gestures and those words that she couldn't understand, but she deduced that Rampa was undergoing the same kind of experiences that she was, with someone else. "Why were Rampa and I separated?" she asked, but Sumpter only smiled reassuringly. Then he pointed to his own ears, to her's, and to the image on the wall. He wanted her to listen to . . . the painted-on man?

Sumpter shook his head, the robe's cowl moving just enough to show the straight black hair that fell to the nape of his neck. He took Ma-ah's hand gently, so as not to frighten her, and ran her fingers lightly over the portions of the wall painting that she could reach. At first she recoiled with uneasy surprise. The oddest sensation began to spread through her fingertips; a tingling. Sumpter just watched, encouragingly.

Ma-ah was caught between wonder and distrust. The lines of the painted figure were giving off . . . sounds . . .

92

that somehow rushed through her hands. Utterly engrossed, she ran her fingers over the broad areas, and these produced a different sensation. The colors had something to do with it, too. Green made long ripples in her flesh, and then long lingering sound-feelings.

The figure's head and shoulders were too high for her to reach. Almost slyly, she sped around and touched Sumpter's robe. It was soft, but no sounds went singing through her fingers. He laughed kindly enough, but she felt that he was making fun of her, or perhaps had even anticipated her motion, or one like it. Her eyes darkened sullenly.

Seeing her reaction, Sumpter touched her robe, the brown one they'd given her, and shook his head with a mischievous shrug as if to say, "See, yours doesn't make any noise either."

Her eyes cleared, but she watched him guardedly. She was under constant surveillance; but apparently she wasn't being restrained. She could look at the cliff walls, or not, as she chose—he wasn't forcing her to do so. No contest of wills was involved. Satisfied, she ran a few steps to the next drawing, a strange large bird squatting on the ground, with people coming out of its open mouth, or belly. She couldn't tell which. The sunlight shone on the bird's folded wings, and the people looked alarmingly alive. How could that be, if the bird swallowed them? And what bird was big enough to swallow whole people?

She glanced sideways at Sumpter. Such things were impossible. She knew what animals and birds were, even if she was ignorant about this hidden valley. So she shook her head and grimaced, then smiled broadly, pointing at the drawing, to show her disbelief.

Sumpter took her hand again and tried to run her fingers across the lines of the bird's body, but she sprang back, frightened that the bird's belly or mouth might suddenly close and swallow her hand, fingers and all.

Sumpter nodded soberly, as if respecting her fear. Then he fingered the painting himself. Only when he withdrew his hand, intact, did Ma-ah follow his example. At first she was very cautious. This could be a trick that she didn't understand. But suddenly her face softened. She tipped her head. The sounds were joyful, filled with exaltation or satisfaction. She laughed up at Sumpter: the bird was singing.

Now it was Sumpter who was excited. She was forgetting herself in the enjoyment of new discoveries, as he'd hoped. She was feeling less trapped. He'd been appointed as her teacher, and she was learning quickly. But how much could she learn? What were her capacities? It was important that he encourage her just enough, without making her feel inferior, faced as she was with so many new experiences.

He walked quickly to a small particularly bright corner of the courtyard, without waiting for her, then stopped. Ma-ah followed readily enough, dawdling along slightly to show that the decision to follow was her own. Good. He wanted to encourage her independence, at least when it wasn't just stubbornness.

But she forgot everything else as she examined this corner of the wall. Here the drawings were particularly vivid, the colors alive and glowing. Some were figures of animals and birds that she'd known in her own world, but others she'd never seen before. Excited, she pointed out those with which she was familiar, feeling that she was showing *him* something for a change. Sumpter was delighted. He waited for her to discover the writing, the simple one-word descriptions beneath.

It didn't take her long. She spied the wiggly ⅂ beneath the bird first, and impulsively fingered it. The sound translation zinged through her fingertips—weak as yet, Sumpter could tell, but she was getting it. It took her only a few seconds to connect the sounds she was getting from the symbol, with the drawing of the bird above.

It would be a while before he could explain that the symbols were embossed with sound—not the drawings themselves, as in the earlier ones she'd seen, because if all the paintings identified thmselves audibly, then there would be no built-in reason for pupils to learn the written characters.

"Boroo," she said, wonderingly, pointing at the bird.

"Bor*uu*," he corrected quickly, almost shouting and smiling at once because she was learning so fast.

Ma-ah loved challenges, but she wasn't about to appear inferior. She frowned, indicated the picture of a hare with its written character, and demanded the sound-word for it. Gently Sumpter shook his head. She sulked for a moment, but then returned to the wall, touched the ⋀ beneath the image, and laughed with renewed astonishment as the symbol automatically gave up its sound to the pressure of her hands.

"Zentu," she said, repeating it. Then she put her fingers to her ears, but the sounds were absorbed too quickly by the skin; she couldn't transmit the sound, like that, to the ears. She glared at Sumpter: Where had the noises gone? Had he taken them from her in some way? He pointed back to the symbol. She touched it, receiving another sound stimulus, and from then on there was no stopping her.

They spent the whole afternoon there. Ma-ah ran from symbol to symbol, picking up the vocabulary incredibly fast, demanding that Sumpter repeat the words for her correctly, sometimes dancing around him when she conquered a particularly difficult sound.

Even when the sun lowered and the courtyard was buried in deep blue shadows, she wasn't really ready to quit. Walking back, she stared down at the floor tiles, calling out the words she could remember as she recognized the corresponding images. Once she got down on her hands and knees and fingered one of the drawings, but these weren't sound-embossed, and she rose, disappointed.

Sumpter didn't want to rush her, but it was time to show her the city, to introduce her gradually to customs and experiences that would frighten her considerably if she were unprepared. He waited until she tired herself out with chattering—in her own language. He pretended not to know it, to give her the impetus to learn the new vocabulary. In any case, he knew many of her thoughts; telepathically she was easy to read, but she wasn't ready for *that*. For that matter, there was something odd in her mental experience occasionally that struck him as incongruous, but he couldn't place exactly what it was.

Now, for example, her thoughts were quite transparent, with curiosity foremost. She was following him agreeably enough. He led her over to the living-wall just on the other side of the courtyard. Two couches were placed at the far end of the room, enough away from the wall so that pupils would not feel trapped or too frightened by what they saw. Purposely Sumpter left the gate to the court open, offering her an easy escape if she thought she needed one. He pointed. She eyed the couch and sat down. Then he pointed to the living-wall, signaled the proper mental sound for activation, and waited.

The opaque wall shimmered, turned milky, and slowly the images emerged, until an entire city street came into view with its sounds, odors, and activity. Ma-ah stiffened, gasped, and eyed the open door. Sumpter watched her eagerly, wondering that his pupil's first reactions still excited him. He enlarged the view. There they were, the tiled paths with their magnificent colors, dotted by islands of foliage; the individual dwellings open to sun and air (all erected with sound frequencies, but using native-Earth materials); one of the model cities that were scattered in suitably hidden areas over the planet.

She was completely engrossed, and he gave the mental sound command for three dimensions. Instantly the scene came forward, leapt out, became complete. He looked quickly for her reaction, expecting that this final clarification might alarm her.

Instead the strangest smile lit up her face, oddly uncharacteristic, unlike any of her other expressions that he'd seen so far.

"Of course," she cried, and jumped from the couch. Instant comprehension flooded her features, giving him the weirdest feeling that she understood something that he didn't; that the scene had a completely significant personal meaning for her that was impossible.

The pupil's gateway to the city was to the left. He hadn't intended to introduce her to the city itself until he'd held several orientation periods, but she rushed to the gate and opened it before he realized what had happened. And why did she run to that one entry which she could not have known led to the city?

It was Oversoul Seven who inadvertently gasped through Ma-ah's lips, and again, impulsively rushed Ma-ah to the city gateway. But Ma-ah's astonishment at the view dislocated Seven's consciousness. She stood amazed, unable to speak. Her look of clear knowing vanished so completely that Sumpter wondered if he'd imagined it, though he knew he hadn't. Instead, Ma-ah just looked dazed and frightened. ("And no wonder," Cyprus would say, later, to Seven.)

Incredulous, Ma-ah found herself staring at three huge triangular objects that towered into the sky. They seemed to have just grown up from the Earth, isolated, not a part of any other structures such as mountains or cliffs. Yet they were made of rock, and she knew they were man-made. Broad at the base, they gradually narrowed to a peak top and were, she saw now, equipped with stairs. Around them, Sumpter's giant-sized people looked like ants as they hurried about, engaged in too many activities for her to take in at once.

Courtyards surrounded the structures, and a series of stone platforms dotted with all kinds of foliage. There were other buildings of various sizes facing several squares. Squinting, Ma-ah suddenly let out a yelp of panic and disbelief. She pointed, trembling, at one of the foundations that had just caught her eye—water shooting up from the ground, instead of coming down upon it, like rain. Water raining up from the Earth, instead of down from the sky! This terrified her above all else she'd seen. It was . . . wrong, impossible . . . against all she knew of nature and the world. Appalled, she stood staring, oblivious to everything else.

"Ma-ah," Sumpter said.

She looked at him, her eyes wide with unwilling sharp perception of her predicament and the power of Sumpter and his people. If they could reverse nature, make rain fall upside down, then she was obviously at their mercy. Sumpter saw that recognition in her taut face as she looked up at him, that grudging awe. But her glance also disclosed an instant intelligence that was shrewd and inventive. Despite it all, she wouldn't be brow-beaten. Already she half-shrugged, accepting her present position but somehow rising above it.

She gave the fountains a sideways defiant look now, took a deep breath, and looked back at the view as if it was, after all, quite usual and nothing to get excited about. Sumpter grinned approvingly, but behind his hand, and with his head turned the other way.

As Ma-ah regained her composure, Oversoul Seven's consciousness came back to itself. He recognized the pyramids, but what else was there that eluded him? What knowledge had he forgotten? A great yearning possessed him. Ma-ah suddenly ran forward, with obvious eagerness, straight brown hair flying, robe in disarray. She wasn't used to running with cloth whipping about her ankles. Several times the robe caught between her thighs, so that she lost her footing, but she regained it and went running on. Bewildered by her contradictory reactions, Sumpter followed. He mused, somewhat disgruntled, that he didn't have to worry about introducing her to new surroundings—she was leading him.

Ma-ah's and Seven's consciousnesses were separate, yet bleedthroughs constantly occurred. Now Ma-ah picked up Seven's surprising sense of familiarity with the people and the pyramids (which she suddenly understood *were* pyramids) and his excited urge to inspect them.

She accepted these emotions unquestionably as her own for the moment—they were so clear and unmistakable. Only later would she question. So she kept running, scattering the people who gathered in various groups around the assorted stone buildings. They looked at her curiously, her small size and darker skin instantly setting her apart. Then they went on with their activities as they saw Sumpter, his violet robe marking him as a prominent Speaker.

And Oversoul Seven felt an exhilaration and joy in Ma-ah's body rhythm as she ran. He was acutely and pleasurably aware of the free integrity of her motion, the smoothly functioning nerves and muscles cooperating in the swift stride. For an instant he and Ma-ah almost knew each other as separate while one, united as they were by that imperative purpose to reach the middle pyramid.

Ma-ah paused, then flew up the steps. They were giant-sized to her, yet she leapt them easily. Sumpter followed, growing more serious and perplexed. They had ascended nearly a hundred stairs when Ma-ah paused to get her breath, and turned, looking out over the city. Now the different areas were clearly visible: the residential sections in a large exterior circle surrounded by foliage and tiled paths; the inter-connecting roads, and in the center the pyramids, temples, and public buildings. The impenetrable cliffs surrounded all.

When had she stood there before? Ma-ah wondered. Why was it so familiar? She leaned against the smooth shining wall for support.

"You haven't been here before, but I think I have," Seven tried to say to her, but now she was suddenly aware of the height, and it made her dizzy. Vaguely the eager run to the pyramid returned to her mind. What was she doing here? Had she run or only dreamed that she had? Never in her life had she stood so high above the ground. She backed away now, toward the wall. Only birds went that high.

Sumpter put his arm out protectively, but his face was stricken: did she know how close she was to . . . the door? She couldn't, of course. Yet she'd run almost like one possessed directly toward one of the most secret of pyramid entries; unknown even to many of the people. Now she stood almost immobile, staring down at the city below, trying to conquer her fear. It was almost as if the fear itself suddenly surfaced, he thought. Certainly it hadn't been present earlier. Yet she wasn't faking now, he was sure of it.

Too late, Seven realized that heights would frighten her. Of course, he should have known. For that matter, he was almost as confused as she was, a pretty state of affairs. She was going to faint. Quickly Seven tried to take over for her, but she took one last terrified look down at the city, and fell in a heap beside Sumpter.

Sumpter picked her up gently, and carried her down. A small crowd had gathered, but the people parted to let him through. A woman brought a sponge dampened with water, and he bathed Ma-ah's face. Her behavior was definitely strange in ways that he couldn't decipher, he thought. Suddenly the words came into his mind: "Once a Speaker, always a Speaker." He knew that, of course, but why did the thought come to him now, under these circumstances? Now the well-known phrase seemed to have a particular significance that escaped him.

Ma-ah was coming to. As she began to open her eyes, Sumpter was suddenly certain that she would end up before the Tribunal, though why he couldn't say.

Chapter Twelve

Ma-ah and the Shining Building Blocks of Sound

"Syllables are the sound equivalents of atoms," Sumpter said. "And atoms compose matter. Syllables can be organized into words, of course. But they can also be organized into sound patterns called no-words. That is, the sounds don't refer to objects or even feelings, and they don't name things in usual terms. Instead the no-words are simply . . . power. They do things, not represent them."

Ma-ah shrugged. "You said we were going to see Rampa this morning. That's all I care about. I can't concentrate. How can you expect me to be interested in anything else, when I haven't seen him in so long?"

Sumpter nodded. She'd picked up their language very quickly, but all morning she'd been scowling and pretending not to understand what he said. Still, he was growing more uneasy. She was learning amazingly well and he resented this . . . encounter that would surely upset her. "Rampa might already be in the courtyard," he said. "We may as well go down now, then."

She jumped up from the stone bench and walked swiftly ahead of him, as usual. She flung the courtyard gate open and went flying across the mosaic floor, with no thought now of the glittering tile patterns that had once so engaged her attention.

Rampa was already there. She stopped suddenly. He looked so different in the robe they'd given him; so distant and oddly unapproachable. Her eyes narrowed. All at once she saw the other robed figure who was waiting for Rampa as Sumpter was waiting for her. Only this was a young woman! Ma-ah swung around and glared accusingly at Sumpter, who'd let her think all along that Rampa's teacher was also a man. She stopped for a moment, then began to walk ahead at a slower pace, almost nonchalantly. But her teeth were suddenly chattering and she had to hold her lips tight together in a forced smile.

Rampa stood silently, watching Ma-ah approach. He was uneasy—she saw that immediately. "How different you look," she said, in their old language.

"You, too," Rampa said. "Is that man your teacher?"

"Sumpter? I guess so. Is she yours?" Ma-ah pointed toward the girl who stood at the other end of the courtyard.

"Yes, my teacher," he said, but there was an inquiry in his answer that Ma-ah didn't understand. She frowned.

"Do you like . . . him, your teacher?" Rampa asked, in the same peculiar tone.

"I like him well enough," Ma-ah said irritably. Rampa seemed confused. He looked past her suddenly at Sumpter. A flash of understanding seemed to pass between them that made Ma-ah unaccountably furious. "Well, what are you looking at him for?" she said. "We haven't seen each other in weeks and you just stand there—"

"I like my teacher very much," Rampa said. "I'm sorry that you don't like yours as well."

Ma-ah glanced past Rampa, over to the girl who stood in the background with her eyes lowered. She was much taller than Rampa, of course; yet Rampa didn't look small by contrast, simply sturdier and more compact. And he'd changed, Ma-ah realized, as she had. There was nothing between them.

Surprised, she looked closely at him. He laughed and mimicked her shrug as he used to. "I don't know what's happened," Rampa said. "What we shared—that life is gone. For all she's taught me, my alliance goes to my teacher. How is it that you don't feel the same for Sumpter?"

Ma-ah didn't answer. She was staring at the girl.

"Her name is Orona," Rampa said.

"Who cares?" Ma-ah flared, automatically. Yet again to her own surprise she realized that she didn't care. They'd joined forces in the old world, and whatever held them together there no longer applied. Rampa smiled when she snapped at him, and she found herself smiling back.

"You agree, then?" he asked.

"To what? . . . To you and . . . Orona?"

"That you and I be . . . separate?"

Ma-ah nodded. He relaxed visibly and said in a softer voice: "They hoped that you would like Sumpter more. They have plans for us, but I don't know what they are yet."

"I'll make my own plans," Ma-ah said with some defiance.

Rampa was silent for a moment. Then he said slowly: "Will you come when they build a dwelling for Orona and me?"

The implications flew through her mind—memories of their being together on the prickly hides, the moonlight through the rock crevices. But she nodded, agreeably, astonished at her own reaction once more. All right, she thought, very clearly. All bonds were cut. She and Rampa in their robes, with their new language and knowledge, were no longer the people they had been. For one thing they weren't half-starved all the time; they didn't have to cling together for protection and mutual help; they didn't have to hide in the cold, forsaken cliffs. All right.

"I'll come," she said soberly. She turned and walked away, but her eyes stung and she glared accusingly at Sumpter once more as they left the courtyard. "So it was all planned," she said. "And what more is planned? I might be heartbroken for all you and your people know or care. It just happens I'm not. But you couldn't have known that—"

"It was hoped that you'd turn to me, as Rampa turned to Orona," Sumpter said painfully.

102

"I turn to no one," Ma-ah said. But when he didn't answer, she grinned to herself: rather than go back to her old world, she'd do . . . well, practically anything. Something in Sumpter's manner made her suddenly realize that he'd hoped she would turn to him, too, in the . . . way she hadn't. Her steps quickened. The realization gave her a certain sense of power. Ma-ah also began to feel very free and unfettered. A mate was just a mate, she thought; important in the old world because men were stronger than women. But here . . .

At that moment, her relationship with Sumpter changed. He was aware of her thoughts, and instantly marked the difference in her attitude. He shook his head; keeping her in line until she learned what she had to learn would take some doing. He was very aware of her swift steps, the swish of her robe, and amused by his own illogical sense of hurt over her . . . comparative rejection. Rampa had instantly taken to Orona. Ma-ah had not been so compliant. And if she did *not* take to him, eventually someone else must be found to take his place. She must have children.

Ma-ah strode ahead silently, but now with a certain amusing arrogance, he thought. She was going to tease him quite purposely.

"Did you take to me at once?" she asked, suddenly stopping and turning to face him.

"Of course," he said.

The simple statement disarmed and infuriated her. Sumpter didn't even seem embarrassed.

"Good," she said, shortly.

At this, he couldn't help but laugh.

Later that day he tried to prepare her to attend the time-of-joining. "Just watch and listen," he said. "I'm not going to explain what will happen now. I want to know how much you'll understand on your own." He told himself that she would do very well, yet when the day of joining came, he was vaguely uneasy. Would her resentment over Rampa and Orona inhibit the proceedings?

Ma-ah, however, was aware of no resentment at all. She stood with Sumpter and groups of his people. A bare spot of land was before them. They all stood staring at it and smiling, splendid giant-sized people with bare heads now, their robes bright and festive. "Watch well," Sumpter whispered.

"Everything is a lesson," Ma-ah said, adding, "some

103

lesson," as she stared over at Rampa and Orona, who stood together in the center of the clearing.

An odd expectant silence fell. Even knowing as little as she did about Sumpter's people, Ma-ah was alerted. Each face was quietly smiling, but no one spoke. Around the clearing chunks of rock were piled haphazardly it seemed, some very large, some hardly bigger than stones. No one moved, yet Ma-ah sensed some change in direction that she couldn't comprehend. Her fingers tingled as they did when she touched the sound-embossed cave drawings, yet she was touching nothing. She heard no sounds, either normal ones or the inner kind that the embossed drawings gave her.

Inquisitively she turned to Sumpter. What was he doing? What were all of them doing? Sumpter's head was thrown back, his eyes oddly masked, secretive, dreamy, yet excited. They glittered. His lips were closed, yet very gently. His throat muscles weren't moving, yet she had the impression that they were. Ma-ah sensed the weirdest kind of rising tension, weird because everyone looked so delightfully relaxed and quiet. How could they stand so still, though, she wondered. Could Rampa? She glanced over at him.

Orona held his hand, and he stood as quietly as all the rest of them, only his eyes were lowered. He and Orona both stared at the ground before their feet, steadily and intently, as if they expected something to happen there. But what? Rampa seemed to know what was going on, though, Ma-ah realized. Irritated—why should he know while she didn't?—she turned to Sumpter and touched his hand. As she did, a strained unsteady sound appeared in the air above her head and she jumped with surprise. She felt as if some . . . sound-shape was up there, invisible and yet shining; and that her irritation had somehow disturbed it, broken it up into . . . known sound? Blushing, she lowered her head. She'd interrupted whatever they were doing, and they knew it, she was certain. . . .

Before she could finish the thought and without otherwise moving, Sumpter reached over and took her hand. Ma-ah would have run away in that first moment, but instantly she was dizzy and astonished. She felt as if a river had suddenly begun to lift her up and carry her along; and the river was . . . the energy or concentration or purpose of the people. They were doing things she couldn't understand again. Her tingling fingers told her that sound was

104

involved, but it was within-sound, not without-sound. She couldn't hear it. But because of her practice with the cave drawings she could feel it now and then; and occasional brilliant images of . . . shaped sound arose in her inner eye. Where they came from Ma-ah didn't know, only that the people were manipulating . . . something. And Rampa and Orona were waiting for it. Did Sumpter smile? Ma-ah thought he did but she couldn't be sure.

Then before her eyes one large chunk of rock rose up seemingly by itself, slowly. She wanted to gasp aloud, but didn't dare to. Her fingers twitched as if they were full of . . . sounds that couldn't get out, or as if she didn't know how to release them. The rock rose higher. It went suddenly flying across the ground, just above it, toward Rampa and Orona. Rampa saw it coming and looked as if he wanted to run out of the way.

For an instant Ma-ah was caught between fear for him —the rock could slam into his knees if it didn't change direction—and relief: she wasn't the only one who was frightened. She and Rampa at least shared that. Rampa's eyes widened as Ma-ah watched, but Orona's hand held his, and he wasn't about to break away if she didn't. The rock came right at them, then about three feet away, its progress slowed. It hung for a moment, then quietly dropped at their feet. Still holding hands, Rampa and Orona took several almost-ritualistic steps to the left.

Ma-ah had been too surprised to do anything. Now she looked to see if some kind of incline could possibly account for the rock's movements. Perhaps her eyes had tricked her; the rock didn't really fly, but only seemed to . . . because of some peculiar aspect of the ground. Her eyes widened with triumph—there was a very gentle incline leading to the area where Rampa and Orona stood. Ma-ah relaxed for a moment, then frowned. The incline just wasn't enough to account for what had happened.

She was used to Sumpter's strange land, with its peculiar characteristics like the fountains. Sumpter had explained how water could be made to flow up from the ground. But . . . rocks flying above the ground like unwieldy, clumsy birds? Some deep part of her was outraged and threatened; and angry. How could you do anything, if the rules kept changing?

Again, Ma-ah's thoughts broke off. For the last few moments the air itself had been developing an unaccustomed

105

feel to it that she'd half-ignored. Now some barrier seemed to break, some hidden but powerful intensity was suddenly released. A dozen rocks lifted at once. Ma-ah's hand flew to her throat. She felt as if a million vowels and syllables rose into the air, all glittering, all . . . alive; like . . . animals of sound, moving beneath the rocks then and moving them, flying with them, supporting them. Instinctively she looked over at Rampa. He stared as unbelievingly as she. But again he followed Orona's example and never budged.

Well, neither would she, then! The rocks lined up, inches from the ground, then gently moved to the bare spot and fell softly. Now the air seemed saturated with sound, but Ma-ah heard nothing. How could that be? Silent sound? Her fingers tingled once more. Then she noticed that her right hand, in Sumpter's, felt different from her other hand . . . lighter, strangely empty yet moving. This frightened her most of all—*her* hand was involved. She was just about to pull away when two things happened almost at once.

First, whole stacks of rocks moved, this time even quicker than before. Without a wobble they whooshed into the air. But even more amazing to Ma-ah was the placement of the rocks. They fell to the ground in such a way that a pattern was obvious. Before her eyes a tall center pyramid came into being, with a half-circle room on either side. Yet no one moved or spoke. Now the rocks piled one on top of the other. No eyes followed their flight but hers. And Rampa's. Again, she thought: they still shared that—they were outsiders.

Then the atmosphere suddenly changed. Ma-ah sensed it at once, even before she realized what was happening. Some massive effort was lessened. A tension disappeared. The dwelling was completed. No—she looked again. A few gaps in the rocks still remained, by the doorway. She was watching the structure, so it was a few moments before she saw the group of children coming from the direction of the courtyard. They were all smiling, obviously excited, hardly able to contain themselves, but none of them spoke.

They made a circle in front of the adults, and as they did so the adults relaxed noticeably; their intense focus was gone. The children looked at the dwelling. Rampa and Orona stood in the doorway. Three stones, small in contrast with the others, still lay on the ground. Were they supposed to go into the gaps in the doorway? Ma-ah stif-

106

fened. The tension was building up again—this time she swore she *heard* it through her fingertips—into a high-pitched whine. Yet with her ears she heard no sound at all.

At first nothing happened. Then one of the smallest rocks rose slowly up but a few inches, wobbled, went up higher, tottered and fell.

The air was so full of extra tension that even Ma-ah held her breath. Then came a single audible sigh of disappointment—the first "real" sound in so long that Ma-ah was astonished. One small girl clamped her hand to her mouth. Those on either side frowned so deeply at the offender that Ma-ah almost cried for her, knowing exactly how she must feel. The girl was about half-grown, but smaller than the others.

Then the child put her hands back at her sides; the look of dismay left her face. Once more everyone was smiling, effortlessly it seemed. Almost at once the same stone rose, fairly steady this time, and flew through the air. It stopped, hovering. Ma-ah grinned herself. The children obviously were trying to move the stone into position. Would they?

A tiny frown began to appear on the face of the little girl who had gasped earlier. Ma-ah knew that in some way a frowning concentration was wrong. "You can do it. You can do it. It's easy," she told the child without thinking. And suddenly the girl's brow cleared. The stone sailed across the ground, landing right where it seemed to belong. Now it was the children's turn to relax.

The air of waiting diminished but did not disappear. Then Orona threw her arms out in a gracious gesture, and the second rock rose and flew into place. One rock remained. Who was to . . . ? Suddenly Ma-ah understood. Rampa was to move the last rock. Of course. The man and woman put in the last two rocks of their own home.

Rampa *had* known about the entire affair, then, and she had not. Ma-ah's cheeks burned. She'd been given no such training. Why had Rampa? But now he threw his arms out in the same gesture Orona had used a moment earlier. Nothing happened. The last stone was quite small, but it didn't budge from its place on the ground. Training or no, Rampa couldn't do it. Maybe only Sumpter's people could. Ma-ah glared at Sumpter for putting Rampa to such a test in front of everyone.

Yet no one seemed worried. There was no impatience.

Rampa just stood there quietly, for that matter, his face quiet and expectant. The idiot, Ma-ah thought; then with a flash of self-indulgent triumph: it served him right. The suspense was more than she could bear. Suppose he failed —in front of his new mate and the entire group?

Memories flew to her mind, of times when he'd helped her; when except for him they might have starved; when except for his strength she might have given in to fear or panic. She wanted so to help him. But how? Suddenly the tingling in her fingers was so strong that she flinched. In her mind's eye she saw the rock rise into the air, then fit into place. It had to! And the actual rock suddenly shot into the air with great jerks and wobbles, flew as if pushed by a great angry force, and slammed into place so vehemently that Ma-ah thought it would crash into pieces.

She almost laughed out loud. Rampa may have been clumsy, but he was effective! She looked over at him, disconcerted: he looked astonished and surprised. There was silence, inside-silence, outside-silence. Then all eyes turned to Ma-ah.

What for? Confused, she swung around to Sumpter—who began to laugh. His laughter was picked up by the others. Ma-ah stood haughtily, angrily. What were they laughing at? It was a great, generous, relieved laughter, almost indulgent, as if she'd done something quite well—considering. Considering what?

Ma-ah looked at Rampa and Orona. They were whispering. For a moment Rampa looked over at her, and Ma-ah saw that he was furious. At what? Why should he be angry when everyone else was smiling at her? "What's happening?" she said to Sumpter, since obviously the ban against talk was lifted. "Why is everyone so happy with me suddenly? And why is Rampa furious? I should be the one who's mad, if anyone. After all, he left me—it's his new dwelling—"

Sumpter looked down at her, so obviously pleased with her that Ma-ah grew even more confused. At the same time she felt terribly left out, not knowing something that was obvious to everyone else. "I'll tell you everything as soon as I get the chance," Sumpter said. "And now your training will really begin. You're ready for it. I'll tell you who we are and how we came here, and where you can fit into our plans." Again his pleasure with her was so obvious that Ma-ah couldn't help but be gratified. Yet despite

108

herself she almost glowered at him: he treated her like an exceptional child, she thought resentfully; just happy because she learned to do something—even if she didn't know what it was.

The crowd had broken up into groups. They were passing around fruits and drinks. Everyone was talking and laughing at once. Now and then someone caught Ma-ah's eye and smiled. The celebrants were making such noise that Ma-ah could hardly hear what Sumpter was saying. She looked around, at Orona and Rampa, who were being toasted; at the new dwelling; at the children who were running and dancing. A great sense of detachment overcame her. She savored it, while resenting it at the same time. Sumpter waited, watching her, the smile gone from his face. Slowly they began to stroll together toward the courtyard.

Chapter Thirteen

Josef's Pictures of Magic and Jonathan's Revenge

Josef eyed his canvas. He was painting a tiled courtyard. When he was finished each tile would be perfect, individually patterned and glowing. The glazes he would use! He almost chortled with delight—and the towering cliff walls, impossibly high, yet somehow right! The scene in his mind was so vivid that he felt a mixture of torture and exaltation as he tried to capture it.

In fact, he was so filled with inspiration that he felt transformed. Only a few days earlier all he could think of was food. Now it was the last thing on his mind. Jonathan left a tray underneath his door twice a day; sometimes it was hardly touched when he retrieved it. Thinking of Jonathan, Josef glowered and stared at the windows. Time and time again he'd begged Jonathan to take the boards down from the top at least, so he could have decent light. The lamps weren't enough.

For one thing, the tiled courtyard was an outdoor scene; he couldn't duplicate that light under these conditions. And what could Jonathan do to him if he ripped the boards down himself? The glass would be ruined, of course, because he'd have to do it from the inside. Josef went back to his painting, forgetting everything else for a while. Then he stood back once more, studying his painting. It was obvious: the light just wouldn't do.

In fresh outrage, he yelled aloud, broke the top window glass with the chair, and banged at the boards that had been nailed up outside. Even the noise he made sounded satisfying. "Serves them right," he thought, enjoying the onrush of energy; grinning as the light came splashing through the room.

He heard the pounding footsteps rush up the stairs, and in a moment Jonathan came in, yelling, when he saw the damage. Broken glass was all over the floor. Jonathan lunged at Josef, cursing. "The glass. The fine, expensive glass," he kept shouting.

"I'll pay for it. I'll pay. I can't work in that miserable light," Josef yelled, fighting him off. Jonathan was so shocked that finally he just stood aside, staring at the glass.

"I warned you," he said, this time in a desperate quiet voice. "This time you've gone too far."

Josef turned back to his painting. "I'll pay for the glass," he shouted again, wearily. "I told you I needed decent light. Before winter, I'll sell these for good prices, and you'll have your precious windows back. Now let me work."

"You're a crazy man. Crazy. Wait till my father gets back from the fields. We're not going to get any glass for *your* windows ever again—"

"Good," Josef said. He laughed out loud and went back to work, leaving Jonathan to sputter and rage until finally he left, slamming the door behind him.

When Jonathan was gone, Josef left the easel, danced in the sunlight that came through the open windows, twirling clumsily around in circles like a circus bear. Then he returned to his canvas. All he cared about now were his paintings. He'd never been so inspired in his life, for any period of time. To work at such a pitch! When you had inspiration, you didn't need discipline, he thought gleefully; or at least inspiration had its own built-in discipline.

111

His paintings came like magic, out of nowhere, or out of a somewhere of dreams or imagination.

The afternoon went so quickly that Josef thought only a few moments had passed when Jonathan returned with his father. Without paying too much attention, Josef was aware of the annoying noise in the hall, the footsteps again; and then Jonathan and Elgren were in the room. The old man gasped, and Jonathan shouted with triumphant spite.

Josef just turned around and looked at them with all the fierceness he could muster. "I warned you that I needed light. I pleaded, but would you take down the boards? No, so it's your fault, for being so stupid—"

"I told you. He's crazy," Jonathan said, with some awe.

Elgren stood there, round, fat, and serious. "There's something here we don't understand," he said, slowly. "Men just don't act like that; not ordinary men."

"That's what I mean! He's—"

For once Elgren motioned his son to be quiet. "The destruction of perfect glass," he said. "Only the finest houses can have such windows. They're the pride . . . the pride . . ." He broke off. "It's demoniac. Wanton destruction. I liked you. Despite it all, I liked you."

"You had a fine way of showing it," Josef shouted, getting redfaced. "Locking me up—"

"For your own good. To make you fulfill your bargain. That was only right," Jonathan shouted back.

"We gave you food again when you started to paint, even though you made no progress on *our* painting," Elgren said, as if his heart would break.

"Thank you. Thank you. I'm grateful, I'm sure," Josef thundered. "And there's your painting. It's started. Begun." He pointed dramatically at the one prosaic, uninspired painting in the room. "The undercoating's done. I'm just waiting for it to dry."

Jonathan ran over and touched it. "It feels dry enough to me," he said. "You just set it aside to do these other crazy paintings; to spite us."

"The window glass," Elgren said, with a deep sigh. "We can just stop feeding you again. You take our food on false pretenses unless you finish our painting."

"I don't care about eating anyway," Josef said. His warm brown eyes filled with vehemence. "I'll just paint what I want, and eat the pillows if I have to—"

"Eat the pillows! I told you, he's mad," Jonathan said.

"There's still something here that we don't understand," Elgren said to his son. "So shut up and let me think."

Josef snorted.

Jonathan paced the room angrily.

Elgren stared at Josef. "We might as well not exist for you," he said finally. "You don't see us at all as us. Just as we . . . affect you and your paintings. We don't exist for you." He paused, struck by his own words, frightened by them even.

"Ahhh, I just want to work, to paint," Josef said, not understanding at all. "You'll get your painting. I'll do it. You see, it's begun. I'll pay for your glass. I'll sell some of these paintings, and I'll pay—"

"He's possessed," Jonathan shouted. "That's it."

"Possessed by nincompoops like you," Josef yelled back. But real uneasiness gnawed at him. Something in Elgren's face worried him, and he realized suddenly that he needed the Hosentaufs. Suppose they put him out and he lost his work space? He was dependent on them right now. All at once he felt threatened, really threatened. Any commotion and his inspiration could vanish—who knew, forever maybe?

He tried to smile pleasantly, feeling the muscles in his face go all wiggly with the effort. "Just let me paint, and you'll have all the fine paintings you want—the one of the house, and the portraits, too—" He blushed furiously, feeling abject, miserable, amazed at the change in circumstances.

He tried to see Elgren as a person, but all he could see was a pompous, fat, funny . . . caricature of a man. Which he was! Which he was, Josef thought angrily. "Ahhh, just don't torment me," he said, in exasperation.

"We'll be back," Elgren said.

"No doubt. No doubt," Josef answered. He glowered at nothing in particular when they'd gone. Elgren was taking him seriously in some way that he didn't understand, he thought. And now all he wanted was to stay here in this room more than anything in the world so he could paint, while only a week ago all he wanted was to get out of it. Somehow that gave the Hosentaufs a hold over him that no one had ever had before. Was he a prisoner of his own inspiration? Where had his freedom gone?

It came to him all at once that he didn't even want to go outside; just to paint and keep up with the ideas that

113

were coming to him so quickly for the first time in his life. They fascinated him. Did they frighten him, too, coming from nowhere as they seemed to? "Bah!" he said aloud. Thinking could drive you crazy. He went back to work. In a matter of minutes he forgot everything but the painting on the easel.

It was early twilight when Elgren and Jonathan returned, and instantly Josef sensed a change in their manner. For one thing, they weren't wearing work clothes; they were dressed for visiting. For another, there was an odd formality in the way they entered the room; quietly, not yelling or shouting at him; soberly. He was still painting, trying to get the last use of the daylight, and he said, impatiently, "Can't it wait? My first day of sunlight. Can't I at least use it all?"

"We'll wait," Elgren said as if he were a pleasant stranger or prospective buyer in to look at paintings. Beside him, Jonathan nodded with a broad smile. Josef was alerted. If Jonathan was smiling, something was really wrong, he thought. He began cleaning his brushes in turpentine; his moustache bristling. He was getting low on supplies, and where would he get more?

"May we sit down?" Elgren asked.

The polite question so alarmed Josef that he turned around too quickly and knocked his palette to the floor.

"I'll get it," Jonathan said, retrieving it, and getting paints all over his hands.

At the sight of this help from Jonathan, Josef plunked himself down on the edge of the bed, threw up his hands, and said, "All right, I give up. What are you trying to do?"

Elgren cleared his throat. "We, ah, had a family conference about you," he began.

"Ahhh," Josef groaned.

"No, no. We've some matters to discuss with you quite frankly. To your advantage—"

Josef wanted to shout, "To my advantage! When have you been concerned with my advantage?" But something told him to remain still. He looked at his hands and pursed his lips. "They must want something," he thought craftily. Otherwise they wouldn't be so nice. Best to be quiet, then, and make them come out with it.

"Yes, a family conference," Jonathan said.

Silence. Josef refused to speak. Elgren began, leaning

forward earnestly. "With all good regards, still you broke our glass and you have no way to pay us for doing it. You can't sell enough paintings now to pay for such expensive glass. And you owe us at least one family portrait, and a picture of the house, for your room and board these months. Instead, you work on other paintings that you, at least, take very seriously—"

"So? So?" Josef said impatiently. They were driving him mad with their politeness.

"What to do honorably was the question," Elgren said. "Throwing you in jail was no answer, though we considered it, because then you'd never pay us and we'd never get our paintings done either. Not feeding you might make you so weak that there'd be no chance of payment for the glass. Putting you out of the house would let you go scot free. And so it occurred to us that you would like this thing settled also, so you knew where you stood."

"Then you could go on painting without worry," Jonathan said quickly.

Joseph scowled. "So this idea of yours, whatever it is, is Jonathan's? He's that worried about my state of mind?" Josef said, thundering out.

Jonathan grinned, smugly.

Elgren spread his hands. "We have problems, like any family. You may be able to help us with one of them, and—"

"I just want to paint," Josef interrupted. "Will you get to the point? Stop torturing me."

"Bianka likes you," Elgren said so quickly and flatly that Josef snapped forward. How much did Elgren and Jonathan know? Had the younger brother squealed? Josef felt his face turning red.

"Don't be embarrassed," Elgren said. "She likes you. So that's a fact that we have to take into consideration. There aren't many young men around here. The farmhands are all right, but she thinks that you're different; romantic, maybe. You know how women are."

Josef didn't dare say a thing. He didn't like the smile on Jonathan's face or the air of absolute earnestness on Elgren's.

"It's time for her to have a husband," Jonathan said, now looking everywhere but at Josef.

"She thinks you would make her a good man," Elgren added. "Now wait—she doesn't like too many young men.

The opportunities are limited around here. It would be different in the cities."

"You hate me," Josef shouted. "Jonathan hates me. Your wife can't stand me. You think I'd marry into such a family? You're all out of your minds." He sprang up, furious, confused, sputtering with outrage—but surprised with himself. Underneath it all, a part of him thought coldly: a guaranteed place to live and work; a woman built-in when he wanted one! They'd have to buy his art supplies, too, or he wouldn't do it. Astounded by these thoughts, he yelled, "No, no. I won't consider it under any circumstances. No. My answer is no."

"These things are delicate. Think about it," Elgren said. "I told Bianka this would be your first reaction—"

"First and final and last," Josef yelled. He stood up and tramped about the room.

"Or we confiscate your paintings and supplies and have you thrown into jail," Jonathan said, mildly.

Josef stopped in his tracks. "That's blackmail! Besides, I'd make a miserable husband—"

"You'd have to help us in the fields in the morning or do the morning chores. The rest of the time you could paint," Elgren said. "Your own painting made me change my opinion of you. You've worked at it steadily now. It consumes you. This is good. It means that eventually you will sell your paintings. A good artist in the family—" He paused and added, "You could do pictures for my relatives, too. That is a fine cultural thing to do."

"You'd never get out of debtors' prison," Jonathan said, "But you can see our point. We have an investment in you. It's only fair that we come to some understanding. And you'd have this room for your studio. I have the feeling that if your painting is so important, you'd be making a pretty fair bargain."

Josef stared; Jonathan was shrewder than he'd given him credit for.

Elgren stood up soberly, again with that unfamiliar formality, and said, "This is how things are done. We've told you our proposition. Think about it. We'll be back tomorrow for your answer."

Josef didn't answer. It was Bianka, the bitch, who was responsible for his getting caught and dragged back in the first place. All she had to do now was tell her father about their romps. Josef was sure Elgren didn't know—though

116

Jonathan might. Elgren thought that his daughter was a prize; not that there was anything really wrong with her, Josef thought hastily. Only that he wasn't about to marry anybody.

The Hosentaufs left. Josef eyed the windows which thankfully were now unboarded, remembering that soon the land would be clear and open. The fairs would be starting in a month or so. In his mind's eye he saw himself jaunty and free, doing sketches for a good price, sleeping in cool fragrant barns. But his eye fell on his unfinished paintings. He had to finish them. He had to have a quiet place to work. What had happened to his freedom?

Frowning, he went back to the easel. He wasn't going to marry Bianka, paintings or no. And all the while that he was talking to himself so vehemently, uninvited mental images came into his mind; Bianka leaving him a tray of food while he worked—Bianka as a model, taking every conceivable pose; and in years to come, Josef the artist, lord of the manor, rich and prosperous while fat sons did all the work in the fields that he and Bianka had somehow inherited.

"You'd better jump out of the window to the shed and just keep going," he told himself, alarmed by these seemingly independent thoughts that glowed so temptingly. Was he being offered an opportunity unequaled where he could work in peace? Or was he in mortal danger of losing all independence? Or both? Or neither? Groaning, he threw his brush down and stared at the wall.

Chapter Fourteen

Proteus's Decision
Window's
Window into the Past
(and Aspect One)

Cyrus and Oversoul Seven sat nonchalantly on a pile of rock on the rim of the hill overlooking the Dig of the Tellers. "I lost myself in Lydia's life, then Ma-ah's, then Josef's," Seven was saying. "It's great to surface again. I'm worried about Josef. I mean, he *is* forming his own reality but he doesn't know it, of course, and he thinks the Hosentaufs are tricking him."

"I take it that Josef is still your favorite?" Cyprus asked.

"Well, no, not really. He's just more like me. Or he seems like me. Anyway, he reminds me of myself more and more. He gets lost in his paintings now, as I get lost in my personalities. And you know, before my examination he didn't paint like that; and I just peeked into my personalities to help them out now and then. I mean—now

118

sometimes I think they own me; and Josef's worried about losing *his* freedom. Well, I don't relish losing mine, either, in their experiences."

"Is that what happens?" Cyprus was smiling.

"Well, it's certainly what *seems* to happen," Seven said, testily. "It's easy for you to talk in your position—" Seven broke off in consternation. Cyprus was gone. "Cyprus? Cyprus?" he called.

"Yes?"

Seven blinked. That was Cyprus's voice, but it wasn't just that she'd dematerialized her image—he could have perceived her presence in any case—

"Over here," she said.

Seven frowned with his fourteen-year-old male face, and swirled around. Cyprus was blinked on and off, or here and there, disappearing entirely *in her essence,* and then returning. Exactly what *was* she doing? Taking herself out of his experience and then reemerging in it? "All right. Come back," he said.

She reappeared beside him, looking rather severe. She said, "When you talk about my position, you aren't thinking straight, as that little performance of mine should show you. Obviously my position is a changing one. It isn't static. And neither is yours. Or Josef's, for that matter."

"I think I understand," Seven said. "But why are we here?"

"Window is going to put on a demonstration for Proteus," Cyprus said. "But afterward, I'll want you to tell me what you think the significance of that demonstration is."

"But Window isn't even one of my personalities," Seven cried. "And if the demonstration is for Proteus, then Proteus should be tested, not me."

"This is a particularly important part of the examination," Cyprus interrupted. "So stop objecting and listen. . . ."

"You have a very adventurous nature," Window was saying to Proteus. "But because you were taught to curb your sense of wonder, you're often frightened of where your curiosity might lead. Story's abilities worry you because you're going to have to open your mind to them, or reject Story—and you don't want to do that either."

"I was brave enough to come here," Proteus said.

"Exactly. So I hope you'll be courageous enough to accept what you find."

119

"Well, I accept you," Proteus said, with a shrug. "And I'm ready to accept whatever abilities you have, as, uh, real."

"That's only the beginning," Window replied. "I'm going to take you on a tour—"

"Story was right. You *are* going to show me around, finally. I was afraid that you weren't, that you were hiding something," Proteus said. He grinned; already he liked Window better than he did his own father, a fact that struck him as very strange. "I've been a little disappointed," he added. "This part of the . . . dig . . . is nice enough, but you've kept me isolated, really." He broke off. He'd also seriously wondered whether or not there *was* anything else to see; and whether Window was lying. Now he blushed, remembering.

Window stood there, ready to leave, when the door burst open. Story ran into the room. "There's another search party coming. I don't know why, but they're more determined than they were the last time. The news came from one of our outposts. I didn't wait to get the details, but now they're beginning to think that Proteus was kidnapped."

Window whirled around. His face was white.

"Did you . . . take him around yet?" Story asked.

Window shook his head. "We were just ready to leave."

"You weren't going to show him all—"

"No," Window said quickly.

Proteus stared at both of them. "You *were* hiding something back, then," he said, accusingly. "I thought you were."

"He has to be found, then. He has to go home," Story said. "He doesn't know what's here yet, and he's got to promise not to tell what he does know. Otherwise, they'll just keep on looking."

Confused, Proteus looked from one to the other. Story was speaking so quickly that it was hard to follow what she said. Proteus spoke as emphatically as he could: "I'm not going home. You can't make me. If you do, then I'll tell them that something strange is going on here, and they'll come back to investigate anyway."

They were paying little attention to him. Story just kept staring at Window. She said again, "Proteus has to be found."

"Or *never* found," Window said.

120

Story shook her head. "That would be even more difficult. He's not able to make the choice."

Proteus was furious. "Stop talking about me as if I'm not here," he said angrily. "I have a right to know what's going on."

Story cried urgently, "Proteus, we're just trying to save you from having to make a decision without knowing what's involved. Till now you couldn't really do us much harm—you hadn't seen anything. At any time you could decide to go home, and we could just abandon you topside and no one would ever find us. But now . . . you're going to have to stay with us for good—never see your home again—or leave at once with a suitable explanation."

"Like what?" Proteus demanded.

"Well, we have the dig above, that they know about. Your could say that you wandered in there. . . . No, then we'd get in trouble for not notifying the proper authorities—"

"Wait." Window closed his eyes. He tried to lose the sense of urgency and desperation that had been closing in on him, and as he did, his inner vision cleared. There were three copters this time. How could one boy threaten an entire project, he wondered wearily, for now he saw that the searchers were far more persistent than they had been. Then he discovered the reason. "Your mother's a member of the search party," he said. "She has some kind of executive position, doesn't she?"

"My mother? Are you sure?"

"Her name is Amanda. She has . . . brown hair, blue eyes and olive skin. She's thirty-nine. She called you Proto—"

"When she thought of me, she called me Proto," Proteus said. "She didn't pay that much attention to me usually."

"Well, she's thinking about you now," Window said soberly.

Proteus was so surprised that he didn't know what to do or say. Window has *seen*—that much was obvious. What Window said was true; so maybe Story's tales were true, but in a different way. He said, wildly, "I could . . . say that I pleaded with you not to notify the authorities; or tell them that your communication system went on the blink—"

"He *could* say that, about the communications," Story said. "It just might work."

"Could we trust you to be quiet about the little you do know, or suspect?" Window asked.

"Of course," Proteus said. "I give you my word."

Story stared at him. "A few minutes ago, that's not what you said."

"I was angry at you, for talking around me. I didn't mean that I'd really do anything to get you in trouble—"

"Then it's your choice," Window said. "Either you return, and we'll still be taking a chance, or you stay. If you leave, we can only hope that your story is convincing enough. I can have our communications cut temporarily, and let *them* come here, where we'll be ready—"

"The men at the dig took care of him till help could arrive," Story said. "That story would work to our advantage—"

To return home! Proteus was almost sick to his stomach with indecision. Despite his resentments, he kept seeing his mother's image in his mind's eye: the green uniform, his mother's image in his mind's eye: the green uniform, and yet . . . "No," he shouted. "I won't be dragged home, even if it means never going back. I won't go unless it's the only way that you'll feel safe, so somebody better think of something!"

"There's only one place where you'll be safe if you stay, and where *we'll* be safe, no matter what. No one knows where it is but the Tellers," Window said. "But if you go there with us, then you'll have to stay and join your fate with ours. Right now there's no time to explain. You'll have to go it blind, if you've really decided." He paused, then said quickly, "They're landing by the outer dig. I see it, mentally."

Again Proteus thought: his mother, so close. He'd decided to leave home once. Now it seemed he was going to have to make up his mind all over again, while knowing that his mother was only a short distance away. Nothing else had offered this tremendous point of contrast. Yet all the deep feelings that had propelled his initial flight now reasserted themselves. "I'm ready. I'll go with you, if you'll take me . . . if I won't cause you more trouble than I'm worth."

His eyes were smarting. Story and Window were already at the door. "All right," Window said. "Hurry."

They ran down the corridor past all the rooms with which Proteus was familiar. The wall at the end of the corridor opened as they approached. Proteus gasped with surprise. He'd been in the hall often, no door was apparent. Now it closed soundlessly behind them. "It's all operated from below," Window said quickly. They were in a very small room with rock walls. Two large rocks moved back. Proteus followed Story and Window inside, and they began to climb down a very steep staircase hewn out of rock.

This time the stairs seemed endless, but the way was illuminated dimly, though Proteus saw no lamps or torches. When they'd walked downward for some time, the steps evened out until they gradually formed a rocky corridor with a downward incline. Neither Window nor Story spoke, so Proteus asked no questions. He was growing more and more excited, even while he realized that they were steadily progressing beneath the Earth's surface. What would he find? What secret . . . project could there possibly be that Window and Story considered so important?

The corridor ended with a final rock door that opened for them automatically, as had the others. Now they were obviously inside a gigantic rock building of incredible age and richness. Here also the walls were lit by that same dim illumination. Drawings of animals, birds, and buildings filled the walls. Proteus eyed them with awe. They seemed alive, waiting.

Window and Story still hadn't spoken, yet Proteus had the strangest feeling that they carried on some inner kind of dialogue. What kind of people were they, actually, he wondered? Story was approximately his age, yet sometimes she acted much older, while on other occasions she was so playful and innocent that she might have been a ten-year-old. And Window? Why did he trust Window so? Proteus shivered slightly. In this odd building, both Window and Story seemed like strangers to him.

He looked down. The rock floor here was smooth and clean, yet the air was filled with a sweet mustiness that was impossible to describe. The cleanliness itself disturbed him; it didn't seem to be fresh, but rather, ancient; a cleanliness somehow preserved from the past. Window and Story turned into another corridor, and Proteus followed. This time Proteus paused briefly. The door before them was heavy and old. Why didn't it creak as it opened? A series of steep upward steps led to a rock landing, and here Proteus stood motionless, unable to speak, amazed. at the scene before him.

He'd taken it for granted that they would still be underground. Now before him stretched a lush valley, ringed by towering cliffs that formed a very wide cone shape, opened, far above. The valley was so enclosed by the cliffs that the only entry seemed to be from the wide circle of sky above. Through that opening the sun poured so brightly that Proteus had to look away, because his eyes were still so accustomed to the dimness of the underground corridors.

"Welcome," Window said, and though he had seemed vital enough before, now he seemed to come truly alive, snap into focus, be himself, in a way that took Proteus completely by surprise. The same transformation came over Story. She smiled at him fully, as she hadn't earlier, her whole pose expressing a deep satisfaction. It was obvious that Story and Window had come home.

Proteus didn't have time to wonder further about the change in his companions. Too much competed for his attention. Everywhere there were tall green trees, grass, flowers, buildings of the oddest designs and all in the richest of colors. Yet in the distance ruins were clearly apparent, in various stages of reconstruction. Piles of rock glittered in the sun. Bright shoots of green licked at them like green flames.

At first Proteus didn't notice the people. Then he saw the figures moving around the ruins, and at the same time men and women began to emerge from the buildings. They came in twos and threes, small groups from the multicolored triangular structures that were arranged in a semicircle around what seemed to be a general square.

It was only then that Proteus thought of turning around. Directly behind him was a pyramid—through which they must have just emerged! "But at the last, we come *up*," Proteus said. "How can that be?"

Window smiled. "We'll explain it all later. For now, meet the Tellers."

"How long has this place been here? Why hasn't it been discovered?" Proteus was so filled with questions that he was in a daze for the next few hours in which several hundred people surrounded them, greeted Window and Story with great warmth, and listened to Window's explanation of Proteus's presence.

Proteus himself began to feel as if he'd also returned

"home." Everything seemed new and unbelievable, yet familiar. It was twilight—twilight on Earth as Proteus had never seen it before, except in his dreams. How sterile and insignificant the floating city seemed by contrast, he thought, remembering the artificial trees and plastic grass. He and Window strolled past the buildings as Window pointed out the sights.

"This place was ancient long before the time of Rome," Window said. "And it's coming alive again. There's so much to tell you that I don't know where to begin. Our discoveries, for one thing. That's a story in itself. We're learning to activate mechanisms that we would never have dreamed of—and they're all here in instructions that date back to the time of the cavemen. This was a fantastic civilization. We don't know yet how it began, but we hope to find out. It flourished while most Earthmen were still savages. We're still learning, finding new records— Look."

Proteus gasped. Above in the wide circle of sky in the center of the cliffs, a few stars shone and a dull Moon. Here before them the valley narrowed slightly into what had obviously been a kind of courtyard. Between patches of grass, broken colored tiles glittered. In several places the grass had been uprooted, baring whole areas of clear shining mosaics, each fitted into the other so cleverly that it was impossible to tell where the divisions were between them.

Window stood there and closed his eyes. "I'll tell you what I see with my inner vision," he said. "Each time I come here and look inward, I see something else, a further detail, another piece of information that tells us where to look, that brings us one step closer."

Window's mental visions shimmered, blurred, then cleared. Describing what he was seeing, he said softly: "This was a courtyard, as you can probably tell. The mosaics covered the whole area, the floor of the valley. The walls and drawings are very important, but while we've discovered some very strange things about them, there's a lot we don't know. They *do* contain a key that's vital; we're sure of that. But wait . . . I'm seeing something new . . . A young woman stands in the courtyard now."

Proteus frowned. Suddenly he felt nervous and uncomfortable. He stared at Window, whose head was flung back, his face expectant and yet passive, his long humped nose sensitive as an animal's. Proteus wanted to interrupt, but didn't dare to.

"She's beautiful, black. She's looking at the drawings—" Window sighed audibly. "She's disappearing. I'm losing my focus."

"I suppose she could be the girl Story told us about—the one who was supposed to threaten the Tellers through me somehow." Proteus spoke resentfully, almost unwillingly. "I wish you hadn't seen her," he said. "Everything was so great. I still think that Story's tale was—"

"Distorted?" Window said, smiling. His eyes opened. "It might have been. The threat she saw could have been the second search party. She could have perceived the black girl separately, and just put the two together. That's possible. She's young, and still learning to use her abilities."

"Well, I just wish she wouldn't practice on me," Proteus retorted. He looked around. Now the ancient courtyard seemed alive and glowing in an unfriendly way. He no longer felt that he'd come home. Sensing Proteus's mood, Window led him back toward the buildings and the people.

Seven and Cyprus stayed. They'd watched the whole day's proceedings. Seven was incredulous himself. "Window saw Ma'ah! Of course," he said.

"Do you understand now?" Cyprus asked.

"Yes, I do!" Seven cried out triumphantly. "Ma-ah and Proteus live in the same physical place in different times, at least they do now that Proteus's journey has taken him there. What a pity that they don't know each other, or see what's happening. I wonder if I could possibly explain it to—"

Seven broke off. He was growing slightly dizzy—or his environment was—he wasn't sure which. Objects seemed to shift focus, become blurred, then become clearer again than they'd been in the first place—yet oddly different. For a moment Oversoul Seven was in the courtyard of the Speakers, standing next to Ma-ah in 35,000 B.C. The mosaics were bright and dazzling. The cliffs shot upward. But there was a difference. What was it? "Ma-ah! Ma-ah!" he shouted.

"Did someone call me? I thought someone called my name?" Ma-ah swung around, obviously astonished.

"It's me, uh, the old man," Seven said. But the ground

126

shimmered once more. Seven could no longer see Ma-ah. The cliffs rose as before, but now the grass covered most of the tiles, and where the rubble was cleared away the tiles were chipped and darkened.

Cyprus was waiting for him. "Now, hold my hand," she said. "And remember, you'll have to answer some questions about this later on."

"I've got some questions now," Seven objected.

"Seven! Pay attention."

Seven sharpened his own fourteen-year-old male image, made the face as elfin as he could—and grinned.

In a flash Cyprus turned into another fourteen-year-old male image and grinned back. The next moment she had the woman's form again. "Now," she said. "Back to your examination. Look at one tile. Any one will do."

Seven chose a chipped blue and orange one, with a design partially showing. The rest had broken off.

"Do you see it clearly?"

"Yes."

"Now, this is the way that the tile appears to your present focus of perception. You must change your focus to see its other Aspects. *You* can stay here. Do you follow me?"

"I'm trying to," Seven said.

Cyprus sighed. "Those in Ma-ah's time use one specialized focus to perceive their reality—and that tile. Do you remember how the tiles looked a moment ago when you slid into Ma-ah's courtyard?"

"I'll never forget—" Seven said.

"Then keep moving your consciousness a notch at a time while watching that particular tile until it looks like the tiles did then."

"A notch at a time?" Oversoul Seven said, frowning.

"All right, if that doesn't quite make sense to you, then do this. Imagine that your consciousness is a light—which it is, of course—and keep turning it in different directions, but very slowly. The rotating light will pick up the tile in its different Aspects. Stop when you think you recognize Ma-ah's tiles—"

"I think I've got the idea now," Seven said. "Now don't rush me." He stared at the tile. How perfect it was in its way, he thought; how unique, even chipped and darkened, the tail of some animal or fish all wiggly set in the stone.

"Blink," Cyprus said.

127

Seven blinked, then looked back at the tile. It wrinkled. It was curling at the edges, diminishing, disappearing at a rapid rate.

"You're going too fast in that direction," Cyprus cautioned. "That's how the tile appears in future centuries, in a manner of speaking. Go back the other way."

Almost in a panic, Seven watched the tile disappearing. He tried to reverse his focus which was difficult, because he didn't know yet how he was doing what he was doing. "Come back," he shouted at the tile. Suddenly he felt a great love for it—how precious it was—yet despite his efforts it continued to wrinkle and diminish. In the back of his mind somewhere, he thought he heard Cyprus's (delightful) laughter. He wondered angrily what she was laughing at, and just then he found the feel of his consciousness, and pulled it back to the left of his inner vision.

Miraculously the tile shimmered, stabilized, then began to grow thicker. Portions of the design began to appear. Then Seven understood. When he saw the design completed, the tile would be as it was in Ma-ah's courtyard.

Then he recognized the right tile, or thought that he did. The design was completed, all the chips restored—a blue fish with a strange long tail. The tile looked new—too new. Before Seven realized what had happened, a brown hand appeared on the top of the tile; laying it, Seven saw, shocked by the hand's intrusion. He was tempted to follow through and go backward before the tile's "time." Instead he backtracked. The hand disappeared, and the tile remained. When it looked right to him again, he held the focus of his consciousness and just observed it. Was Ma-ah near? "Ma-ah?"

Instantly he was dizzy again. In the same instant he saw Ma-ah quite clearly, standing only a few feet away. Enlarging his inner vision without being sure how he did so, he saw the ancient courtyard; but unmistakably, vividly, and simultaneously he also saw the courtyard as it existed in the twenty-third century A.D. The tile in the same physical place showed its two separate Aspects at once, not one before the other. And as his vision widened, the two courtyards were transposed one upon the other.

Cyprus's voice seemed to come from a great distance. "This is just one hint of what's possible," she said. "But the same is true of you, Seven, and your personalities. You all exist in your own Aspects, at once, each separate yet a

128

part of the other . . . occupying the same 'place' which isn't a place at all . . . like the tile. Lydia, for example— her experience is yours, even if you aren't conscious of it. And your experience is hers, if only you can help her realize it—"

Cyprus paused, and said, "Even now she's translating your experience in her own way."

"Yes, I see," Seven cried, and the courtyards—both of them, disappeared. He was Lydia, yet she was herself, distinct, an old woman strapped in a wheelchair, staring with drug-filled eyes into the faces of her adult children.

Chapter Fifteen

Lydia's Children Grow Backward in Time and Tweety Delivers a Message (Aspect Two)

Lydia sat staring petulantly at her grown children. She'd been in the Medford House for a week. If was Sunday, visitor's day, and she sat propped up in the wheelchair like an ancient doll, powdered and perfumed, and dressed in one of the few dresses she owned. They'd thrown out her slacks and dungarees. Her eyes kept drifting off to the right, and she kept trying to bring them back into focus.

"We have her all fixed up for visitors. Doesn't she look nice?" the nurse said. Like Lydia's children, the nurse was in her fifties. "Shit!" Lydia said under her breath.

The nurse, Mrs. Only, smiled indulgently and chuckled. "Don't pay any mind," she said to Lydia's daughter, Anna.

"Mama, you're looking well," Anna said nervously. She

was a big woman with a large bosom; well-educated, at a loss as to what to say.

Lydia just stared.

"She's tranquilized," Mrs. Only said.

Roger, Lydia's second son, grinned: "Any particular reason?"

"She got upset the other day and threw her milk glass across the room. Then she cursed everyone out, ran down the hall, and was heading for the stairs when we caught her."

"I'd do it again if I had the chance." Lydia tried to say the words clearly. They came out garbled, slurred. It was the damned drugs. She strained to get out of the chair.

"See, she can't articulate," Mrs. Only said. "The blood thinners should help bring more blood to the brain, but her condition is really irreversible."

Lydia threw them a fantastic scowl this time. How could she get them to understand that she knew what was going on quite well? And who wouldn't try to get out of this stupid place?

"Mama, what is it?" Anna asked. She took off her hat and gloves, laid them carefully on an empty chair, and came closer.

In her mind, quite sanely, Lydia formed the mental words: "Get me out of this hellhole. And stop calling me Mama, as if you were ten." But all that came out was a mess of gibberish, with a few recognizable words mixed in. Worse, something else happened. Before her startled eyes, Lydia saw Anna quickly change from a stout woman in her early fifties to a woman in her . . . thirties . . . to —Lydia gasped, no longer able to keep track of the rapid transformation. In the next moment she saw Anna, aged approximately seven, standing there in a starched yellow dress. Lydia trembled in recognition and shock. The dress —she'd just ironed it for Anna's birthday.

"Mama, tie my sash," Anna said.

"Say please," Lydia said automatically.

"I said please, didn't I?" Anna asked.

"No, you didn't," Lydia said. "But come here and stand still."

"She said quite clearly, 'Come here and stand still,' " the grown-up Anna said to Mrs. Only and Roger.

"Well, do it and see what happens," Roger said.

131

The grown-up Anna came close to Lydia's wheelchair, and stood there with a silly I-don't-know-what-to-do look of embarrassment. For Lydia, the two figures merged one into the other. "Not you," she said irritably. It was terribly difficult to separate Anna Young from Anna Older, and Anna Older didn't need her at all. Why didn't she get out of the way?

"Come here, honey," Lydia said, coaxing, to Anna Young.

"Okay."

Lydia smiled. By working . . . something just right, she could block out Anna Older entirely and tend to the child.

"You look lovely, honeypot. Happy birthday," she said, glad now that she'd ironed the yellow dress after all. "You smell all nice and clean and starchy."

"Mama, it's me," Anna Older said, near tears. "It's not my birthday. Is that what you said? Who are you talking to?"

"She's living in the past. She probably thinks you're a child or something," Mrs. Only said. "They go on this way. She might come out of it in a minute."

Roger didn't know where to look. He shook his graying head, adjusted his glasses, blew his nose, and tried not to look around at the other old patients. He had the oddest feeling that they were all staring. But when he took a quick look out of the corner of his eye, he saw that no one was paying the slightest attention.

Anna Young pirouetted. "See how far out my skirt goes when I turn 'round and 'round—"

" 'Round and 'round," Lydia laughed, delighted to be so young herself. God, how beautiful the child was; and even the kitchen—the leaves through the window all waving and alive. The ironing board stood there with the iron upon it, splashed with sunshine. She bent over, saw her own face reflected in the iron, and the smell of freshly ironed clothes rushed to her nostrils. What a fantastic day—the birthday cake on the table—the small guests shortly to arrive.

"Oh, Mama." Anna Older suddenly bent down and took Lydia's hand. Lydia's eyes had been hazy only an instant earlier. Now she stared, with an angry superclear glance, it seemed to Anna, that quite pierced her through. "Go

132

'way." The words didn't quite come out clearly, but their intent was plain.

Lydia's hand gripped the wheelchair. When she focused on Anna Older, then the child Anna disappeared, and the kitchen. Anna Older was in an incredibly dreary hospital-type room, surrounded by old people who looked half like mummies, half-dead, strapped in chairs; and Anna Older was clearly no beauty herself. Lydia tried to blot out the vision and return to the kitchen, where at least she could cope.

"She doesn't want a thing to do with me," Anna Older said, with half a sob. "Roger, you try."

Lydia frowned. There they were, at her again. Now which Anna was that, and where was Roger?

"Aw, Ma, it's a girl's party and I don't want to go," Roger said, coming into the kitchen. He wore dirty sneakers and torn jeans.

"Don't, if you don't want to," Lydia said calmly. This kind of remark always disarmed him.

"They're all little kids, besides. I'm ten," he said.

"And one day you'll be eleven," she laughed. But somehow she knew she was on dangerous ground. One day he'd be eleven, then twenty, then forty, then fifty—

"It's me, Ma; Roger," Roger Older said. He was perspiring. He'd never put in such an afternoon in his life. He didn't know if he could bear to come back again.

But Roger was Lydia's favorite. Nonplussed, she looked about. Roger Young and Roger Older were each there; the boy in the kitchen, and the man in that awful hospital-type room. Her head throbbed. First the kitchen would disappear, to be replaced by the other room; then the reverse; then, dimly, both would exist together again.

Roger Young was on his way to the dining room desk where Lydia kept all her poetry, notes, books, and papers. He was carrying a glass of pop. She didn't want him to spill—"Don't spill that on my things," she called. "And get away from my desk—"

Lydia broke off, seeing Roger Older's face suddenly transposed on the boy. And Roger Older looked hurt. He thought she was yelling at him. Oh, dear. What was he saying? She strained to hear.

But Roger Young yelled, "Okay, Ma," and turned toward the kitchen, grinning; he was going to . . . going to . . . "Oh! no—"

"What is it, Mama?" Roger Older asked, bending down. She tried to say, "I can't tell you now. You're going to spill—"

"Oh!" Lydia cried. The pop spilled all over her papers. Were they ruined? She had to clean it up before the party. Her arm swung out, knocking a glass of water off the tray that was attached to the wheelchair.

"Oh!" Lydia cried again. The wetness shocked her. "Look at what you did." She scowled at Roger Older. Again her words were garbled. In the hospital-like room she couldn't make her tongue work right, although in the kitchen she had no trouble.

Anna laughed, almost hysterically. "I *think* she's bawling you out for spilling the water—"

And Lydia thought: what the hell is going on? She'd seen this room before, but hadn't realized that she was in it. Yet she was. Of course: she was seeing it through the eyes of the old woman in the wheelchair. But how could this be, when she was simultaneously a young woman in the kitchen, just before the birthday party for Anna? Her own thought made her grin. Now just how did you put a kitchen *before* a birthday party? Or in front of a birthday party? The party, then, had been years ago. Yet it was going on now. If she could do . . . what she'd been doing —whatever that was—then she could catch the party in progress.

"Don't you know me, Ma?" Roger Older asked.

She glowered at him. Of course she did. What a stupid question. If he'd just stay one age at a time, it would make things a hell of a lot easier. Here she was, trying to figure out what was going on, and he wanted to know if she knew him. Just like him!

If she was losing her mind, she was certainly losing it in the craziest way, she thought; then she realized that she wanted a cigarette. "Smoke." The word came out in a croak after she tried to say "Pall Mall" and "cigarette" without success.

They all stared at her. Ninnies. Patiently she made pantomime gestures of smoking. God, they were stupid. Didn't they understand anything?

"You can't have a cigarette," Mrs. Only said, finally. "You might burn yourself."

"Even if we watch her?" Roger asked.

"Well, all right."

Roger—bless his heart—gave her a cigarette. Her fingers just wouldn't do what they were supposed to do to hold it, though.

"Look out—she'll burn herself," Anna cried.

"Oh, shut up!" Lydia said in disgust. For once the words came out clearly. Anna recoiled.

Someone next to Lydia chuckled. Lydia's normal vision returned. She swung around. An old man with half of his teeth gone was strapped in his own wheelchair a few feet away. He caught her eye.

"That's Mr. Cromwell," Mrs. Only whispered to Anna and Roger. "Don't be frightened. He can't help slobbering like that. He's all right; just, well, you know—"

"Afternoon," Cromwell said brightly. He spat through his teeth, just missing the toe of his right foot. Anna blanched. Lydia tried to say, "What manners!" But this time she couldn't get her tongue to move right at all.

"Nice day," Cromwell said, leering at Roger.

"Why, he knows what's going on," Anna said, horrified, to Mrs. Only.

"Be quiet. He can hear you," Roger whispered back.

"I think it's time for us to go, Mama. We don't want to tire you out," Anna said nervously. "We'll come back next Sunday."

"Don't rush," Cromwell said, to no one in particular.

"He's . . . malicious," Anna whispered.

"Oh, no. He doesn't really know what he's saying," Mrs. Only said.

"Bye, Ma," Roger said.

Quite suddenly and simply Lydia put out her hand, almost formally; and Roger took it, feeling foolish. He wouldn't be coming back—Lydia knew this in a rush, without knowing how she knew. He was scared of becoming what she was, or what she seemed to be. But she didn't really understand him too well, even if he was her favorite, and she could get Roger Young back if she tried to. He had all kinds of great things going for him. Had Roger Older gone? And Anna? Lydia supposed they had.

"Your kids, huh?" old man Cromwell said.

His raspy voice was so intrusive that she jumped.

135

"Gotcha all doped up, huh?" he said sympathetically.

Lydia ignored him. For one thing, she wouldn't associate with old men who spat through their teeth; what a nasty habit. For another, she kept seeing Roger and Anna as they used to be, and somewhere in the back of her mind a birthday cake glittered with candles.

"Blow them out. Make a wish," she said gaily. In the dining room, her voice was lovely and clear as a bell. How odd!

"I want to be a doctor or an artist when I grow up," Roger said.

"You can't wish. It's my birthday," Anna said. "You shouldn't even be here, anyhow. You're a boy, and it's a girls' party—"

"Now, don't be that way, honey," Lydia said. But now she couldn't figure out if she was the old woman in the wheelchair, or the young woman cutting the birthday cake. For example, she thought: Now what did Roger grow up to be? And she didn't know *who* thought that: the old woman or the young one. Then the answer came. Roger grew up to be the manager of a chain of department stores. Now *who* knew that? The young mother couldn't. But miraculously Lydia realized that she was both—and now the young mother, looking at Roger, also knew what he grew up to be.

But Lydia in the wheelchair thought: what a pity. Not that she had anything against department store managers, but suppose she'd encouraged Roger's drawing more when he was little. She thought she had, then, of course. Still. . . . Desperately she tried to remember. What games had they played that day? Pin the tail on the donkey, hide and seek. Suppose she stepped in and made a change. Could she? Well, it was never too late to start.

"Roger . . . is going to make pastel sketches of each of you!" she said quickly. "Just like a real artist. And you can take them home—"

Roger said: "Wow!" and rushed off for his materials. Odd, that only now she remembered how crazy he used to be about art. He used to copy the funny papers for hours.

Now she was all mixed up again. Was she changing the past? And if she was the old lady and the young mother at the same time, then had she changed the future, too? Would Roger be different? Of course, he might not respond

136

to the encouragement, either; she might end up not helping him at all—if that would be helping him. And had she
done enough, or would she have to keep it up, inserting
encouragement in suitable places in the past?

Someone said something to her in the hospital-like room.
She tried to see who it was, but when she went back to the
woman in the wheelchair again everything got foggy.

"Time for our pill," Mrs. Only said. "We have a new
nurse coming late today. We want to have our medications
all taken care of, so she can just relax and get to know
everybody."

Where the hell had the nurse come from? What was she
chattering about? Lydia scowled again. What was real and
what wasn't? Could she get back to the birthday party?
She certainly wasn't going to stay here with that madden-
ing, condescending . . . person.

"Now, now," Mrs. Only said.

Lydia was quite exhausted. She stared at the nurse, or
tried to. Her eyes kept going to the right again. Mrs. Only
put the pill in Lydia's hand and gave her the water. Lydia
swallowed the pill resentfully, and went on with her own
thoughts, lost in them; but as the medicine took effect
everything became blearier.

She dozed. Once the weirdest thing happened. She felt as
though she was slipping sideways out of herself; then her
body shook and jumped as if she'd fallen back into it, but
from above. "Doped up," she thought irritably. "The pills.
Next time I won't take them."

Then she saw the birthday party, but from a great distance; and felt motion so fast that she couldn't follow what
was happening. Briefly it stopped, and she thought that she
saw herself sitting in the wheelchair. Instantly the motion
started up again. It was accompanied by odd sounds, rustlings, as if tissue paper was being crumpled right next to
her ears, and static. She glimpsed a body in a casket—hers?
Then a young girl appeared, about twelve years old. She
said something like, "Lydia, I'm Tweety. Tweety." And she
almost felt as if she knew who the girl was. Then the motion and the noises came once more.

The next thing Lydia knew it was dinnertime, and she
kept dropping her head into the mashed potatoes.

"We can cut down on her dosage, I guess," Mrs. Only
said to the new nurse. "It takes a few days before we can

137

figure out just how much they need. I don't think she'll turn violent again, anyway. She's been with us a week now."

A week? Lydia thought. She tried to focus her eyes. When was the birthday party?

Chapter Sixteen

Ma-ah's Signature
in Stone and
Sumpter's Surprise
(and Aspect Three)

While Oversoul Seven was perceiving the tile in two of its many Aspects, and Lydia was slipping back and forth in time, Ma-ah stood in the courtyard of the Speakers. "Who called me?" she asked again, and again she received no reply. She shrugged, and looked up to see Sumpter walking purposefully toward her. Coming close, he smiled and pointed at the tree drawing on the wall nearby.

"Mamunsha," he said. He squatted down easily beside her, a habit he'd recently taken to, to minimize the difference in their sizes.

"I thought *sanoraja* was the word for tree," Ma-ah said, in her new language.

He grinned. "Sometimes it is. Sometimes tree is *arumba* —that's a tree at night, when there's no moon. *Lidata*—

that's a tree splashed with sun. *Kadita*—that's a tree with leaves dancing." He was laughing now, but serious. His laughter disconcerted her. It reminded her that he had feelings. "Look at that drawing, and make up a word that fits it," he said.

Ma-ah stared at him uneasily.

"Go on," Sumpter said.

"Brambeda."

"Then that's what the tree drawing is in this moment."

"But I just made it up." Despite herself, Ma-ah was laughing, too.

"Exactly. When you force certain specific words onto objects, you limit them and their reality to you. So we have certain words which you've learned for the purposes of classification. But we never make the mistake of confusing the object with the name we've given it. All objects are changing constantly. No one word could ever express the entire reality of any one thing in all of its many aspects."

She liked him best now when he was teaching her. In that role she could accept him and not feel threatened. Now she shook her head, laughing back at him. "But you are Sumpter. That's a name."

"It's the name I gave you as mine at the moment you asked me," he said, soberly.

"You mean it isn't your name?" Ma-ah was scandalized.

"It is sometimes. I call myself other names, too—"

"If you don't have the same name, how will people know who you are?"

"My face tells them," he said. "At different times my friends call me different names, too. And I call myself what I please—"

She didn't like the odd warmth in his expression as he spoke: it had currents of coolness in it, too, but also a lazy, frightening invitation. "I call you Sumpter," she said, almost angrily.

"That's because you try to limit my reality for your own purposes," he said, without rancor. "You try to limit your perception of me, too. But right now I call you by two names—Sorana and Marunda. These names and words suggest two parts of you, seemingly in conflict at this instant."

"I'm Ma-ah," she said, irritated. She sprang up and paused. Sumpter made no move to follow her. "What two aspects?" she asked in spite of herself.

"The desire to control and the desire to surrender," he said.

Her thighs felt warm and her head felt cold. The remark was so true of her in so many different ways that she just stood staring down at him.

"We're called Speakers because we try to speak inner knowledge," Sumpter said softly. "Often we put it into words for people who need them. But otherwise we free ourselves from words. The people in the world you came from are just beginning a long journey into discovery. We came here to help them because that's our purpose." Sumpter suddenly looked away. Ma-ah watched him, curious. He seemed almost uneasy.

"We're beginning to mix our race with yours. Already on other parts of the Earth, this process has begun. You're a part of this, Ma-ah. It's time for you to mate. Since you're with us and don't want to return to your old world, then you should choose a man from the Speakers."

"Choose you," she said vehemently. "That's what you want; or what I was supposed to do—"

"Choose whomever you will," Sumpter said. "But you must join your stock with ours, or return."

"Why? I won't go back," she shouted.

He smiled, yet she sensed a great impatience beneath his manner. "You've been a good pupil," he said. "You learn quickly. Your race will take centuries to learn what we've managed to teach you so far. But we can't stay here forever, for reasons I won't go into now. You must pass on what you're learning to your own people, and the mixtures of our stock is important."

The sun was hot on the tiled courtyard floor. Ma-ah stared down as Sumpter talked. The shadows of night would soon be falling, and she shivered. He was giving her an ultimatum and she had the sudden feeling that she had to come to a decision before the evening came.

"Some of our knowledge is written in our blood," Sumpter said. Her soberness was upsetting Ma-ah more and more. "It's become a part of our physical stuff," he went on, watching her. "It will be passed on, latent, but full of potential. It *will* emerge, time and time again."

He didn't stand up, but she had the impression that he was standing; beneath his words she was dimly aware of other nonverbal meanings. She thrilled to it, and was frightened at the same time.

141

"Knowledge exists in every form possible," Sumpter said. "What you've learned is written in your soul, which is independent of your body. But it's also written in the body you inherit from the Earth, in the cells, and that knowledge is passed on, whether or not it's ever consciously recognized or used." He paused, and added, "I want you to have a child . . . with that heritage. . . . I want you to mix your stock with mine."

Ma-ah's eyes flew wide open. Until now he's always said "our stock" or "your people." Now he was saying "his stock," and "I want *you* to—" Suddenly she thought of the drawing of the strange bird, with all the people emerging from its belly. "You weren't . . . born here. You weren't, were you?"

"No," he answered, watching her face.

"You came from . . . that bird in the drawing. I used to think that it was a real bird, but it must be something different—"

"It is something different. But I can't discuss that particular subject with you yet . . . not until you take the part that you must take if you stay here."

Ma-ah frowned. "I won't go back. That's all there is to it. Not willingly, and I know enough about your people to know you wouldn't use force. But I don't like to do something because I'm supposed to, either. I know how animals mate. Rampa and I have done that often, if that's what you mean. You say children come that way, but Rampa and I had none. If I had any, they'd be *mine*. So I'm not sure what you want me to do. If it's what Rampa and I did, why didn't you just say so? That's only natural and makes you feel good all over. But you must mean more than that in some way I don't understand, or you wouldn't be making such a fuss about it."

"What you and Rampa did, will do then," Sumpter said, very formally.

"That's all you wanted?" Ma-ah was astonished.

"Why did you and Rampa stay together?" he asked quietly.

"Why, we needed each other. It's much easier to hunt for food—and we helped protect each other. Why else?"

"No other reason?" Sumpter asked carefully.

"What other reason could there be?"

"Did you feel toward each other the way Rampa and Orona seem to feel now?" he asked.

142

Ma-ah's face darkened. "No." She paused and said, accusingly: "You feel that way toward me sometimes, though, and it makes me uneasy. I thought that you wanted me to feel . . . that way too, whatever that way is. I didn't understand that you just wanted me to do what Rampa and I did, or I'd have said yes at once. I haven't done it since I've been here, and I've missed it, too."

She expected Sumpter to laugh, now that the matter was cleared up. Instead, some hope seemed to drain away from his face. He looked up at her and said, "I'll never threaten your sense of . . . emotional freedom. I'll settle for what you can give me now. And the mating, hopefully, will bring a child. You're much healthier than you were."

Ma-ah looked up, startled, to see that the shadows were beginning to fall. There had been no decision to make, then! Yet she felt oddly cheated, as if there had been a decision that she hadn't seen or recognized—and should have. "Just mate, as Rampa and I did?" she asked again.

"Yes, Ma-ah," Sumpter said quietly.

"Well, let's do it now, then." She threw herself down on the ground, laughing. "I'll never understand why you just didn't say so. You made such a fuss that I got the idea something more was involved, something I didn't understand." Then, at the expression on his face, she cried, "What's wrong?" Yet all the time she felt that she knew without knowing, and that he knew. Knew what? "You've got that look again," she said, accusingly.

"And you're . . . Sorana and Marunda again," Sumpter said.

She sprang up, grabbed a loose stone, shouted defiantly: "I'm Ma-ah!" and scratched the symbol for her name into one of the floor tiles as deeply as she could. "There!" she shouted triumphantly. "Now do we mate or not?"

"The part of you that can mate now will mate," Sumpter said. And he thought: she was unpossessable . . . like the world from which she'd come; innocent, splendid, shrewd, and perhaps terrible in the same way that a storm was.

Ma-ah began to slip off her robe.

"Not here," he said quickly. "The tiles are too hard. . . . We'll use one of my private couches—"

She shrugged. Now at least she thought she understood what was wanted. It was something she wanted too. There was no conflict. She ran along beside him quite happily. She considered the whole affair so matter-of-factly that

143

Sumpter was deeply troubled. So far, emotional feelings weren't connected in her mind with sex at all. He'd suspected as much, but he wondered what to do with his own longings for the part of her that even she had not yet discovered.

"I'm walking on the tiles' faces," Ma-ah said. Now she felt anticipatory and carefree.

"Yes," he said.

"Wait . . . why, the tiles are shifting." She cried out in alarm and ran ahead of him.

Sumpter caught her arm. "Of course they aren't. See? They aren't moving."

"I saw them. I was looking down and they began to . . . crawl . . . yet they stayed in the same place." Ma-ah shivered.

"Well, they're not moving now," he said.

"No. But when they moved, I got frightened. They made me think of things. If we mate and I have a child, then it will live and come and go, and be forgotten like a wolf cub. That's what I thought when the tiles moved. Or maybe I just thought they moved. But something shifts and we die. I've seen dead animals, and eaten them and never thought about it before."

"Our child, if we have one, will have many birthdays," Sumpter said. "And live to grow old."

But Ma-ah stood there, still startled. Her feelings had erupted; feelings not connected with hunger or necessity, free emotions welling up as she remembered them doing only once or twice before in her life. Astonished, she said, "Feelings . . . *move* inside people."

"You've felt emotions before—"

"But I didn't have time to know what I felt," she said wonderingly. "I never had feelings before that I didn't have to do something about right away. Well, once I did, watching a storm when I was safe in a cave. Or maybe a few times that I've forgotten. I don't know if I like this kind of feeling or not. You can't do anything about it."

"Something shifts," Sumpter said, echoing her earlier remark. "Strange." He refused to read her thoughts, though he could have easily. But he knew that something had happened to her. In some way she'd changed, opened. She walked pensively now, beside him. Quite unaccountably he felt sorry for her. The birth of feelings, and feelings' reflections, he thought.

144

And into Ma-ah's mind rushed memories of her earlier life, in the world of cliffs and hunger, light and night's un-mitigated darkness. The contrasts had been so brilliant and demanding that there'd been no time to think. They'd just seemed given, and she'd accepted them without questions. Now she discovered her memory clear and unblemished—yet there was no reason to remember. The memories just came. "I won't go back there," she said, in a hard voice.

"You won't have to—" Sumpter broke off, realizing that for the first time, perhaps in her voice, Ma-ah had given him a real glimpse of her life before she came to the Speak-ers. She'd told him all the details before, but in such a matter-of-fact way that her emotional response to the en-vironment never came through. With all he knew about her, she gave little of herself.

They were almost at his quarters. It was a humble enough stone structure, with a single unit—the basic pyramid-shaped center shabia or center room, with two smaller rooms on each side. The tiled floors were covered here and there with small white wool rugs, and the walls hung with tapestries in bright, glowing colors. Sumpter led her to a side room, with its wide windows and low couch.

The dwelling was much like the one the Speakers had given her.

"I've never mated where it was protected like this," Ma-ah said. And suddenly she was uneasy and shy. "Usu-ally we just mated when we felt like it, on the spot. All this talking—" She began stalking about the room.

But Sumpter didn't want to just take her, though she seemed quite ready, and his own attempts to give her time were apparently making her nervous. "Sit here for a min-ute," he said. "Once we mate, I'll have much to tell you about the Speakers' background; how we came here, tradi-tions we hope to pass on. But we maintain this place in ways that you don't yet understand. One day all of it will be yours; it will belong to the children of matings such as ours. Still . . . we'll vanish from the face of the Earth as we are. Mingling, we give up certain qualities that we'd retain if we kept our stock pure—"

Ma-ah sat there listening, wondering if the Speakers really mated or only talked about it. At the same time Sumpter's voice had a soothing hypnotic quality that she enjoyed, and a liquidlike fluidity of feeling rose and fell within her as she listened. "We'll retain our most character-

145

istic natures," he said. "We'll go truly inward, though, reaching men in the dream state, where words are really only symbols—"

She suddenly looked truly curious. "Why, that's like the old man, I suppose," she said. "I see him in my dreams often. Or I did. I can't remember seeing him lately."

"Speakers appear frequently in people's dreams and sometimes they *are* seen as old men. Why didn't you tell me earlier?" Sumpter stared at her, amazed.

"He's just the old man," Ma-ah said. "He isn't a Speaker because he isn't as tall as your people—"

"Is he always an old man?"

"Of course," she said firmly.

"Are you aware of him at other times?"

"No. Well, sometimes there are thoughts that don't seem to be mine, so I suppose they're his. I don't know why— like the time I ran up the pyramid steps. It was like having a dream while I was awake."

Sumpter's face grew so serious that she broke off. "What's wrong?"

"Nothing's wrong—"

"Well, then. I feel better." Ma-ah started to throw the robe off, this time with mischievous haste. Sumpter stared at her. She was there, offering herself so carelessly, yet he had to meet her on the terms she offered now. After what she'd just told him, a meeting of the Tribunal was a necessity. Only for the moment he had to relate to her as the person she thought she was, and try to forget the person he suspected she might be. She was right: something happens and reality begins shifting. And most important, Ma-ah had been . . . that "someone else" the day she went running up the pyramid steps.

Chapter Seventeen

Seven's Blackboard
in the Sky
(and Aspects Four and Five)

Josef stared at his painting uneasily. It had the oddest kind of mobility. The mosiacs seemed to jump up; move out of place; shift, as if the painting didn't want to stay on the canvas—as he didn't want to stay in one place either. Why should he? If he pretended to agree to Elgren's proposal, they'd allow him some freedom; then he could escape easily enough, he thought craftily. Bianka would be furious. He grinned: what a man-trap she was, and she knew it.

Now he sat on the edge of the bed, relaxing, eyeing one painting after another, enjoying the warmth of the sunlight that splashed through the windows onto the wooden floor. He'd been painting for hours. What a great day's work, he thought. What a perfect studio. Who could ask for more? He almost dozed, his muscles relaxing in the summer heat.

In his mind's eye he saw the room cozy in wintertime (without the windows boarded like last year), a rug on the floor to keep his feet warm (he'd insist on it), and a bright coverlet for the bed (Bianka could damned well make one). But there would also be her room—ah hah! *their* room—for sleeping and romping. And he'd gone scrambling through the countryside for the last time, half-starving, peddling his talent. This time he'd done himself well, outdone himself, set himself up for good.

The sunlight moved over the tiles in the painting. Josef watched, nearly hypnotized, dreaming of the comforts of the "good life." Then he caught himself. Not that he intended to go along with any of it, of course. He was just playing around with the idea of staying before turning it down; exaggerating the benefits so he could feel doubly virtuous (and twice as crafty) when he finally got out of there, regained his freedom, and left the Hosentaufs more or less the way he'd found them. There was no doubt in his mind that he would leave as soon as he got the chance.

A small ladylike knock came at the door. Josef's face lit up exuberantly. "Come in."

Bianka came into the room with the new shyness she'd developed since the "arrangement" arose for discussion. She left the door open—and at this, Josef laughed out loud.

Her face clouded. "Mama's orders. Papa's, too. It isn't funny. They don't know about us . . . last winter."

Despite himself, Josef remembered the two of them hot and sweaty beneath the covers, though the room had been chilly enough. He said, "Well, come in anyway. *You* can come in, can't you?"

She looked at him as demurely as she could manage under the circumstances. She had to show him that she could make a wife as well as a bed companion. Now she couldn't afford to be bold.

"If you don't stop trying to be such a grand lady, you'll explode," he said.

"Oh, shut up!" she said, before she caught herself.

"That's better. Now close the door and let's go to bed—"

"You know I can't." She was honestly scandalized. "If we're going to get married, then it's not right."

"Good. We'll go to bed and forget marriage."

"You think I'm trapping you."

"You? How could *you* trap me? I do only what I want to do!" he shouted.

She sat down next to him, averting her eyes, not yelling back at him as she used to do, and it worried him. She stuck her legs out in the air parallel to the bed, under her long skirts and petticoats, and wiggled her booted feet in small perfect circles. Her hands were in her lap. "That's a pretty picture," she said, looking at the courtyard scene.

"Say what's on your mind," Josef said, uneasily.

"You could go right inside that picture and walk to that yard or whatever it is, and no one would find us." She giggled softly. "The picture's big enough. We'd just disappear."

He stared at her. "I didn't know you had such an imagination. I didn't know you liked that painting, either." He paused. "Come on, let's talk about something else," he said. He didn't know if he liked the idea of Bianka having imaginative qualities or not. He was growing more uncomfortable every minute. The room seemed to be waiting. It had an unreal clarity to it; extraordinary, he thought. If he could only duplicate those colors! The sunlight almost had a . . . texture: there were variations in transparency so that one moment he could see through it and the next moment it became heavier, though without any suggestion of weight . . . thicker, moving in golden columns of air.

"You look so funny," Bianka said.

He turned and saw that the room's transformation affected her also. The brown hair was an intricate thick and lovely webwork about her face. Her eyes seemed built up of deepening layers of color, not isolated but flowing one into the other—the pupils small pools sunken miraculously in the eyesockets. The cheeks cast rich purple shadows that echoed the firm jawline. The face was a living landscape— he saw it, filled with these soft hills and valleys of flesh, with Bianka's moods illuminating it from within, flashing across it like clouds or sun emerge and disappear in the sky above the Earth.

"Don't move. Don't move an inch. Just sit still—" He was rising. Everything was shifting, he felt: room, sunlight —everything in precarious balance. He had to get her just right, this moment, before it all changed forever. One canvas was prepared for painting. He grabbed it and began to sketch her face. She stared at him, filled with awe. He was like one possessed, she thought. Not daring to move, she sat until her muscles ached.

"No, no. Don't move," he said.

"I've got to rest," she protested.

"Not now. You can't." But he saw then that she was losing the pose, the muscles were quivering like shadows underneath the skin. "All right, all right," he said. "Take a rest, and then return to the same pose."

"But I can't just sit like a statue so you can paint me."

"Why not? Of course you can. Think about something else."

"Let me see what you've done." She sprang up.

"No. No. Not now. Later."

At his insistence she sat back down and they resumed. They went through the same routine three times when Josef finally put his brush down. "The light's no good now. Come back tomorrow at the same time."

"What? Besides, Mama may not—"

"Tell her I said to send you, dammit!" he thundered.

She backed away, and he realized with amazement that he'd frightened her. "Bianka, I didn't mean to yell. It's just that my work is important. You're a good model, a great model. I don't know why I didn't realize it before."

"Could I see what you've done, then?" she asked.

"Yes, yes. Anything to mollify you," he said.

She stood in front of the easel. The canvas was barely covered, yet the face seemed to be appearing from within the canvas, peeking out, emerging from some hidden dimension. "It's spooky, looking at my face, unfinished like that," she said.

"You think it's spooky, do you?" he said, laughing now, in great good spirits.

Bianka stared at the painting and then at Josef. Then she made one of the shrewdest moves of her life. If he saw her like *that*, she thought, then she had no worries. "Mama's resting," she said. "Papa and my brothers are in the fields. If you want, you can leave. I won't tell or give warning. If you go west from the house, no one will see you. I don't want you to feel trapped. I thought I wanted you any way I could get you. Now do what you want."

At first Josef didn't believe her. She stared at him again, then turned toward the door. "I'll go downstairs. You can only have an hour or so to get clear. When Mama wakens, I'll keep her busy in the kitchen for as long as I can. If you're still here by suppertime, well then, that's your choice." And she was gone.

Damned good of her, Josef thought. At least she was

150

sporting. He wondered what he could manage to take, and what he'd have to leave. Once he'd left with only the clothes on his back and a few extras; now he had seven paintings in various stages of completion. The exuberance was at him again. He threw some belongings in his knapsack. Free again! Wandering the villages and the fairs—the outsider, with his canvases and paints! He started to hum. The sound vibrated satisfactorily through his teeth.

His travail and imprisonment were over. Aha! But even as his mouth hurt from grinning so broadly, he avoided looking at his paintings. He tried to pretend they weren't there. And all the while he wondered: would he really leave? When he turned around and saw the paintings, would he be free to go? Of course he would. No one was keeping him, after all. He went on thinking and humming, because no matter how loudly he hummed, the thoughts wouldn't go away. If no one was keeping him, then what was? What kind of a game was he playing with himself? Had Bianka unknowingly—or shrewdly—called his bluff?

Lord, what nonsense went through a man's mind at times. Of course he was leaving. He was half-packed.

And he turned. His paintings stood there like living entities materializing out of paint and canvas. The sun and shadows within them now seemed more real than the sun and shadows within the room itself. He couldn't leave them. And he couldn't take them. Some were too wet; he didn't dare roll them up; they'd crack and be ruined. For a moment he felt really frightened and more imprisoned than ever.

But what a great technical job he'd done on those tiles. He bent closer to the courtyard painting. The way he'd applied the coats of lacquers so that the transparent colors lay clearly one over the other, without muddying—

But suddenly it was as if the various layers of color somehow represented his own emotions. Not physically, but mentally he felt himself falling through the coats of lacquers, only in doing so he was falling from one emotion to another. The feelings had been opaque. Now they were so transparent that he saw them with childlike brilliance, but the dizzying physical sensation of falling through them remained, though he knew he was standing quite solidly on the floor.

They were *his* emotions! First there was his desire to leave. He felt this so strongly that his stomach ached with

151

longing. But then he fell through that feeling to the one beneath. This one was a combination of relief and shame so closely bound together, glued, that the feelings were like fabric and he fell into the soft slippery folds of unsuspected shame.

His real emotions, buried, denied, now caught him. He was really so glad to have "a place," so really delighted not to be wandering half-hungry, that he was ashamed. A man should be free, not tied down to one family, one room, one woman. Tears ran down his face as he fell through the shame to the emotion that had been beneath.

The anger felt like a thick red web that enveloped him. He stormed about the room, feeling the web grab at him, catch his legs in a tight grasp. Even this gave way, and he tumbled headlong into the fear that had given the anger its strength. He tossed a chair across the room and threw his knapsack at the wall.

For this was what had been bothering him, beneath all the other guises. The fear—he'd tried to avoid it—but it was too late, of course. The inspiration that he'd wanted so desperately had come—and it had somehow betrayed him. It was forcing him to care, to feel, to become attached. Even while the inspiration seemed to come from another world, it was forcing him to relate to this one— and he hadn't wanted to. Even the Hosentaufs were becoming real to him. They were no longer caricatures that he could make fun of, or ignore.

The superclear light bathed the room again. Or was he only imagining it? He turned. Amazingly, Bianka stood in the doorway; staring. He hadn't even heard her come up the stairs. She was different too, he saw—uneasily. She was no longer just someone to romp with, or the model for his latest painting. She was . . . herself, whatever *that* meant, with a reality of her own apart from his . . . alive with the same tormenting complexity of emotions that he'd just experienced, and usually tried to hide.

"You didn't leave," she said. This time she closed the door.

She looked so splendid—she might have just stepped out of one of his paintings, he thought. Grinning at him, she went over and waited for him by the bed, willing to make *some* compromises now that matters seemed sealed. They threw their clothes off, shouting happy obscenities at each other. In his mind's eye, Josef saw the two of them lying in the courtyard on the hot tiles, and staring from the painting out into the room.

Actually, Proteus stood in that precise spot in the real courtyard, with Window beside him. And Window could have seen into Josef's room—he was staring in the right direction—as far as space alone is concerned. But instead he was concentrating on Proteus's discovery.

"I'm sure of it," Proteus said. "We were standing right here talking a while ago. Remember? Then we walked back to talk to more of your people. I was upset because you 'saw' that black girl, and you were trying to divert me, I think. Then we drifted back here. But that one tile! Earlier you were staring at it as you told me what you were 'seeing,' and it didn't have that sign or symbol on it then. I'm positive."

"It could have been a different tile," Window said.

"But it wasn't. I know it's the same one. I kept staring at it because you were. And that mark wasn't on it."

"If you're right, then someone had to do it while we were gone."

"But look at it," Proteus cried angrily. "Get down and see for yourself. That's what's so unbelievable. It isn't a fresh mark. It's old. It's been there for ages, *yet it wasn't there a few moments ago.*"

Window knelt down, examining the tile. The blue fish with its lost tail sparkled even in the dim light, and a small symbol was clearly visible just above the fish's eye. "You're right. So it must have been there earlier, and we just overlooked it," he said.

"But it's almost dark now. It would have been easier to see when we were here before," Proteus said impatiently. "You're the one with all these abilities. Find out where the mark came from—"

Rising, Window smiled. "All of a sudden you sound like Story defending herself against your skepticism. I don't remember seeing the mark earlier, either. But in this case, common sense tells us that we just missed seeing it for some reason—"

"Now I *do* know how Story felt," Proteus said. "And I don't like it. Maybe there's no explanation, but I know you're wrong and something about that symbol is important."

Window said. "Either the mark was there and we didn't see it, or it was put there while we were gone and in such a way that it *appears* old. The first explanation is certainly the more reasonable one."

"I don't care; it makes me uneasy," Proteus said. "This arouses my curiosity more than any . . . demonstration of your abilities or Story's just because it happened to me, I suppose. No matter what you tell me, I know the mark wasn't there earlier. And I'm going to find out where it came from, one way or another." Proteus straightened up, his voice ringing with such intensity that Window couldn't help teasing him.

"This is our pragmatic Proteus?" he asked.

"See," Cyprus said to Oversoul Seven. "Each of your personalities interpreted your experience with the aspects of the tile in their own way. Lydia used it to feel her own identity in the midst of 'shifting time'; Ma-ah and Josef used it emotionally too, perceiving to some extent the many aspects of their own subjective reality; and Proteus is letting it open his mind to new possibilities—"

But Oversoul Seven was staring at the symbol that was indisputably now set in the tile. He turned to watch Proteus and Window as they walked away, and then shook his fourteen-year-old-type head: "Proteus is right. That symbol shouldn't be there; at least Proteus shouldn't be able to see it. When I traveled to Ma-ah's time, the sign wasn't there in the tile in *her* courtyard. It's her signature, the sign that she scribbled just now in the tile—defiantly— when she got angry at Sumpter—"

"Exactly," Cyprus said.

"Exactly what?" Seven cried excitedly. "What do you mean?"

"I've told you before that everything happens at once."

"Yes, but—"

"And that time is open-ended—"

"Yes, but—" Oversoul Seven felt on the verge of a great discovery, but he couldn't quite get it. His predicament was so obvious (and to Cyprus, amusing) that she started laughing.

"Stop it," Seven said. "I'm distracted enough. Let's see. Everything happens at once, so while I had my experience with the tiles and how they exist in 'time' . . . then each of my personalities did the same thing, but in their own way. I understand that much. In Earth terms, my experience rippled out in all directions—"

"An excellent analogy," Cyprus said.

"Yes, but . . . new things happened. I see what Lydia did or tried to do. . . . She went back in time and realized that the past and present are happening at once, so she tried to change the present by changing the past. But there's a big difference between that and the other thing that happened. Ma-ah signed the tile, but Proteus saw it in his present where it hadn't been a few minutes earlier. And it wasn't there in *my* Earlier either—"

"Of course. Go on," Cyprus said.

"Go on? I can't. That's where I get lost," Seven said dejectedly. "There's something that's escaping me."

"There certainly is," Cyprus said, smiling. She kept changing from a man's form to a woman's so swiftly that Seven said, "I don't mean to be rude, but couldn't you stop doing that just for now?"

"It's supposed to remind you of something," Cyprus said. "But you're too involved with this particular problem right now to pay any attention," and she steadied down to the woman's form that she used as a matter of convention.

"You don't have to sound so superior either," Seven said angrily. "I never had an examination like this in my lives, any of them, and I hope I never have another like it in the future, if you'll forgive the term."

"Oh, dear Seven, do calm down and try to understand," Cyprus said. "The so-called past is a source of fresh action and constant creativity just like the future or present—"

"I know *that;* that isn't the part that confuses me—"

"So Ma-ah signed the tile *now* and affected Proteus's present," Cyprus said. "A few moments earlier she hadn't done it in the past, so it couldn't appear—it hadn't happened—"

"Ah, I caught you," Seven cried. "I was always afraid that I would, some day, but I wanted to, too. Now that it's happened, I wish that it hadn't. I've caught you in the worst kind of contradiction."

"Don't look so . . . soulful," Cyprus said softly.

Seven didn't even smile, he just threw Cyprus a reproachful look and said, "You said that Ma-ah hadn't

155

signed the tile *yet*, so it couldn't appear in Proteus's twenty-third century. But, Cyprus, that doesn't make sense, not if everything happens at once!"

"You can scowl just like Lydia," Cyprus said.

"All right, take Lydia. She went back and did something new in the past," Seven said, scowling even harder. "I understand that, I think. Yes, I'm sure I do." Suddenly Seven got so excited that he blinked off and on until he even made Cyprus dizzy. "I'm getting it, I'm getting it. I think. New things can happen in the past, right? Even as the present happens and keeps happening, the past keeps happening and new events can happen in it. Oh, no, that's not quite what I mean—"

"You're getting closer, though," Cyprus said, excited herself. "Make up an analogy if you have to."

"An analogy! This entire examination is an analogy, if you ask me," Seven exploded. But the next thing he knew he had an analogy so real and vivid that he was astounded.

"I must be making it big, so I can see it clearly," he apologized, grinning. For written across the entire sky in towering, shining letters was the following message:

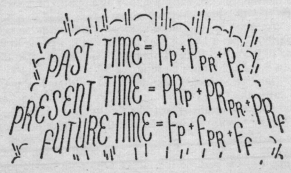

$$PAST\ TIME = P_P + P_{PR} + P_F$$
$$PRESENT\ TIME = PR_P + PR_{PR} + PR_F$$
$$FUTURE\ TIME = F_P + F_{PR} + F_F$$

"Since this is an examination, I'm using the sky as a blackboard," Seven said proudly. "An extra touch that should earn me a few extra credits, I hope. It's put rather simply, so I'm sure that it's clear. Just look at that."

He'd really outdone himself. The glowing letters covered the sky from horizon to horizon. On second thought, Seven gave the letters shadows that now covered the tiled floor of Proteus's twenty-third-century courtyard so that the tiles and grass were full of contrast and brilliance. "How do you like that?" he cried triumphantly. "Now that's a landscape and skyscape no one is apt to forget—"

"Breathtaking," Cyprus said. "Would you mind giving me your interpretation of the letters?"

"Can anyone else see it?" Seven asked. "It's a pity to create something so spectacular, and have it more or less go to waste."

"Seven," Cyprus said, with at least a touch of severity.

"All right. I made an analogy so I could understand, and I made up my own formula to express it. All time *is* simultaneous. There isn't any contradiction, thank heaven. But while we're at all attached to ideas of time or people who believe in them, then certain contradictions *appear* to exist. Actually, they're not there. They're only the result of limited perception. So I made up this formula to explain the contradiction that isn't there—"

"Must you be so wordy?"

"All right. It's as though there are three kinds of time, perceptionwise: Past Time, Present Time, and Future Time. Look—" As he spoke, Seven demonstrated, and in the sky above the letters, three boxes appeared, like this:

"Excellent," Cyprus said, concealing a smile. "You certainly are inventive."

"Now listen," Seven said, impatiently. "I put those kinds of time in big letters to show that they're the main divisions. But there's a past, present, and future in Past Time; and a past, present, and future in Present Time, and a past, present, and future in Future Time—"

"I see what you're getting at," Cyprus said.

"So the *past* has its own present, past, and future in

157

small letters, like this," Seven said. And he added the letters in the boxes in the sky, thus:

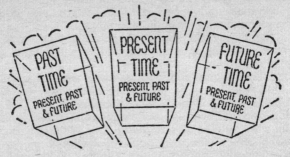

Seven was so taken with his own creation that he stared with awe at the giant boxes and the huge sparkling letters. "There's so much I haven't got yet," he said. "But I'm getting it. For one thing, that middle box, marked Present Time, is particularly intriguing—"

"Seven, you're getting very close to something very important," Cyprus said. "Whatever happens, remember: *You create your own reality.* You're apt to get lost in your own analogy. Be careful, Seven. There are implications—"

"Careful? Why? I'm fascinated," Seven cried.

"Don't be *too* impetuous!" she cried.

But Seven was muttering: "That middle box. Lydia's Present Time is in it, with its own present, past, and future. But so is Proteus's, isn't it? And Josef's and Ma-ah's? It's according to . . . But no, Lydia certainly thinks it's her Present Time—"

"Dear Seven, please. You must remember. *You create your own reality.*"

But it was too late. Seven felt himself drawn up toward the middle box, analogy or no; and into its mosaic-like structure. There were cubes within cubes within cubes, endlessly it seemed. And in one Lydia waited.

Chapter Eighteen

Out of Body, Out of Mind
Lydia Takes a Journey

Sweet Young Thing was the patients' name for the newest nurse. She'd been there three days now. She handed Lydia her pill and said, "There, let's just open our mouth and swallow this, and we'll feel so much better."

Lydia's thick tongue pushed out dutifully and the cracked lips opened; but craftily, oh craftily, Lydia made swallowing motions while holding the pill in her cheek. When the nurse turned away, Lydia spit the pill out and waited.

Old Cromwell, in the wheelchair next to her, leered his approval but kept silent.

Tranquilized, Lydia had more trouble than usual concentrating, but she knew now that she could do what she wanted to, if she only tried hard enough. She'd been "out," as she called it to herself, twice now. She mumbled irritably; she was bored rotten. To hell with it, she thought. She closed her eyes and imagined herself out of her body, standing right beside it. At first she made all kinds of mistakes, straining her physical muscles instead of using the peculiar inner tension that she'd discovered only the other day. A few times she swore under her breath. If her body moved too much, some troublemaker might come in and think she was trying to get out of the wheelchair. Then they'd add more restrainers, or strap her in tighter.

"Out, out, out," she kept saying to herself.

"Old Lydia's talking to herself again," Sweet Young Thing said, passing by.

"Poor old Lydia, my foot," Lydia thought angrily, and in that moment she was out. In a snap, a real snap, she felt as if rubber bands went zinging too far, and then broke, and there she was. Oh, God. Unbelievingly she saw the really wild old bony body, the sly face with the eyelids closed, hiding such great secrets—*her* body in the silly robe and pink slippers, and that stupid little-girl bow they'd put in her hair, so condescendingly. And there the others were, all of them, in the stark room, the propped-up half-empty bodies. The shock of seeing her body almost made her hysterical, but she caught herself at the sound of her first crazy chuckle. She didn't know how long she could stay out of her body yet, or what she could do. Could she, for example, just sneak away from it, and not come back? And if she did, what would happen?

"If you ain't the tricky one," a voice said. She swung around. Old Cromwell stood a good three feet off the floor, tipped sideways, grinning at her. Startled, frightened even, Lydia's eyes flew to his wheelchair. His body sat in it, as quiet as you please, fat and funny in its flannel pajamas and feet stuck in mismatched socks.

"Thought you were alone, and had it all to yourself, huh?" Cromwell asked. She gasped. He looked like an off-balance kewpie doll, floating in the air like that. "Come down on the floor," she commanded. Lydia's composure returned. She certainly wasn't going to be intimidated by toothless Cromwell. "Come down this instant," she said.

"Haven't got myself properly organized yet," he said. "But I know more than you do. You're new at it. I've watched you. I can get out of this place, and you haven't figured that out yet."

160

Lydia blinked up at him. "Out of what place?" Actually she was almost disappointed. She'd felt so beautifully isolated before. Knowing Cromwell could leave his body, too, almost spoiled it all.

"You just follow me and do what I do. It ain't going to hurt none," he said.

"*Isn't* going to hurt *any*," she corrected, automatically. A surge of dismay filled her. "Oh, Cromwell, why you?" she asked, half in amusement now and half in tears.

"You want to waste all your time yakking?" he demanded.

"No. No. You mean that we can get out of this . . . infirmary?" Lydia was embarrassed at the urgency in her voice; or was she actually talking? She touched her lips, wonderingly. Yes, they were moving.

Cromwell jumped up and down, watching her, holding his fat sides. "Sure they work. Your lips work, your arms work. Everything works."

"You crazy old coot. Stop laughing at me," Lydia shouted. This only made Cromwell laugh louder.

"Sorry," he said. "But you beat all. Here you are, finding me out of my body, too, and all you can do is correct my English and check to see if your lips are moving any. Never mind, come on, follow me now."

She tried, but she had difficulty navigating. She wanted to walk along the corridor, with dignity, but she kept rising up in the air, bouncing up and down, and once she even floated sideways. They passed Sweet Young Thing in the hall. The sunlight through the window fell on her hair. So breathtaking was the light that for a moment Lydia forgot everything else. "Come on," Cromwell called, looking back.

He went into one of the empty visiting rooms off the hall, walked over to the window, and went right through. There he was, bobbing up and down like a balloon, only in the air three stories above the ground. "I must be out of my mind, not out of my body," Lydia thought with a pang of panic. "They're right. I'm just senile, quite mad." The sight of Cromwell lolling out there enraged her.

"What the hell is it now?" he asked, and impossibly he was beside her again.

Lydia pulled herself up to some semblance of dignity. "Old men don't go strolling through the sky in the middle of the afternoon," she began.

"Would you like it better if I was a young fella?" he said stiffly. "What's bugging you more: looking funny, making an ass of yourself, or are you just plain scared?"

She'd hurt his feelings. "I'm sorry. Really I am, and I guess I'm scared. I just can't do it, just step out like that through a window three stories up—"

"Okay. Go back to your body," Cromwell said. "I thought you had some guts. They said you raised Cain right up to the last, but I guess that's all left you now. Be like some of them others if you want, afraid to get out even when they know they can."

"Besides being a crazy old coot, you're a cruel one," Lydia said.

"And you're a stubborn old idiot," he said, grinning.

She looked out, debating. Suppose she fell and died? Then the humor of it hit her. Everything was so outlandish that the word *death* didn't really mean much any more. How could it when her body was all folded up by itself in the other room, while she was here? At her age, what the hell did she have to lose?

Lydia almost gave Cromwell a coquettish smile. "I might as well die trying to fly as any other way. It's better than being drugged to death," she said.

"Now!" he shouted. He floated up several feet and just walked through the window; the glass just seemed to part to let him through, though at any time Lydia expected to hear the whole thing crash into pieces. She kept her eyes on him, rose, approached the window, put her hands out, closed her eyes tight then—and went through! Hardly believing, she found herself looking down at the yard. Below sat other old people, in less advanced stages of senility, those still allowed outside privileges. How she used to envy them! "Cromwell, I'm doing it, I'm doing it," she shouted. She felt free and weightless as the air itself. Already the two of them were moving so that the building itself became a blur.

"Oh, God, how I wish I were back at my desk, writing all of this down," Lydia thought. And suddenly, with no transition that she could remember, there she was in her study. A notebook and pen were in front of her on the desk. She felt the wood, her fingers trembling. Was the desk real? It was. Wasn't it? It certainly seemed solid. But her furniture had been sold. She knew that.

Yet each object in the room stood out with the most

162

intense brilliance. Even the air itself seemed to shine. A bouquet of violets stood on the coffee table. Her favorite flower. It was spring, then? It was! The scent of lilac came rushing to Lydia from the garden below. Then she looked down at herself, half-terrified, half-filled with exaltation. Her body was a young woman's; hers, as a young woman. She was wearing a long-forgotten lovely blue-flowered dress.

What was happening to her? It was fall, not spring, or it had been. "I won't stand for this confusion," she said, suddenly furious. "I'm an old woman in a home for the aged," she added, sternly, determined to hold onto whatever reality was left.

And she was. Lydia opened her eyes. She sat in the wheelchair. Her bones ached. Her hand was sore, and clenched. She opened it. The tiny tranquilizer fell out and rolled to the floor. The nurse would find it. Desperately she tried to reach it with her slipper, so that she could shove it underneath her chair.

As usual, when she tried to move her physical body correctly, her arms flopped like two scaly fishes, their mouths where her hands should be. Fascinated, she made her fingers move, or what felt like fingers, and watched the fishes' mouths open. A napkin lay there. If the fish swallowed the napkin, and if her hands were the fishes' mouths, would her arm digest the napkin? Marvelous! Delightful. She could experience her hands as hands, or as fish. Reality was slippery.

But Lydia's eyes fell on the tranquilizer again, and she sobered. If they realized she hadn't taken it, they'd shove the next one down her throat. She'd seen it done to others, and had already resolved that she'd bite down hard if they ever tried it on her. Teeth and biting reminded her of near-toothless Cromwell, and the entire episode with him rushed back into her mind. She turned as far as the chair straps would allow, to get a glimpse of his face.

Two things happened then, almost but not quite at once. First, Sweet Young Thing's voice came from the hall; she was obviously approaching. Lydia's eyes flew to the pill again, where it lay out in plain sight. Next, Cromwell did . . . something . . . that she couldn't put her finger on. She just sensed the quickest, most eerie feeling of some kind of communication going on between him and Mariah, whose wheelchair wasn't strapped to the wall as theirs were. In almost the same instant, with nothing being said, Mariah wheeled out to the center of the room. The wheel of her chair went crunching over the tiny pill, smashing it into the smallest of pieces.

"La la la la," sang Mariah, wheeling back and forth in the same spot, never looking down. Now the pill was white powder, scattered so thinly as to be invisible. "La la la," went Mariah, with her tongue lolling. She looked over and gave Lydia a broad wink. Cromwell chuckled, yes, chuckled quite sanely, Lydia realized. Then Mariah banged on the chair so that it made a defiant, satisfying thud.

"My, my, what a lovely song," Sweet Young Thing said, entering the room. Lydia's heart sank, but the nurse didn't even look at the floor. Mariah kept chanting, "La la la," sounding quite like the senile old lady she was supposed to be.

Sweet Young Thing said, "Now let's wheel you over to the window, out of the center of the floor so other people can get by. There! I'll turn the television set on, so you can watch before supper." Then she left the room.

"Got lost, huh?" Cromwell said. His words were slurred, as they usually were. He had the same old white bib tied about his neck in case he salivated too much and dribbled. His hands danced around each other as if they had a life of their own. Yet his eyes were crafty, amused, and in a strange way guileless.

"You got a bib on too, ya know," he said as if reading her thoughts.

"What? What?" Lydia's voice was harsh. She could hardly hear what he was saying above the television program.

"When we was on our flying stroll you just plinked out —you got carried away somewhere—" The words ran together, but made sense.

"Hush, hush," she snapped. "They'll hear you." She glanced quickly, fearfully, all around. "Sometimes I think I *am* batty," she cried.

This sent Mariah and Cromwell into gales of laughter. Mariah wheeled herself up close to Lydia and screeched: "Fly, fly like a bird. Tweet. Tweet. Tweet. Tweety." She waved her arms in the air and made a face, giggling all the while.

Then, exhausted, she fell back in her chair.

164

Sweet Young Thing came bustling in. "Now let's not be so noisy. Who's making all the racket?" This time there was a slight edge to her voice. Lydia watched her, thinking that she was young and sane at least, and could be depended upon. "N . . . Nn . . . nu . . . nurse—" she said, furious with herself; when she wanted most to speak, often she couldn't. Worse, the nurse didn't even hear her. She reached out, and this time the floppy right arm just lay there, refusing to move. But . . . an arm reached out. Briefly Lydia saw it . . . and felt it . . . and then it came back into her body and disappeared.

She was nearly in a state of shock. Sweet Young Thing turned, saw her face, and said, "What is it, Lydia? Are you trying to say something? What do you want?"

Lydia meant to say, "I know this sounds crazy, but I swear I went flying about this afternoon." Instead, all she got out in a raspy voice was: "People fly."

"Of course they do," the nurse said cheerfully.

Cromwell had a coughing spell. The nurse said, "What next?" and left to get him water.

Everyone in the room stared at Lydia.

"Fear you notch," Cromwell said, meaning to say, "Fear you not."

"They don't know nothin'," Mariah said. She grinned like a three-year-old and rolled her eyes.

For an instant Lydia rallied. "They don't know *anything*," she corrected, but when she tried to speak again the words didn't make any sense.

But her thoughts did. It came to her quite clearly that even while she couldn't speak properly, she *could* concentrate. And just as she was beginning to learn about these odd new movements in her . . . inner body . . . she was aware more and more of an inner straining, as if words from outside were trying to form in her mind.

Chapter Nineteen

The Speakers'
Dream Tribunal
(Ma-ah)

Sumpter slipped out of his body easily and stood up. He always felt more truly alive and alert, lighter and more exuberant when he cast his physical body off. Not that the Earth form wasn't marvelous, he thought, because it was, and he couldn't manipulate in the environment without it. Still, he felt more in his natural element whenever he slipped out of his skin.

Ma-ah was on the couch. He went in, moving quietly in the moonlight that splashed through the window. Her body was sleeping but Ma-ah was obviously gone; her form showing that peculiar vacancy that was apparent when the person-consciousness deserted it. Well, he had plenty of time, and he had a good idea where she was. Smiling, he remembered the nights that he'd followed her down to the courtyard, and found her studying the cave drawings and inscriptions. In the morning she never recalled their meetings, though now her dream memory was improving constantly.

Still, as he left his quarters, he wondered how she would respond at the Dream Tribunal; and what they'd learn. An unaccustomed nervousness was at him—she obviously knew so much and yet so little. He had the feeling that the Tribunal would discover information of great import to all of them. But as he went along, his native sensitivity drowned out his speculations. The night was so perfect that he felt honored to be a part of it.

He paused by the private dwellings. The Speakers' bodies were all sleeping, men, women, and children alike. But the Speakers themselves were up and about. The having just finished the children's nightly dream training; adults would soon be heading for the Dream Tribunal, and the children were playing. Groups of them went rushing by, playing tag, and Sumpter grinned indulgently as he watched.

The children ran laughing and shouting in their dream bodies—straight through trees—usually the biggest ones they could find, emerging gleefully on the other side. Their games reminded him of his own early training: the joy of learning to use the dream body and the great freedom of discarding the physical one. Then, of course, there was the contrast, equally delightful, of slipping back into the physical form. As children, they used to compare the two bodies for hours at a time.

He found Ma-ah at the courtyard as usual. He approached slowly, calling out when he was some distance away. She still had some difficulty in controlling her consciousness when she was out of her body, and he didn't want to startle her.

"Who is it?" she asked, turning.

"Sumpter."

"Oh. Funny. I thought it might be the old man."

"You might even see him before the night is out."

"What makes you say that? Do you know something I don't?" she asked. "Besides, this is another dream, isn't it?"

He paused. It might be best if she thought that the whole thing was just a dream, at least for a while. "You might call it that," he said, "but there's someplace I want you to go. I told you that most of the Speakers' real work was

167

done at night, and this evening the Tribunal is being held. I want you to go with me, and please try to remember what's happening."

She shrugged. "A dream is only a dream. I'll stay in this one as long as it's happy." Laughing, she took his arm as she never did in the day, and they walked down the path together.

At least Sumpter walked down the path. Ma-ah still bobbed along. Sometimes her feet were on the ground, and sometimes she floated gently above it. A few more children passed, and she frowned: "Look at them. They navigate better than I do. This is like learning to walk all over again."

"Just tell yourself that you want to stay on the ground, then forget it," Sumpter said.

"That might work for you, but I keep bobbing—"

"You're trying too hard. Forget it," he said. "If you were in your physical body, you probably wouldn't even see those children, you know. The place would look empty."

"Will I remember any of this in the morning?" she asked. "Anyway, do you think I will? I'm getting better. During the day bits and pieces of our dream activities keep returning."

"I hope you will," Sumpter said. "Tonight's Tribunal is very important, and I've tried to prepare you for it."

They were nearly at their destination. The robed Speakers were congregating in a small natural cup of the valley. Seeing them, Ma-ah said, "They're part of my dream, then?"

"What's happening now is an event. A dream event is as real as a so-called waking one. You know that."

Ma-ah nodded; but the colorful robes of the Speakers blended with the landscape, and now and then one of the figures would disappear, then reemerge. She shook her head, and blinked.

"Your consciousness is fluctuating," Sumpter cautioned. "Remember what you learned a few nights ago. Get the feel of your consciousness again. Mentally swing it around until this entire scene comes into clear focus. Then hold it."

She did as he directed, grinning up at him because the instructions worked so beautifully—when she remembered to follow them. Now she could make out the individual

168

faces of the men and women who seated themselves on the grassy banks of the circular hill. Sumpter walked over to the center of the natural arena, and stood there. Ma-ah sat down, to his left. The people quieted, and Sumpter began to speak.

He said: "It's written that all events occur at once, and as Speakers we know this. Yet past, present, and future seem to exist. So a prophecy has come down through the ages in our records about a woman who would come into our midst from the outside. She would learn our customs with great rapidity, and be a pivot point of energy in a way that even she would not understand. Her actions would deeply affect our work, opening up new probabilities that would appear in Earth time as it is experienced, pulling together the future and the past. She is here, now, among us. Of this I am confident."

He was silent for a moment. The Speakers stirred expectantly. Sumpter went on, with a certain dryness. "She has mated with one of us. Our stock will be reflected through hers. Though she appears in this present time as predicted in the apparent past, we know that in other terms, this has already happened—and yet is still to occur. So what we discover here will affect all other realities and times in which we are in any way involved."

He paused, looking into the faces of his people. "Many of you have met Ma-ah in day-life, or in our dream-training periods. She's learning our ways very quickly, as predicted, and before coming here she had some basic understanding of out-of-body consciousness, an unusual achievement for one of her background. But many important questions remain unanswered, and these I hope can be resolved before the tribunal is over."

Sumpter turned to Ma-ah. "Will you tell them how you came here? Tell them how you found the cave—the part of the story that you didn't understand yourself, and only remembered recently."

She stood up slowly; suspicious, quite stunned. "You're saying that I was meant to come here? Why didn't you say something to me about this?"

"I wasn't sure until yesterday," he said soberly. "And according to the prediction, you weren't told until the Tribunal was held."

Ma-ah looked out at the Speakers. Now they seemed to blend in with the trees that dotted the hillside, or some-

169

times they disappeared back into the grass itself. She tried to readjust the focus of her consciousness. Again everything came into clear brilliant focus, and she found herself speaking.

"I can't remember much," she said. "Rampa and I were half-frozen. We'd wandered too far that day and I knew we had to find some kind of shelter. Then something like a dream happened. I kept feeling as if the old man was talking in my head, giving me instructions, telling me to go in a certain direction. I've told Sumpter about him. I used to see him when I was out of my body; he helped watch for me before I came here. I don't know why I haven't seen him since, unless he knows that my body's safe here when I leave it. Somehow through him, I knew there was a refuge nearby. When we got to the cave I fell asleep or fainted, and when I came to, Rampa and I were both inside."

"The two-faced door." The words rushed up almost in a chorus from the Speakers.

"What does that mean?" she asked.

"It's symbolic, but also quite practical," Sumpter answered. "The door that leads inward or outward. We have several secret entrances—and exits—to our territory. They're almost impossible to just come upon; but I'll explain that to you later. Tell about your experience the day you ran up the stairs of the third pyramid."

"All I can remember is—" Ma-ah broke off. Portions of the trees began to fall apart and fly away. She felt dizzy. The images of the Speakers began to disintegrate at the edges, and her side vision kept closing until all she could see was a circle of light surrounded by darkness. Involuntarily she yelled out.

"It's all right. Don't be frightened." She heard Sumpter speak, but couldn't find him. "I'm right in front of you," he said. "You've lost your focus again, that's all. Relax. Don't worry."

His voice reassured her. For a moment she felt held in a soft blackness. Sumpter said, "You know what to do. Feel around now with your consciousness until you begin to see us—"

She gasped. The scene instantly cleared. The Speakers were smiling and nudging each other. "She's still learning," Sumpter said.

"I'm back in the dream again," she said, astonished.

170

"Remember, dreams are events as real as waking ones," Sumpter said. "Now—the pyramid."

"Pyramid?" She'd forgotten.

"Tell about climbing the stairs of the pyramid," he said gently.

"Why can't we do all this in the day, with my usual consciousness?" she asked, suddenly irritated.

"One kind of consciousness is as normal as the other," Sumpter said. "And this way we'll be able to find out far more, as you'll see. Now go on."

"I was with Sumpter, and I saw the three pyramids, only then I didn't know what they were. Then again I fell into a dream or something like one. When I came to, I was standing way up the stairs that lead to the top of the middle pyramid, and I was scared to death because I'd never been up so high. Then I realized that the old man had done it somehow. . . . The pyramid was familiar to him, but not to me. But even this vanished from my memory until a few days ago when I suddenly remembered it again."

When she finished speaking there was such a silence that Ma-ah was frightened. Though she still saw the Speakers, she had the oddest feeling that they'd withdrawn in some way that she couldn't fathom, or disappeared into some inner dimension where she couldn't follow. Disconcerted, she turned to Sumpter—and stared. The same thing had happened to him, or he was causing it to happen. All those people there, in plain sight, and she felt completely . . . alone.

"We just switched our awareness to another level for a moment," Sumpter said. "Forgive us. It isn't very courteous, but it was necessary. We've decided to tell you more about the prediction, and see if you can help us."

Ma-ah frowned. "It wasn't my imagination then? Well, it frightened me. I'm going back to my body and forget the whole thing. What good is it if I hold my consciousness at the right level, and you go off someplace else?"

Some of the Speakers smiled. She glowered back at them. "It's uncomfortable being with people who know more than you do all the time," she said angrily.

"No one is trying to make you feel inferior," Sumpter said softly. "You aren't. You're more important—and your presence here is more important than you know. Try to understand. You didn't come here accidentally. It's probably no coincidence that you were even in the area. You were led here. By whom? You ran unerringly to the third pyramid, stopping just outside the invisible third door. Its real significance is known only to a few Speakers.

"And there's more," he said. "In our records it's also written that the woman would have a twin; a psychic one, of the other sex. We don't believe that he's the old man. From talking to Rampa, we don't think he's the one either. So we have two questions. Do you have any idea who the twin could be? And what do you know about the old man?"

She looked sideways at him, grinning. "You didn't tell me that you talked to Rampa about this. Anyhow, I don't know the answer to either question. I know that this is an important dream event, and I'm determined to remember it. But I don't see how all this is connected."

"Neither do we—yet," Sumpter said. "Ma-ah, can you find the old man? Have you ever called him?"

"I never went looking for him. I wouldn't know where to look, or how. But why is it so important?"

"Learning the answer to that question is part of the importance."

Her eyes widened. Suddenly she felt frightened again, but excited at the same time. "Wait," she cried. "I do remember something else. The other day in the courtyard, I thought I heard someone call my name. No one was there. For a moment I felt it was the old man's voice. Is that any help?"

"It might be. Perhaps the courtyard is a focal point." He touched her hand and imagined the courtyard. Instantly they were there. Ma-ah was aware only of a whirr of sound like wind rustling through very dry grass. They'd traveled that way before when out of their bodies, but it always confused her.

Now she rubbed her eyes and looked about. The Speakers stood on the sidelines, so that their figures seemed to blend in with the drawings on the cliffs, as if the people themselves constantly moved in and out of the stone. The moonlight was brilliant and the tiles glittered.

"Think of the old man. Keep him in your mind," Sumpter said.

She tried to do as he directed, but there was no response, and unaccountably she became frightened again. "Maybe he's gone, or in trouble," she said.

172

"Just keep thinking of him, picture him," Sumpter said. None of the other Speakers made a sound. To Ma-ah it seemed that the world was waiting. Then she said calmly, "Lydia is dying."

The sound of her voice startled her. "What did I say? Did I say that? Who's Lydia? Sumpter, I'm frightened. What are we trying to do? What's happening? What do you hope to find?" Then she felt as if she was falling steadily downward. The last thing she remembered was Sumpter's voice saying, "Don't worry. I'll follow you if I can."

Then the scene vanished. She was tumbling, helpless it seemed, into darkness.

Chapter Twenty

The Speakers'
Dream Tribunal
The Night of the Soul
(Seven and Lydia)

Oversoul Seven began to fall headlong into . . . himself or his personalities . . . or something, yet he was losing himself at the same time, being dispersed. Into what? Frantically he tried to recall Cyprus's last words, but they eluded him. He kept feeling the separate essences of Lydia, Proteus, Ma-ah, and Josef. They were gaining a soul and he was losing himself—was that it? No, he thought, it couldn't be. I'm each of them, yet more, he told himself. I'm the portion that makes them what they are—not the product of what they are. "Aren't I, Cyprus?" he called. But there was no answer.

Even his thoughts began to slide away in the most insidious fashion. He felt his consciousness break apart into specks of energy, yet he was aware of his being in each of them—even as they fell away from each other. "Come back, come back," he cried to his multitudinous parts. For an instant there was just . . . nothing, and even Seven's terror was lost. Then he was in the midst of an incredible silence. There was no reference point within it. He seemed to be everywhere equally, yet nowhere in particular.

It was impossible for him to say, "I'm here," or "Here I am," because *here* and *I* had become impossibly synonymous. He could almost say, "There is no here and there is no I," except then who was thinking?

And then even his thoughts ceased; or if he thought, he was not aware of it. Instead he felt dragged down, drugged. Even the *I* who had been doing the thinking lost itself, until only nonverbal emotion remained. Seven fought against falling. He struggled against this great power that seemed to push him down into some indefinable blackness.

"Souls can't die." Once, from somewhere within him, the thought surfaced. He tried to anchor himself to it, but it fell away into meaninglessness. All the while he kept falling, and fighting against it, and the harder he fought the faster he seemed to fall, the further down he was dragged, and the weaker he became. Once again he managed to cry for Cyprus. At least he heard his own mental call, and again there was no answer. Nothing seemed to exist but this terrifying descent into darkness.

At the same time he felt that Lydia was falling too, surrendering; and in a different way, Proteus and Ma-ah and Josef, all together. Suddenly in the background of his wavering awareness, he thought he heard someone call, "Old man, old man," and he felt that the words must have a significance, though at the time they were meaningless. He couldn't tell where they were coming from. For that matter, the concept of *where* quite eluded him.

The word *Cyprus* seemed once to hang in his mental vision, and he knew only that Cyprus was someone he needed desperately to reach. And in that moment he realized that someone else needed him. There was someone he had to help, and only by helping this other . . . someone could he rouse himself. He was falling with someone, for someone, because of someone . . . who was also in great danger. The need of that other consciousness became his own, was his own: he became it, looked out through its eyes; through the drug-filled eyes of Lydia.

175

The eyes saw nothing but the blackness in which all objects were swallowed. Then the falling intensified. But Seven knew that he looked out through Lydia: that this was Lydia; he had a reference point and he tried to collect himself about it and save them both. It was her fear of death and dying that had trapped him, that must have come upon her with great suddenness—or had he just become aware of it because she had? It was impossible to tell.

"Lydia. Lydia." He said her name over and over as calmly as he could, even while the darkness rushed past them both and engulfed them in the chasm of her panic. "Lydia." It was no use, he realized. She didn't believe in life after death, or *the* soul, much less her own soul—he could never reach her that way now.

"Lydia," he said again. This time he mimicked Lawrence's voice perfectly.

Their descent slowed. He caused an image of Lawrence to appear in the blackness. Somewhere in it he could feel Lydia's surprise—her hope; and a small pinpoint of light appeared. Now Seven felt stronger. He caused Lawrence's image to appear in her mind and said, "Lydia darling, don't be frightened. It's all right—"

"Larry?" Even mentally she could hardly form words.

"You're having a terrible nightmare," he said. "That's all. Concentrate on my voice and it will be all right."

"Larry?" This time her lips moved.

"That's the name of a . . . friend of hers who died," Lydia's daughter, Anna, said to the nurse, Mrs. Only.

Lydia's terror released her enough so that one clear circle of consciousness formed.

"Relax," Seven said, as Lawrence. "Your own fear is causing the nightmare, and it stops me from helping you."

"But I'm dying." Lydia's words rang through her own awareness and fell crumbling into the room.

"No, no, you're not," Anna said. "Don't say things like that."

"She knows," Mrs. Only said.

Lydia heard. Frantically Oversoul Seven tried to calm her. Where was the real Lawrence? Why wasn't he here? Seven tried to call him, but there was no answer. Where were Lydia's parents or her husband? Why was there no one to help her? But Seven had no time to wait for answers. Lydia's fear was mounting again, and she'd have a difficult time adjusting if she died believing that her consciousness was really annihilated. He still had to fight against her panic, but he gathered together all of his strength to capture her attention. He needed a suitable vehicle. . . .

Suddenly he knew what to do—if he could do it. Slowly and at first in miniature, he built up the image of the old camper-trailer in her mind. She began to focus upon it; it roused her interest and curiosity. As it did, Seven built up the image, enlarged it, brought it into focus—and then projected it outward until it enclosed them. And he adopted the image of Lawrence.

"Lydia—"

"What?" She looked around, spun around. She was in the camper-trailer, in the front seat. Lawrence was driving. Greenacre, the cat, was on her lap and Mr. George was in his goldfish bowl on the wide shelf under the windshield. She closed her eyes deliberately, then opened them again: everything was still there. The sun was bright through the green treetops by the side of the road, and the air was soft and warm. It was early fall. Her right arm rested on the open window, and the air moved the tiny hairs on her skin. Everything was very real.

"We don't have far to go," Lawrence said.

She looked over at him. He looked great, like pictures she'd seen of the aging William Saroyan: funny, philosophical, his dark moustache bristly, his eyes grave and amused all at once.

The hair at the nape of her neck prickled; she felt an odd sense of foreboding, yet she felt more alive than she had in ages. Yet . . . "Larry, I had the worse nightmare," she said. "I dreamed that you'd died and I was dying, and that I ended up in an old people's home after all." She shivered. "It was so real . . . yet here we are, our trip uninterrupted . . . going on as if nothing happened."

"You *were* sleeping, snoring too, but I didn't want to disturb you," Lawrence said. "If I'd realized you were having a nightmare— But maybe it was something you ate."

"Mmm," she said. "But what a strangely lovely day. I mean there's something positively unearthly about it. And

177

you even seem different, more sure of yourself, maybe; decisive or something; wiser."

"That's just my natural superiority," Lawrence said. "I didn't know it showed."

"*Honestly,*" she said. But she felt uneasy. Her gaze flew about. She turned and craned her neck to see the back of the camper.

Inside his Lawrence image, Seven was nervous, too. The camper was a duplicate of the real one. He'd placed everything as carefully as possible, but undoubtedly he'd forgotten something. Nobody was perfect. The ruse had to hold until she was safely dead, to protect her from that panic—and if she found just one item wrong or missing, it could make her question the entire episode. Not that it *would,* he thought hastily. He could always think up a good explanation. Still he wished that she'd stop looking around like that. "Why don't you read me a few of your poems and practice for your reading?" he asked. "We'll be there soon."

"I left my notebook in back."

"No, it's behind me," Lawrence said. He reached around the seat and brought out the freshly materialized book.

She was smiling. Oversoul Seven was so relieved that the Lawrence image was grinning from ear to ear. Seven felt much more like himself now, and far ahead somewhere it seemed to him that he heard Ma-ah calling.

Lydia laughed, and pulled her visor cap further on her head to shield her eyes from the sun. "This is one of my children's poems. It came so easily that I can hardly lay claim to it, really," and she read:

> The future rises up
> Like a camel's hump,
> A part of the beast
> Like his ears or his feet.
>
> Who rides the present,
> Wiseman or dunce,
> Rides future and past,
> Aha, all at once.

"A great little poem," Lawrence said. "And true, too."
"Is it? Yes, I suppose it is," she said. "I did a series of

children's poems and called them *Sumari Songs for Children*. I don't even know why I called them that. The title just came to me. I always considered them odd in some crazy fashion. The book sold amazingly well, too. My own kids were young when I wrote them. Funny, as I said that, I had the feeling that Anna was upset. Now, I mean. I heard her voice way back in my mind—"

"I'm sure she's all right," Lawrence said.

"Mmm. I suppose." She looked out. "Strange that there isn't much traffic. We seem to have the road to ourselves."

"She's sinking," Mrs. Only said to Anna.

She had minutes left. Lawrence said, "We're coming to a tunnel. There's a terrific place on the other side that I want to show you."

"Oh?"

Seven materialized the tunnel quickly; because Lydia's physical senses would be experiencing their final darkening. She shouldn't be aware of it now, yet the final severing might possibly alert her to the physical situation and renew her panic.

"Oh, how dark it is," she cried, astonished.

"Tunnels are," Lawrence said.

"Mr. George won't even be able to see the sides of his fishbowl," she said.

For some reason this reminded Seven that he'd forgotten to materialize the second cat. Hastily he did so, placing him in the rear of the camper.

"This place I mentioned," he said. "I know the people will really appreciate you giving a poetry reading. They're poets too, in their own way."

"Do keep talking. This tunnel makes me nervous. I guess I'll take off my sunglasses."

"We're coming out of it now. There's the light at the other end. See?"

"Thank heaven. Poor Mr. George will think he's gone blind. Greenacre couldn't care less, of course. Cats can see in the dark." She broke off. "Oh, Larry, how lovely!"

"She's gone," Mrs. Only said to Anna, who started to cry and blow her nose, and look for her kleenex and sinus drops all at once.

"The landscape's changed. Look at that," Lydia cried, quite delighted.

Inside Lawrence's image, Seven grinned; the landscape

was an excellent job if he did say so himself—soft hills, early twilight—but now he had to let it merge with the quite real environment, because he knew now where they were, and what he had to do. "I might have to leave you for a minute after I introduce you to these people," Lawrence said. "I'll be back shortly though. It's in the nature of a surprise."

"A surprise?"

"Yup." He stopped the camper, got out, dapper and chipper, and opened up the door for her. She stretched and turned around. Lawrence was gone. An old man stood beside her instead. He looked vaguely familiar though she couldn't place him, and he wore a brown robe that suggested a monk's garb or an unconventional academic gown.

"Lawrence had to leave for a while. He'll be back. He turned you over to me, and I'm to take you to the poetry reading. I'm . . . Oversoul Seven."

"What an odd name," she said. "Well, if you're a friend of Lawrence's, I'm sure it's all right." After all, she thought, Larry knew an awful lot of far-out people; he used to travel around selling his leather goods off-season. She looked around. "Is this a . . . commune or something? Did you buy leather from Lawrence? I mean, do you know him well?"

"I know you far better," Seven said, grinning. She was seeing him from a memory in her mind of an aging sophisticated college professor—a roguish sort of would-be philosopher, but a kindly, well-meaning man to whom she'd once been attracted.

"Now what does that imply?" she asked. "I'm sure I don't know you, though you remind me of someone. At least, I think you do."

"You'll remember," Seven said. "But here is your audience. In a moment the poetry reading can begin."

Lydia blinked. In the background there were groups of people, obviously waiting. Where had they come from? She hadn't been aware of them before. Nor did she know how it was that she suddenly was standing in front of them, with the old man at her side. Politely Seven materialized a chair for her, and she sat down. As she did so, her poetry book appeared in her lap. What was happening? First everything made perfect sense, and the next moment

180

none of it made sense at all. She was about to say something when a lovely black girl in a long gown left the audience and came up to the platform.

Lydia gave the peace sign, but the girl ignored her.

"Well, at last you're here," Ma-ah cried to Seven. She saw him as her version of the old man, with a white beard, black skin, and clear piercing eyes. "I don't know what's going on, but it's very important," she said. "And I've had an awful time trying to find you. I fell into a terrible nightmare and kept falling and falling, and Sumpter had to get me out of it. All that to reach you," she finished, accusingly.

Sumpter came forward and paused deferentially. He bowed to Oversoul Seven, perceiving him as a giant-sized Speaker of superior bearing, wearing the sacred purple robes. "We're honored to have you here," he said.

"Honor yourselves as well," Seven said. "Tell me, do you see me as an old man too?"

"As a prophet, sacred Speaker of old," Sumpter said.

Seven shrugged. "I'm Oversoul Seven, a learner and a wanderer. I'm not physical at all, but if you want to see me as an old man, that's your business."

"Now, stop that. You *are* an old man," Ma-ah said angrily. "And the Speakers want to know how I got here. You had something to do with it, that much is certain. My guess is that you know more than you're telling."

Sumpter frowned. "Ma-ah, this personality is One Made of Many, as our records say. Be more courteous."

"She always talks to me that way," Seven said. They all looked so serious that suddenly he grinned and added, "Well, I guess I'll leave now. You're all so profound that I feel out of place."

"But you can't," Lydia cried, from the platform. "Where's Lawrence?"

Seven sighed. "You certainly all get yourselves in messes," he said, but suddenly he knew that the examination was nearly over. Memories that he'd purposely put aside now returned to consciousness. There was a job to be done.

"Some time you'll see me as I am," he said to Ma-ah. "But you'll have to see yourself as you are first. In the meantime, the necessary answers must come from you and

181

Lydia. The whole must discover its parts, and the parts must discover their whole—"

Sumpter stood back, smiling. "Yes, I understand now why I see you as I do. My interpretation, of course. But you *are* who I knew you were."

"Am I?" Seven asked. "But there's someone I want to introduce. Please ask your people to be quiet and just observe." And Seven called Lydia. She looked down at herself with some surprise. She was wearing a lovely softly folded gown that she remembered wearing years ago, as a young woman. Confused, she said politely to Ma-ah, "How do you do?" As soon as she spoke, the Speakers stirred with sudden understanding.

"I've seen you someplace before," Ma-ah said. "But how can that be?" She frowned. "Maybe in my dreams. But I'm sure that I know you."

They stood staring at each other, astonished by the warmth they felt, and then Lydia gasped: she was . . . growing younger, there was no doubt of it. "Something strange is happening to me," she said, in a whisper. "And besides that, the funniest things are coming into my mind. They're pictures of *your* life," she said to Ma-ah. "I know they are. They're your . . . memories. They're certainly not mine."

The same thing was happening to Ma-ah. She saw Lydia as a child, as a mother, as— Quickly Ma-ah dropped her eyes, for the pictures in her mind showed her something else—Lydia's death. And she understood in a flash that Lydia didn't know. A great, almost unbearable love went through her for this . . . woman, this girl, this *dead* old woman? Confused completely, Ma-ah turned to Seven.

"Lydia is going to read some of her poetry," he said.

"Oh, do," Ma-ah cried quickly, for who would tell Lydia that she was dead? And what did the whole thing mean? How long could a dream last, if this was a dream? But suppose it wasn't? "Sumpter?" she said, but Sumpter took her hand and motioned her to be silent.

The Speakers quieted. Lydia opened her book. "This is from my *Sumari Songs for Children*," she said, and she began to read:

The wind remembers tomor-
row.

182

Children, hear its voice.
It speaks through the voice of
    the singing leaf
That dangles in time's corner.
All at once is evermore.
The leaf in the moment knows
It is present and past and tomor-
    row now,
And even a leaf is wise.

Sumpter's face showed such utter surprise with the poem
that Lydia broke off. "What is it?" she asked. The Speakers murmured. Expectancy was on each face.

"Please read another poem," Sumpter said. Ma-ah
couldn't believe what she was hearing. She just kept staring at Sumpter, waiting for an explanation.

Lydia looked around again. She was more confused
than ever, but not at all frightened. Her poetry had never
affected an audience so strongly, and she felt more exuberant each moment. Once more she began to read:

No one comes to the land of time
Without wandering the fields
Of the hours,
Plucking the minutes that grow
Side by side,
And climbing the trees of the
    months.
Very high.

Lydia got no further. Ma-ah ran forward. She recited
the following so quickly that the words all ran together:

De li a ne bo,
Fra se igna mambra.
Sor ju anda
See far barde nee um
Lar breatum tes mu
Ze to.

"Not yet. Don't say it yet," Sumpter said, urgently.
Seven just stood there, feeling freer and freer, beginning
to understand the events that would unfold.

183

"I don't understand," Lydia said, appealingly, to Ma-ah.

"Do you write poetry for adults?" Sumpter asked.

"Why, yes, but I don't think I can remember any of them all the way through, and I don't seem to have that book."

"You can remember, Lydia," Seven said, gently. She gasped again; his eyes seemed to unravel her memory.

"How odd. Yes, I *do* remember. Yes." And she recited:

Thought-Bird Song

The birds outside my window
Are your thoughts sent to me.
From the nest of your brain
They come flying; fledglings.
I feed them bread crumbs
So they do not go hungry.
Then they perch on the tree
    branch
With beaks open, singing:

"We have come from the nest
Of yesterday and tomorrow.
God bless our journey.
We have flown from the inside
To the outside world of your
    knowledge.
The cage door is wide open.
We burst out, singing.
We fill all the treetops.

"Splendid and glowing,
Tiny as tree bells,
We dance on the branches
Of night and day always.
Listen to us. Feed us.
We are your thoughts winging
Out of the nest
Of the birth cage
Into summer and winter.

"Our song is your heartbeat.
We move with your pulses.

You send us out
Perfect and shining,
Each living and different
To populate your kingdom.
We sing outside your window
And line up on the rooftops."

As Lydia finished, all the Speakers arose. They began talking excitedly together. Many rushed up to Sumpter. He raised his arms for silence and everyone quieted as he began to speak.

"Lydia's poems, as you now know, are translations, somewhat distorted, of the Sumari verses we teach our own children, in which truths as we understand them are passed on through the generations. Ma-ah has been learning these precise verses as a part of her training." Sumpter paused, then continued. "I assume that our telepathic translation of the poems was correct, but I was astonished that Ma-ah understood at first. Then I remembered the connection between Lydia and Ma-ah that was apparent when they met—"

"But what *is* the connection?" Ma-ah asked. "And what was the last, longer poem? I didn't understand that one—"

"The last verse was also from our Sumari records," Sumpter said, "But your training hasn't extended that far yet. Again, the poem is one of many in which we transmit the truths of existence to the best of our ability. That's one of the reasons we're called Speakers—we try to put inner Sumari knowledge into verbal terms for those who have a need for words. The word *Sumari* is Lydia's translation of another word that refers to a particular 'family' of consciousness. All of us here are Sumari, for example."

"But where did I get the poems, then?" Lydia cried. "And who are all these people? I've never had such a dream in my life. I'm beginning to doubt it's a dream at all. But if it isn't, then what is it?" She turned to Oversoul Seven and said, impatiently, "And where is Lawrence? You told me he'd be right back, and that was ages ago. Oh, I'm so nervous. I need a cigarette."

"Here," Seven said obligingly. He materialized a cigarette of her favorite brand from the folds of his robe, and lit it for her. She puffed at it with great vigor and stared at him suspiciously. "Now I'm not to do another

185

thing or move an inch until you tell me where Larry is," she said.

Seven sighed. Pretty soon he was going to have to tell Lydia that she was dead.

Chapter Twenty-one

The Speakers'
Dream Tribunal
(Proteus and Josef)

Who was Lawrence? Proteus was having the most dis-
jointed dream. Nothing in it fit together. Yet for a moment, like now, he knew that he was dreaming, and this
only confused him the more. The whole thing was somehow connected with that symbol he'd found in the ancient
tile—he knew that much. Groggily he wondered what he'd
eaten to bring on such a dream. But then he fell back into
it again. This time he dreamed he was traveling backward
in time to the original civilization that the Tellers were
studying; in the exact location; and the tiles were new, or
nearly so.

Proteus could even feel his feet on the courtyard floor.
He looked about. How curious! The place was mobbed
with robed figures, with everyone listening to someone who

was speaking at some kind of podium. It was a brilliant night. He'd never had such a dream. It seemed so real. Proteus shook his head, shrugged, and made his way up front so he could hear what was going on.

Suddenly he stopped, almost thunderstruck, recognizing one girl in particular. He was certain that she was the one Window "saw" and described to him, the one Story said was connected with him in some way she couldn't understand. At least she was black and beautiful. Proteus stood there a minute, trying to decide what to do. Should he speak to her? If this was a dream—which it had to be, of course—it didn't make any difference what he did.

But suppose it wasn't a dream? The girl was several years older than he was, too. He didn't want to make a fool of himself. As he stood there trying to make up his mind, Proteus saw Window—or he thought he did. Window? Proteus scowled: what kind of a dream was this, anyhow? He pinched himself, and it hurt. What did that mean? That he was awake, which was impossible? Or that he dreamed that he pinched himself and it hurt? He decided he'd rather take his chances making a fool of himself with a man than with a girl, so he approached the man who looked like Window.

"Window?" he asked.

"Yes?" Sumpter answered.

"Oh, I'm glad it's you. You didn't find out how that symbol got on the tile with the blue fish yet, did you? That still bothers me." Proteus wanted to ask if they were both dreaming or not, but he was too embarrassed.

"Why, Ma-ah did it, but how did you know? Who are you?" Sumpter asked.

"What? Don't you know who I am? I mean, you *are* Window, aren't you?" Proteus began to blush. "You look just like him . . . but no, you're much bigger. Of course you're not! I don't understand. Are you a Teller?"

"No, I'm a *Speaker,* is that what you mean?" Sumpter asked. "But how did you know about the tile? No one was there but Ma-ah and myself when she did it."

Proteus closed his eyes and opened them again. Sumpter still stood there, along with all the rest of the people. Proteus tried again. "I saw it yesterday. And it doesn't make sense because it wasn't there a few moments earlier. It just appeared. And why did you answer to Window if that isn't your name?"

"Names are just designations. I answer to just about anything anyone wants to call me," Sumpter said.

"So you finally got here," Oversoul Seven said, coming over. Proteus also saw him as an old man. He struggled to wake up. Everything began to blur, but Seven touched him on the arm and the scene cleared.

"Who are you?" Proteus demanded. Dream or no, now he was determined to find out what was going on, and hold his own.

"Don't you know me at all?" Seven asked, disappointed. "Never mind. At this point I suppose it doesn't matter. You're back in the good old times you were always dreaming about. Doesn't that make you at all happy?"

"This is only a big dream!" Proteus shouted at the top of his lungs.

"Well, make it a quieter one and stop yelling," Seven said. "I've lots to explain to you. Come with me." Then he called to Ma-ah and Lydia. The Speakers retreated so that they seemed to be only shadows cast by the late moon.

"Proteus, what time do you live in?" Seven asked.

"What do you mean? It's 2254," Proteus stammered, as Lydia and Ma-ah walked over beside Seven.

"And who are the Tellers?"

"Why, they're . . . archeologists of a sort, living on the ruins of an ancient civilization—"

"Oh! This one!" Ma-ah cried. "The Tellers are . . . the—"

"He's got to find out for himself," Seven said quickly. "But you're doing very well; you're picking up part of my knowledge."

Despite herself, Lydia joined in. She was growing more excited. Even Lawrence's absence seemed unimportant in the face of what was happening, or seemed to be happening. "And my poems?" she asked. "They came from here. Did I get them from Ma-ah?" Her mind was working with great clarity. She turned to Ma-ah, who now seemed like an old dear friend, except that now she felt too young to have felt that way about anyone.

"In some way. I'm not sure," Ma-ah said, smiling back.

"I hate to admit it, but this is spooky," Proteus said to Ma-ah. "If I'm thinking straight at all, then you and I live in the same place, with me in the future and you in the past—"

"Well, you're *not* thinking straight," Ma-ah retorted. "I

don't live in the *past*. What do you mean?" she said, staring at Proteus.

Sumpter looked, amazed, at Seven. Indicating Proteus, he said :"The twin . . . Ma-ah's twin . . . in our records—"

"I suppose it isn't important, but I wish Lawrence *would* come," Lydia said, to no one in particular. Ma-ah took Lydia's arm quickly and said, "I'm sure he'll get here. But there's something I want to show you first. Look at that cliff wall. That's the way those poems of yours look in the language of the Speakers. See those symbols? And the drawings?"

Oversoul Seven was more than delighted with Ma-ah's concern over Lydia. He nodded at her vigorously, then said to Lydia, "If you'd been interested in art rather than poetry, you might have tuned into the drawings instead, as Josef did."

"Who's Josef?" they all asked.

"Oh, I've been so busy, I forgot," Seven apologized. "He has to meet you all, too." Seven was growing younger himself, more buoyant, as the bits of the puzzle began to come together for him, and suddenly it occurred to him that . . . they saw him as an old man when . . . in their terms, symbolically, he felt like one. What was it that Cyprus told him to remember . . . her very last words? "Well, no matter," he said. "Watch."

Mentally he called Josef's name so clearly and truly that it echoed through Josef's sleep. "What? What is it? Oh, it's you again," Josef said. He sat up, out of his body without realizing it. Bianka was sleeping beside him.

"Follow my voice. We're, uh . . . having a party," Oversoul Seven said.

"Can she come too?" Josef asked.

"No, there's too many already," Seven said.

"I don't know, then. I'd hate to have her wake up and find me gone."

"Your body will be there," Seven said, reasonably enough, he thought.

"My body!" Josef cried.

"Hurry, we haven't got all night," Seven said, with just a touch of severity. And in the next instant a blinking Josef stood with all the others. "What? What? How did I get here?" he asked. Then he recognized the courtyard. "This is my painting. . . . What are all these people doing in my painting?"

190

"Is that Josef?" Ma-ah asked.

"Why, he's the boy we followed down the tunnel that night," Josef yelled, pointing at Proteus. "There was a man there, too, with a funny name—"

Proteus turned white. "Window? Was that his name?"

"Right. Right. It was Window," Josef said. "Does he appear in your dreams too?" he asked, indicating Seven.

"Not in mine," Lydia said. "My, you look familiar. I'm sure I've seen you before. If only I could remember. . . . Are you an artist? I had a son sometime or someplace . . . who could have been an artist. I wonder how he is—" Lydia broke off. Suddenly she was looking into Roger's bedroom, and she knew quite clearly who he was. Memories of her life, but not of her death, rushed back to her. Roger was grinning, looking very relaxed and boyish for a man of fifty. He stood painting at an easel set up by his bed. The easel seemed quite incongruous and out of place compared with the white ruffled curtains at the windows. It seemed to be very early in the morning. He was talking to someone in the next room, through the open door. Lydia was quite astonished. Roger, *painting* before going to work in the morning? Roger—who had let his artistic ability just vanish through the years?

"Funny," Roger said. "Since Mother's . . . well, anyhow I've been remembering things I'd forgotten for years; how mother encouraged my painting even when I was a kid, for example. And I just remembered an incident I haven't thought of for a long time. It's so clear now that I wonder how I ever forgot it."

He paused, squinted at his painting, and went on. He was in his pajamas still, and Lydia smiled: the pajamas were a riot. Roger always did have lousy taste as far as clothes were concerned.

"There was a birthday party, for Anna, I think," he said, "and Mother had me do pastel sketches of the kids. They thought I was great. Maybe that buried memory was responsible for my taking up painting again, who knows? I feel as though I've found something I lost. I can even remember what Anna wore: a yellow starched pinafore." Roger stopped and turned as his wife entered the room. At once she burst out laughing. "What is it?" he said.

"I don't know. You just looked so funny for a minute, standing there in those crazy pajamas—"

The scene vanished.

191

"What is it, Lydia?" Ma-ah cried. "You look as if you've seen a ghost."

"Why, I don't know. I just saw my son as clear as life," Lydia said. "But . . ." Her eyes widened incredulously. "He was fifty, and I don't look nearly that old. Look at me, I'm not nearly that age. And there was something else; I'm not certain; he started to say something about Mother's—something, and he didn't finish. But it gave me goose pimples."

"Why don't you tell her?" Ma-ah said to Seven.

"Someone else wants to, but I will if he doesn't get here," Seven said.

"I'm here," Lawrence said, suddenly appearing. He carried Mr. George in the goldfish bowl, and a picnic basket. "Come on," he said to Lydia. "I promised you a picnic and we're going to have it. It's almost daylight and we'll watch the sun come up."

"It's about time you got here," Seven said, with a mixture of irritation and relief. "What kept you, anyhow?"

"I'll explain when I see you again," Lawrence said jauntily. He took Lydia's hand. "We're going to have a long talk. Here. I brought you a pack of cigarettes in case you were out."

"Well, I'm certainly glad to see you," Lydia said. "I thought you'd never come back—" She paused. Then she gave Ma-ah the peace sign, and she and Lawrence vanished.

Proteus and Josef stood side by side, staring.

Sumpter came forward. The Speakers moved softly out of the shadows. "I don't mean to interrupt," Sumpter said to Oversoul Seven. "And you've certainly given us some education in a short time. But there are still so many questions important to us. Why did you bring Ma-ah here? How did you know about the third pyramid's secret door? And are the Tellers really the Speakers? I mean, does the name mean the same thing?" He paused, then said quietly: "Perhaps most of all—are the ruins in the future the remains of our culture?"

Seven started to reply, unsuccessfully. For one thing, he didn't know all of the answers. For another, an acceleration seemed to be happening all about him. His consciousness started to whirl faster and faster—swirling upward as swiftly as earlier he had been swept downward; yet, again, up and down were meaningless. For an instant Seven felt suspended just above everyone else, moving in the same

192

spot so quickly that the others seemed motionless by contrast, caught in midactions, almost frozen into position.

The next moment everything vanished.

Cyprus stood there.

Seven stood there.

They were in the courtyard of the twenty-third century A.D. Above them, Seven's huge letters blazed in the sky, with their boxes carefully marked.

"See? You got caught in your own analogy," Cyprus said. "You just plunged headlong into the middle box, the one that you marked Present Time, and experienced some of its ramifications—"

"But—"

"The Dream Tribunal is over," Cyprus said. "At least, in terms of *your* experience."

"There you go again," Seven cried. "Qualifying. And when I've got something very important to tell you. Lydia's dead. Lawrence just came for her. What kept him? And there was no one to greet her—I had to do it myself—"

"Lydia didn't believe there would be anyone. You create your own reality," Cyprus said. "That's the last thing I told you to remember. You forgot to examine your beliefs."

"*My* beliefs?" Seven exploded. "Lydia's the one who didn't believe she had a soul—"

"And you let *her* belief sweep you under," Cyprus said. "You accepted it, and that belief drastically reduced your energy and effectiveness; and drained your vitality. You weren't able to use it because you accepted Lydia's belief as your own. One of the most important jobs of an Oversoul is to instruct its personalities—not to fall prey to inferior beliefs; to become part of their experience but not to lose sight of your own nature."

Cyprus broke off and said with very gentle severity: "Seven, for a split second you didn't believe in yourself."

"But what saved me?"

"I believed in you," she said. "But the examination isn't over. Proteus and Ma-ah and Josef are in physical reality, you know. There's some important questions that you must learn the answers to; then I want to see how your personalities apply what they've learned—or almost learned."

But Seven felt crushed, and disappointed with himself. He glowered impatiently and erased the letters from the sky.

"Any Oversoul can make a mistake," Cyprus said. "And

sometimes we make mistakes on purpose, to teach our-selves something important. . . . Oh, Seven, stop it—"

He'd changed his image to that of a little, angry old man, and started pacing up and down. "Oversouls are supposed to be dignified and . . . well, Window or Sumpter look more like souls than I do," he muttered irritably. "Physically speaking, that is. And they looked up to me so down there, and I tried to help Lydia; and here all the while I'd made a big error and didn't even know it."

Cyprus immediately changed into a clown and started laughing. "See, examine your beliefs again," she said. "Souls are full of vitality and energy, and if people want to think of them as being dignified and longfaced, then it's up to you to change their beliefs, not accept them." And Cyprus rolled into a ball and went bouncing over the tiles.

Seven was utterly astonished. Still in the old-man image, he went rushing after her, trying to keep up. When she stopped he said: "I never thought I'd see you do anything like that—ever—for any reason. I'm . . . scandalized. . . . I mean, well, you shouldn't act like that."

"Why not?" Cyprus said, adopting again her more conventional woman form.

"Why, just because," Seven started to answer. Then he got it, and blushed.

"You're learning," Cyprus said dryly.

Chapter Twenty-two

Proteus Gets a Few Answers from Window and Learns That Window Doesn't Know It All

Proteus awakened. He felt lonesome, which was silly, he thought. Still, he'd had that crazy dream about all those people, and he *missed* some of them: the girl called Ma-ah, for instance. He grinned, rubbing his eyes to get the sleep out of them. She was so spendidly . . . insolent in a way; well, maybe not insolent, but— Actually, though he tried to remember it, most of the dream was disappearing. Wait. He sat up, feeling that he was about to recall something very important. But he lost it. Anyhow, he thought: it was reality that counted. And he had a million questions for Window.

The Tellers, for example: how strange that this second dig wasn't discovered from above. It was protected by the cliffs to some degree, but it wasn't underground. And Window'd said nothing about the rest of the planet. Was it populated? And why had Window been so certain that search parties wouldn't find him here? What was there to stop them?

Something about the dream itself made him determined to get some definite answers. He got up and went barefoot, looking for Window. He was also ravenous, so he went to the eating hall first. (He kept wanting to call it an eating nodule.) Window was there, and Proteus sat down beside him.

"You're gaining weight," Window said. "It must be our sun and food."

Proteus grinned. "My stomach's finally getting used to the bulk, instead of synthetics. Window, where did your people learn to grow all this food? Any of it?"

"It's given," Window said, with a half-smile.

"Given?"

"It's aleady here. The Earth produces it. We harvest it and plant the seeds that the Earth gives; and cultivate the soil—"

"What about the rest of the planet?"

"It's in pretty poor shape. It's been stripped, but it's recovering, now that most of the people are gone. Even the animals are coming back. There's no question, though, that this particular area is amazingly productive." Window spoke slowly, and Proteus thought that he was holding something back. He was tempted to pursue the subject further, but there were too many other questions on his mind.

"Why don't the Floaters know about this dig?" Proteus asked. "They know about the first one."

Window stood up. "We don't know," he said. "You tell me."

"You don't know? You're joking, aren't you? With all of your knowledge, you don't know?"

"You can't even get in here except for the way we took you in, through the pyramid," Window said. "We suspect there may be other secret entrances but we haven't found any. No animals come in either, unless we bring them. Of course, the cliffs make a natural barrier, and there aren't that many animals yet, still—" He lowered his voice, almost in embarrassment. "A few times we saw planes go over. We thought for sure we'd been discovered, but nothing happened. The truth is that this place should be easy enough to spot from the air, yet it escapes the observa-

196

tion cameras that are aimed constantly at the Earth from the floating city. And we don't know why."

"Maybe the Floaters *do* know, but aren't letting on," Proteus said.

Window shook his head. "We're sure they don't."

"Well, maybe you can't answer my next question either, then. I never thought of that. But your abilities seem shared to some extent by all of the people here. Where did they come from?"

"We've developed them," Window said. "Living close to the Earth seemed to arouse long-forgotten tendencies in us, for one thing. We tried to encourage the Earth to come to life again. After everyone left, we explored the land as well as we could. This area was the least damaged, the most fertile. I'm second-generation. A few, like Story, are third. This work was begun by our fathers. But I'll have to show you something in order to really answer your question. Come with me."

Window took Proteus to another building he hadn't been in earlier. "Here's a videotaped record of the day the Tellers first found this place," Window said. "The narrator is Joel Bradwick. He was my father's brother. At the time he was fifty-seven. He lived to be a hearty eighty-four. The cameraman is Story's grandfather—one of the reasons I've taken such an interest in her development. Here we go." He darkened the room, and he and Proteus sat down to watch.

Window said, "Actually, after they found the valley, they went back for cameras and so forth. Bradwick waited here. When this video begins, the other members of the party had just returned."

The video glimmered.

"Incredible," Bradwick said. Watching, Proteus caught his breath, feeling that he was intruding. He was embarrassed for Bradwick, a man long dead, he reminded himself. But Bradwick was so obviously awed. He looked full-face at the camera and said, "I've never seen anything like this in my life before." He was so moved that his eyes looked bleary. There was sweat on his forehead. His thick mobile lips seemed uncontrolled.

"It's just chance that we ever came on this place," he said. "God knows how long it's been here." He paused. "I'm going to sit on this rock and narrate while the camera roams the nearby area. I've been here alone while the rest

197

of my party went back for some equipment, and I've discovered some astonishing things." This time the camera showed him full-figure, and Proteus saw that he limped, and was taller than the earlier shots made him appear.

Bradwick went on, excitedly explaining the video scenes. "This whole valley is surrounded by those high cliffs. You couldn't climb them—it's impossible—so we must have gone under them through the door we found at the first dig. And we thought that we had a find there! Twentieth- and twenty-first-century ruins. But this! This is the greatest archeological discovery of the century. Any century!" The video showed the wide expanse of sky, then moved in for a shot of the cliff walls.

"The cliffs incline forward as if on purpose, to protect the valley and keep it hidden," Bradwick said. "But more than that, the ancient drawings and signs on the cliff walls are in excellent condition, which is amazing when you realize that this place isn't underground. The later ruins at the other dig are in far worse shape. I found records stored on blocks of stone here, thousands of them, in inner rooms. Who knows what they say, or if we'll be able to decipher them."

The camera took a closeup shot of one cliff section, and involuntarily Proteus yelled out.

"What is it?" Window asked.

"I don't know. Can you hold that shot?"

"Of course."

Proteus stared. A small section of the wall held his eye. On it the following appeared:

$$\Delta \quad \daleth \quad 2 \quad 4 \quad 5 \quad \jmath \quad 1$$

$$/ \quad 3 \quad (\quad \Delta \quad 4 \quad c \quad)$$

Window said again, "Proteus, what is it?"

"I just don't know," Proteus answered. "My pulses are really racing, I'm so excited. Yet I can't tell you exactly what it is, because I don't know. But I had the wildest dream of my life last night, and the dream has something

198

to do with those symbols. I only remember a little. There was a girl in it, a black girl. It struck me as odd, since Story spoke about a black girl and then you 'saw' a beautiful girl with black skin the day that the symbol appeared on that tile. And in the dream someone was giving translations of ancient verse. When I saw those symbols just now, I thought that—" Proteus broke off, embarrassed. Then he continued, almost despite himself. "Well, I thought that I knew what the symbols meant; or rather, I thought I saw them translated into words of a sort, but in a different language. Yet I've seen symbols like that on the cliff walls here and never felt anything like that."

"Maybe you tuned into some kind of unconscious knowledge in your dream," Window said. "That's quite possible, you know."

"No. I really think that I just had the dream because that stupid symbol on the tile bothered me so. The dream might have been an imaginative solution to the questions I had or something—"

"Do you want me to go on with the tape?" Window asked.

Proteus nodded. "Yes, go ahead with it."

"Words can't describe this place," Bradwick said. The camera showed the entrance to the courtyard and played over the tiles. "How this place remained undiscovered through the centuries . . . I just don't understand it." Bradwick shook his head. "Until the end of the twenty-first century, this planet was literally covered with people. Yet no records mention this place. The ruins are obviously ancient, yet they're right here—out in plain sight—with no later ruins on top. It just doesn't make sense." Bradwick's voice was so filled with amazement that it was shaking.

"It's terribly difficult to recapture the sense of wonder those men felt when they found this place," Window said. "That's why these films are so valuable, to remind us. We're so used to it here."

"I just don't get it," Proteus said. "No later ruins? I don't suppose that somebody dug these out from under later ones?"

"Not unless they made them disappear completely," Window answered. "And there's no evidence of anything else having been here."

"The Floaters have complete records of the entire Earth," Proteus said. "Are you sure that—"

Window interrupted, smiling. "Our men went over all those records. There were various towns and small cities here, particularly in the last centuries of Earth's habitation—and no ruins of them in this particular spot. The first dig checks out perfectly, for example. There are a few possible explanations, but they don't hold up.

"Remember," he continued, "buildings in the later centuries weren't made to last, for one thing. Civilization was remaking itself, tearing itself down at an ever-increasing rate, and rebuilding. They destroyed a good deal of evidence of their past, so that only records or pictures remained. The whole so-called Urban Renewal Era began in a small way, but it ended up so that few cities were ever in decent shape or in stages of completion at any given time. They ripped down the old buildings to put up newer ones to house the greater numbers of people. But the new buildings seldom lasted over ten years. Material got low, until finally there was nothing else to do. They left for the floating cities and these took nearly a century to complete—"

"But Earth's been under observation all this time," Proteus said.

"Yes, but the race has concentrated all its attention and energy on off-Earth survival. Actually, there haven't been any real overall systematic explorations of the planet since man left. For so long it was just stripped bare, they had to let it rest. Portions are still scarred, maybe permanently, by radioactivity from the nuclear skirmishes of the early twenty-first century. Even many of the old famous ruins were destroyed. The Greek and Roman edifices are completely gone, for example. But here, I'll switch the video back—"

The picture came into focus. Bradwick said: "The thing is, these ruins have no right to be here. You get the insane feeling that they're . . . fresh. They're ancient, of course, but you think in terms of . . . freshly created age, or some such. And they're too complete—"

As Bradwick spoke, the camera ranged around the area once more. The three pyramids came into view. "That middle one is the one we emerged from when we got here," Window said.

Bradwick's own voice was more controlled now. A touch of resolution hardened his tone. "It's occurred to us that we might be able to keep this our secret," he said. "We've declared the first small dig, but so far no one knows about

200

this place to our knowledge. There's an unequaled opportunity for me and my entire party. We could spend our lives here deciphering what we find—"

He paused, then smiled ruefully. "I really don't know how we could get away with it, but the idea is worth considering. Women rule the floating cities now with an iron hand. Men have the least important jobs. It's only because this type of exploration is low on priority lists that no one bothers us. They think there's nothing valuable to be found. If they discover the importance of our finding, they'll take it completely out of our hands."

Bradwick looked away from the camera as if unwilling to meet the eye of any subsequent observers of the film. "This may be a rationalization," he said, "but the race needs one spot on Earth where maybe it could start over—one spot where we can be Earthlings, not Earth men or Earth women but Earthlings. This place could present us with the opportunity to begin a small living experiment of our own." Bradwick's voice was unsteady again. He said, "It's almost as if we were led here."

Window stopped the soundtrack. "So that's what they ended up doing," he said. "It took all kinds of subterfuge, though hardly anyone comes down to the surface as a rule. Planes are obsolete, no good for the Floaters' above-atmosphere conditions, though a few are stored on Earth, and copters are carried in the skylevators for use here when necessary. But still—both have gone over and still this place remains secret." He added soberly, "That's why you put us in such a predicament. We didn't want any attention drawn to this area at all—much less a search party looking for a citizen from one of the floating cities. They must think you're dead by now."

Proteus listened, but he wiggled uncomfortably in his chair. Portions of the dream kept returning, particularly the image of Ma-ah. He colored and looked away because the mental picture of her was so vivid. He realized that he wanted to meet her again, which was really impossible, he thought, because the whole thing had only been a dream. Some of his thoughts were so confusing that he tried to keep them even from himself.

He'd always wanted to be a girl because they had the positions of power, and the girl in the dream was exactly the kind of a girl he would have liked to be, for instance. On the other hand, he wanted her the way a male was supposed to want a woman—and in the way he *didn't* want Story, though he thought that he *should*.

The half-buried thoughts brought up another that surfaced suddenly, with strong emotional vitality. "I just remembered something," he said. "In the dream it was the girl who made the symbol in the tile. And she was supposed to live in . . . this particular spot, right here . . . but back in the past, when it was all new." The memory almost made him dizzy—because if this was so, then the girl in the dream *was* imaginary, beyond all doubt, and he'd never see her again. Either that, or she'd been dead for centuries. How could she have seemed so alive? How could the dream have been so real? "I just don't understand it," he said.

Window smiled sympathetically. "You had a dream that explained something that had worried you," he said. "Natural enough. And at your age, so is a dream girl. And you got the idea for her from my description of the girl I 'saw.' "

"I know. But just suppose that I did see an actual girl and it was the same one? I know it's not really possible, because she'd be dead. But if you can see things in your visions, then why couldn't I, in a dream?" Proteus frowned. "I don't believe it, but—"

"You could, of course," Window said. "But you haven't had the advantage of our training, so I suppose that didn't really occur to me."

"There, now, what training? You've kept so much from me because you were afraid that I'd be found, and tell it all. But since you don't even know how this place remains secret, I don't blame you. But I know something, I'm sure of it. That symbol on the tile is a key. That much is logical. There's a tie-in."

"In what way?" Window looked troubled. He turned the video off and turned to Proteus. "Maybe Story's insights weren't distorted as much as I thought they were, and you *are* connected with all this. Tell me what you mean."

For the craziest moment Proteus felt that he should drop the whole thing, that he was dabbling in something dangerous, that this very instant had a significance beyond any he could imagine.

"Well?" Window asked, and Proteus looked the other way.

"I've always liked you, Window," he said. "But I feel

closer to you now than I ever have. I'm embarrassed, I guess. I have the funny feeling that what I'm going to say will change our lives—not just yours and mine, and Story's —but the Tellers too, as a group. Yet I don't know why I feel that way."

"Just trust what you feel, and say whatever it is," Window said.

"That's just it," Proteus answered. "What I have to say just doesn't sound that important at all. Listen: this is all there is to it. The symbol on the tile appeared suddenly. No matter what we tell ourselves, it wasn't there and then ten minutes later, it was—fresh and new, yet ancient. And watching Bradwick on the video, I realized that in a bigger way, that's what happened with this whole dig. He found this place—obviously ancient, yet it hadn't been here earlier—or at least there were no records of it. The same thing as the new-old symbol on the tile, only on a larger scale."

Proteus lowered his voice. "But the important thing is that the tile symbol just happened a few days ago. So whatever is going on *is still happening*. No matter how crazy it sounds, the same thing *just* happened, and we almost saw it take place. If we'd been there at the precise moment the symbol appeared, what would we have seen?"

Window just stared at Proteus and didn't answer.

Proteus rushed on, carried along by the intensity he was feeling. "You've been here so long, Window, that you take lots of this for granted. But I don't. If you'd tell me about the training you've been speaking about, maybe it would help. Maybe I'd be able to see things that you can't, just because of my different perspective. And you've kept so much from me. Where does your water supply come from? Where did you get the model for your civilization, small as it is?"

Window said, "I'm afraid that I've relied on my inner seeing, and ignored some things that were right in front of my physical eyes. Forgive me, Proteus. Maybe you *can* be of help."

"Not only that," Proteus said. "But the tape showed me so many things. Those men began just the kind of experiment that I dreamed of for years as a boy: setting up natural life on Earth again. But you've really stopped asking the kind of questions those men asked. You've even stopped wondering why this place is still undiscovered.

Only my question brought the matter to your attention again. But finding the answer is important."

Window stood up. "You're right, of course. In a way, maybe we were afraid of learning too much," he said slowly. "A lot of this has to do with the training. We do many things because of it that we don't understand. We've been content to do them, and let it go at that, I suppose. We began the training—or it was begun—about three years after the original party arrived—and in a most peculiar manner.

"Wait a minute," he said, "And I'll show you another tape that you'll find even more informative." He paused, then continued. "Proteus, your attitude had a lot to do with our secrecy, too. You were upset enough about your own situation, of course: running away, the search, the new surroundings. But more than that, you were shocked by the little you did learn about us. Your reaction to Story was a good example. We knew you were uneasy about our abilities, and I 'saw' that you weren't ready."

"I'm sorry I was so skeptical," Proteus said. "I didn't mean to hurt Story's feelings."

"That's another thing," Window said. "I had her to think about. She's in the middle of her training, and she's never come up against doubts like that before. They *can* be ruinous. But here—this is a later tape. Three years later."

The sound and video returned. This time Bradwick stood in a room lined with stone slabs piled sideways on rock ledges. Bradwick was obviously older, yet in another way he looked more vigorous. His voice had an added assurance. A baby about two years old sat on the stone floor. Just as the camera focused on Bradwick, the child began to toddle about.

"The date is June 17, 2211," Bradwick said. "We all know it—I doubt we'll ever forget it—but our descendants might be interested. To save equipment we only tape on the most important occasions, and this is one of them. Rather than tell what happened, I'm letting my brother's child unknowingly demonstrate. At least we hope he'll do what he did earlier in the day. Please watch. The camera will be aimed at the baby. And just a hint here. We've left some of these stone tablets loose on the floor We're hoping that the boy will go over to them as he did about an hour ago."

Proteus watched expectantly and somewhat impatiently

while Window sat there smiling quietly, and offering no information. The baby crawled about, half-stood, fell down, got to his feet again, laughed, got up. "What does he do?" Proteus asked. "Just tell me so I'll know what to watch for."

"There. All right. Watch closely now," Window said. The child saw the stone slabs, went over, sat down, and put his chubby hands flat on one of them. The camera came in closer, and Proteus could make out the symbols on the stone quite clearly. The baby seemed disappointed. He put his hands down flat on the symbols and scowled. Out of camera range, Bradwick chuckled encouragingly. Proteus almost snapped, "Be quiet." He'd completely forgotten about Bradwick in his intentness.

The child turned, yelled, "Da!" and grinned, apparently at Bradwick.

"What does he *do?*" Proteus demanded; then he bit his lips, staring. While he'd turned to look at Window, the baby had returned to the stone tablet. Now the camera zoomed in. The small fingers were clumsily following the outlines of the symbols. Proteus noticed that the signs themselves were larger and more pronounced than the others he'd seen. At the same time the baby laughed with delight When his fingers ran off the symbols he stopped, looking disappointed again and ready to cry. This happened twice. Then, whether his fingers just happened to return to the symbols or what, the baby seemed to be—

Proteus turned, startled, to Window. "What's happening? He looks as if he's . . . listening through his fingers? Or hears something through them?" But before Proteus finished speaking, the baby stood up unsteadily, and then went back to the floor, this time with his ear to the stone. Nothing happened. The child looked outraged. There was a rich, loud laugh—Bradwick's. "Just exactly what he did earlier," Bradwick said.

"Sssh," Proteus said, and Window laughed.

The baby fingered the symbols again, and began jabbering excitedly as if he was trying to . . . repeat sounds he was hearing through his fingers from the stone? "Gibberish?" Proteus asked, not taking his eyes from the screen.

"That's what Bradwick thought at first too, but watch now—"

Bradwick squatted down beside the child. "My nephew has given a beautiful demonstration of his earlier per-

205

formance," he said, with obvious pleasure. "I didn't know what to make of it in the beginning. He's often in here while I work. Curious, I examined the tablet and almost dismissed the whole thing, but something—his aura of discovery, maybe—wouldn't let me. What did he find so fascinating? Then I thought of repeating his actual motions—"

Bradwick paused significantly, then looked directly at the camera. "When fingered a certain way, those symbols give off sounds that are carried through the fingertips. In this case, the symbols themselves give off the vibrations, but there are other variations, as we've already discovered in the last hour or so."

Window turned the sound off. "I can tell you this part," he said. "They were so excited that everyone tried fingering the symbols, of course. After several weeks it was apparent that the tablets were arranged in a certain order. In the first series, for example, simple pictures gave off an audible 'word' that described the object shown. Later ones added the symbol so that you had the written version. . . . Proteus, what's wrong?"

Proteus stared, white-faced, at the silent screen. "Turn up the sound, hurry," he said.

Window turned up the volume. The screen showed the following:

$$ 7 \cdot S \, \Gamma \, L \, \wedge \, \_ 7o $$

Bradwick was running his fingers over the symbols. "In sounds, these come out like this," he said. "Sa or ne ba tu om."

"It's impossible," Proteus cried.

"Proteus, what?"

Still watching the screen, Proteus said, "Don't say anything. Just hear me out before I lose the thread of my thought, or think it over and decide that the whole thing is too ridiculous. Before you tell me any more about the training you undergo, let me tell you more about my dream—and *your* people. Then tell me if I'm right or not. Your people discovered verses, too, that were supposed to . . . carry truths from generation to generation. Some were for children, some for adults. And the cliff drawings

206

are tied in here, too. I wouldn't be surprised if they gave off sounds in the same way—"

"Proteus, that's all correct," Window said, staring at him. "What else do you know?"

"That's it, I *don't* know. I didn't know I knew that." Proteus was dazed himself. "I thought it was just a dream. But those symbols looked so like the ones I saw last night that startled me on the first tape you showed me. But in my dream, someone told me what I just told you—or I saw it, or something. But I definitely recognized the sounds just now, the words or language, or whatever it is."

Proteus paused, trying to remember more of the dream. "There's something else important, but I'm not sure what it was. Something about the sounds themselves having the power to . . . do things; that's entirely apart from their meaning . . . I just can't remember."

"Give yourself the suggestion that you will, and you will," Window said.

But Proteus frowned. "I've lost it. But I'm more excited than I've ever been in my life. You've got to let me take that training. Maybe we'll discover how this place has remained secret—you never know. But you have to send out expeditions to other parts of the planet. *We* have to. Suppose there are other places like this that we don't know about. They'd be hidden, too, from us. Unless we find out what conceals this dig, we'll never know if there are others like it or not. Maybe there's several, for all we know, all waiting to set up new life on the surface of the Earth."

"Maybe," Window said. "But Proteus, don't be too excited. We may be the only ones, you know. What makes you think there may be others? This is an amazingly complex—"

"I don't know," Proteus interrupted. "But I'm sure that there *are* others. And I don't know how I know."

207

Chapter Twenty-three

Ma-ah and Sumpter
In Which Ma-ah Speaks
Through Proteus

Sumpter said, "Ma-ah, how much of the Dream Tribunal do you recall?"

"How much do *you* remember?" Ma-ah asked, grinning at him. "I have the feeling that more happened than you counted on."

"Ma-ah, be serious," he said.

"Don't 'Ma-ah' me that way, or I won't mix your stock with mine. What a confused baby I'll have. He won't know if he's awake or asleep-awake."

"He? And anyway, you already have—"

"But nothing's happened yet." She grinned at Sumpter seductively, on purpose. "I think we should do it again right now, just to make sure." Then she laughed uneasily and shook her head. "I remember the old woman who turned young, I'll tell you that. She was dead, and didn't know it. I guess I remember that most of all because in a queer way I almost felt like I was her—or a version of her. I can't explain it—"

"You're doing very well," Sumpter said. "You recalled that with no distortion; that is, without any hallucinations of your own. You seem to have those under good control."

"Is that what happens when I lose the right focus of consciousness?"

He nodded. "What else do you remember?"

She closed her eyes to think. "A boy, a few years younger than me. But he said that I lived in the past and he lived in the present, and we almost argued about it. He seemed so smug. I said that I didn't live in anybody's past. I lived now." Unaccountably Ma-ah found herself growing angry. "Why should he say that I lived in his past?"

"He lives in your future, Ma-ah," Sumpter said softly.

"Do you know him?"

"No. I've never met him before, but he's connected with you, and someday you'll realize how. I can't tell you."

Her eyes darkened. "Why not? I'm always in the position of your knowing more than I do. Why can't you just tell me?"

"Because I'd rob you of something important."

"Not if you have my permission," she laughed.

"Ma-ah," Sumpter said. "How can you give it, when you don't know how invaluable the thing is you'd be giving away?"

"Oh, all right," she said, only half-convinced. "But tell me one thing. Does that boy really live in the future? That's impossible in one way because he wouldn't be born yet." She frowned. "When I was in the outside world, before you found me. I would never have thought anything like this was possible. I mean, everything was Now. If I wanted to I could remember past nows, but I never thought of a future now." Ma-ah's eyes widened. "Why, that would mean that there was a future-now me to remember me, and you, and all of this. Just saying that gives me the strangest feeling."

"The now part is the truest statement," Sumpter said. "But you have to go through the past and future stage of thinking to understand it."

"Well, I'm more concerned about something else," Ma-ah said. "If I'm going to bear your child, I have a right to

209

know about your people; that is, if what you tell me is true, and a child comes from both of us."

"It's true," Sumpter said gravely. "But what about your own people? How much do you remember of them? So . . . mysterious in a way, that your stock grew out of the Earth itself like the trees, literally emerged from the womb; everything, men and animals, coming from the rich body of the planet, and physically at least returning to it. It's still such an alien concept to me."

His eyes were half-lidded, and his tone frightened her. She said slowly, "Sumpter, did someone give you . . . training on how to go *in* body? I mean, on how to live *in* one, just as you train me to live out of it, and remember?"

He stared at her. "Ma-ah, sometimes *you* frighten me. After showing the greatest ignorance of your own body mechanics and the birth of children, then you perceive something that I've . . . tried to keep from you, at least for a while. I shouldn't have said what I just did. I was swept away by your own beauty, as I often am. Then to think that this planet of itself produces such fantastic channels through which consciousness can express itself—" He broke off. "We still haven't discovered how you knew your way here."

"The old man, I remember him now, too," Ma-ah cried. "And I know he's somehow different than I thought he was. That's another thing. He's the one who directed me here, I'm sure of that—"

"And knew of the secret pyramid entrance, too," Sumpter said. "The connections are important in terms of what happens to the future of this settlement. And in some ways you're a key to the knowledge."

"Stop looking at me like that. I don't know anything I haven't told you. The old man does, though."

"Do you want to try an experiment?" Sumpter asked. "I have an idea—"

"No. Suddenly I'm nervous. . . . Rampa and Orona will have a child, too, won't they? Born of your people and mine." Ma-ah looked at him quickly, shrewdly, out of the corner of her eye. "Are there more children like that?"

He waited before answering. "No," he said. "For several reasons I can't go into right now, it . . . hasn't happened before."

She didn't know what to say, the implications of his answer were so startling. "You mean, our child could be the first; or Rampa's? According to who gets pregnant first, Orona or myself?"

Sumpter nodded.

Ma-ah said slowly, "Our child won't even know what it was like, outside in my old world, will it? I've almost forgotten myself. I try to put it out of my mind, I suppose. It was so terrifying. But I didn't have anything to compare my experience to before I came here. Then, I just accepted it." She paused and said: "Maybe I should go back sometime. I'd be frightened now, in a way I didn't used to be. But perhaps I should do it anyhow."

Sumpter stared at her. "Once you said you'd do almost anything to stay here."

"But it occurred to me: I don't even know what my heritage is. I call the people out there my people. There are bands of them, tribes. Rampa and I came across them but they were leery of us, and chased us sometimes. But their children will know that world. So awful in a way. Yet I feel almost frightened right now because I'm so safe and isolated. My people will go their way, and I'll go another—" She couldn't look at him.

"You're not really thinking of leaving?"

"I probably wouldn't even have the courage. But I'd like to see it again."

"If you left, you'd change everything," he said.

"Oh, why did such an idea come to me? It spoils so much," Ma-ah said angrily.

"What I said about my awe of Earth did it, I'm afraid," Sumpter said. "I emphasized differences—"

But suddenly an idea came to her; a way out, a compromise. "I have to do something tonight," she said. "Please don't ask me what it is. I have to do it alone and I don't want you to follow, even to help. Maybe the Dream Tribunal had something to do with all this. It made me realize how different we are, you and me; how easily you manipulate in ways . . . I find difficult. I'm still an outsider in your world."

"But your world *is* on the Earth. This is the Earth. It's not something apart," Sumpter said. "Look—trees, grain, flowers—everything is inside here that's outside—"

"But maybe I was meant to go through . . . whatever my people have to go through before they end up with this: your buildings and pyramids and cultivated lands. Maybe I was closer to myself in a crazy way when I was

211

half-starving. I have to do what I have to do, or even staying here wouldn't work."

"You can't go outside alone. You don't know the way—"

"I know it," Ma-ah said. He could read her mind easily and see what she'd planned, but she knew that he wouldn't.

Sumpter looked at her quietly for a moment. "I suppose you want me to leave you alone now."

She nodded. "I want to think. And I want to sit here and look at the courtyard awhile."

There was nothing for him to do or say. He nodded soberly and walked away.

Ma-ah waited until after sundown. She wanted to be back if possible before midnight, when the Speakers would be up and about in their dream bodies. Now she was frightened but determined. Could she remember the mechanics of out-of-body travel well enough to do what she wanted to? Could she master them without Sumpter around to help? Could she set her destination, reach it safely, and return?

It wouldn't occur to Sumpter that she'd try to go back out-of-body, because he hadn't given her instructions yet on going so far from her physical form, or pinpointing destinations. Ma-ah hoped she remembered enough just from hearing him talk about it at various times. She frowned again: physically she didn't even know how to get outside, but unconsciously she must know. And Sumpter had mentioned once that unconscious knowledge could be used to direct you to otherwise unknown destinations.

Still pondering, she walked back to their private dwelling. When you went "out" spontaneously, things often took care of themselves—she thought—but all kinds of hallucinations could happen, too, if your body was still sleeping. Yet to grab control consciously as she was going to do, and direct the journey, *you* had to do the things that were automatically done for you in a spontaneous dream projection.

Ma-ah lay down on her couch and closed her eyes. Will power alone wouldn't get her anywhere, yet she didn't want to fall asleep and drift into a dream, either. Instead, she started saying mentally: "I want to go outside, to the precise spot where I entered this place." Nothing happened. She wasn't being clear enough, she thought. She tried saying instead: "I want to stand outside, on the other side of the hidden rock door." At the same time she tried to visualize the spot as clearly as she could, from her hazy memory of it.

Suddenly her body felt as if it was rocking from side to side. Then she felt as if she was rocking inside her body. There were odd rustlings of sound, like words scrambled or backward, then loud whooshing noises like wind. "Be calm. You have to stay calm," she told herself, even while the sounds became louder. What caused them? Later she'd ask Sumpter. The wind became a roar, the rocking motions quickened. Something snapped at the back of her skull with an almost sickening thud—

And her eyes snapped open. Everything was quiet. She was outside; it had worked. At first she just stood there, staring. So much, yet nothing. The area was full of prickly shrubs and dry high grass. There were no high trees, just cliffs on one side, behind her, and mountains in the distance. The mountains contained caves—she and Rampa had used them for shelter often.

Her eyes stung—her dream-body eyes, she reminded herself. Her physical body was on the couch, back inside. She and Rampa had traveled from one full moon to another many times without meeting any of their own kind. Why hadn't they even been in one of the tribes of men, women, and children? They'd been alone together as long as either of them could remember. Then so suddenly— they fell apart from each other when the Speakers found them! Why? How dreary everything looked, she thought.

She took a few hesitant steps. She could stay on the ground easily enough if she simply told herself that she would, she found. But if she forgot, she'd begin to float upward. But she wanted to walk, to feel the Earth against her feet. She stopped: she wasn't doing something right because while she could see and hear, she wasn't feeling; not the air against her face, or the grass against her feet.

She concentrated on using all of her senses. Almost at once everything intensified. It was just as if she was in her physical body. She was home! The air had a different aroma somehow, she thought, fuller of wild roots and bushes, but how strange—the air itself had a loneliness in it, an odor of waiting . . . of suspension. She shook her head, unable to put what she felt into words. The air felt as if it was waiting for . . . people. For an instant Ma-ah felt close to men and women who *would* come, to that very spot. Unseen but felt voices seemed to murmur around

213

her as if, unbeknown to her, she was surrounded by people in other times, close enough to touch, but divided by some invisible barrier.

It was as if . . . here, outside . . . she could sense people happening but not formed *here* in this particular focus. But there was activity all about—as there had been activity and tribes all around Rampa and her, though they'd never come near enough . . . never . . . Ma-ah felt close to some personal revelation, and again she was frightened, overly excited. Yet another part of her was very calm, just waiting for the ignorant parts to understand.

She was outside, she thought. When she and Rampa had lived there before, how lonely they'd been. They'd never questioned their isolation, they'd just accepted it. Now she was shaking· Just who were her people? Where did she and Rampa come from? Why couldn't they remember? And this Outside, how far did it go? They'd only traveled so far in it. The Speakers' settlement had definite boundaries. How was it that she and Rampa had never wondered about that in the past? Or had they? Did they know and had they forgotten?

As she stood there a wind began to rise. It was gentle enough, yet it, too, had odors in it that she couldn't place. How odd, she thought. She looked up at the sky and gasped involuntarily. She'd come from the sky! She knew it, could feel the rush in her belly as she made the descent from far up, down through the clouds.

It was impossible, of course; people didn't come from the sky. At first Ma-ah thought that her consciousness was simply confused, but her thoughts were clear and distinct and her reasoning was functioning. The odd impression continued:

She came down.

In something like a round bird with open eyes on all sides, from . . . some large settlement . . . far above the clouds; she descended in a bird of metal that detached itself from something else—

And this place now where she stood was different . . . yet the same. She knew that—but suddenly Ma-ah was floating and her consciousness fluctuated. She saw glimpses of ground . . . then a tunnel underground. . . . There was a small dog running ahead down crumbled, dark stairs. She was dizzy; where was she, and where was her body?

Then she saw someone who looked like Sumpter. Mentally she called out to him, but it wasn't Sumpter at all.

This had to stop. It wasn't making sense. She was coming out of the pyramid's hidden door now, but the pyramid was no longer as high as it was, the hill was gone from beneath. She was back inside the Speakers' settlement. Relief almost made her cry; then she held her breath. Everything was wrong. Half of the buildings were gone, or crumbled, or . . . just not right.

Ma-ah sat up.

Sat up?

Who sat up?

Everything was out of focus. Proteus was terrified. He'd been examining the sound-embossed drawings in the courtyard; he'd grown dizzy or dozed for a minute—he wasn't sure which, now—then he sat up. And everything looked wrong. He tried to stand up but he couldn't. What happened? The Speakers' settlement was in ruins. Such an unutterable regret and sadness filled him that he felt literally sick.

But at the same time he kept thinking: What's the matter with me? I know these are ruins. And why did I say *Speakers,* instead of *Tellers?* Yet no matter what he said to himself—or to this other part of him who was so astonished by the ruins—he was still overwhelmed with bewilderment and the deepest desolation.

And the part who was so bewildered said: Of course, the Speakers told me how to get here when I came down from the sky. That's how I knew!

And Proteus said to himself: What am I talking about? The Tellers directed me here after I left the skylevator, but what of it? And why did I say *Speakers* instead of *Tellers* again? "I'm arguing with myself," he said, aloud.

Ma-ah shut off her thoughts. She was back in her body but someone else was in it—at least other thoughts were in it that weren't hers. It was the oddest feeling. Or had someone moved her body? Because what she was seeing through the eyes wasn't right at all. Or was her consciousness just confused? She stared—the ruins were still there. Had some catastrophe taken place while she was out-of-body? But no—these were old ruins, not new ones. . . .

Of course they're old ruins, Proteus thought angrily; that was the intriguing thing—the old ruins and the symbol on the tile—

215

The tile, Ma-ah thought, where was the tile with her sign on it?

Proteus shook his head. Why did he want to look at that stupid tile again? It was already driving him out of his mind.

There it was. Then this had to be the right place, Ma-ah thought. But she'd left her body on—

"Window! Window!" Proteus cried.

Window had been working nearby. Hearing Proteus's call, he came running over.

"Something's happened. I don't know what . . . I don't know if I can separate myself from what I'm getting—"

Window squatted down, and nodded, but he was alarmed. Proteus's eyes had an uncharacteristic expression, as if they were reflecting another personality entirely. "Proteus—"

"Listen," Proteus said. "I'm trying to do something . . . but it's so hard . . . listen, and see if I can do it." He paused long enough for Window to become even more alarmed, then said: *"Tellers* is another name for the *Speakers.* This was their . . . settlement. This place is inside in a funny way . . . I don't understand. . . . There's an inside way to get here, besides the way I came . . . not a physical way but a real way— Oh, I don't know if I can keep this up. . . . The tile *was* signed in the distant past. . . . No, it was three days ago," Proteus said, in a quite different, feminine voice. Window bent closer. "Proteus?" he asked.

"I'm Ma-ah," the voice said. "Where am I? I signed that tile a few days ago. Who are you? You look like Window—"

Like Window? Proteus thought, way in the background somewhere. In his dream there was a man who looked like Sumpter. And the name Window was familiar. He tried to speak, but the odd voice kept saying other things instead, and he couldn't seem to control his own vocal cords.

"Be calm," Window said. "Speak slowly."

Proteus managed to get control. "Who said that?" he asked, dazed. "Did I?" Then the other voice immediately cried out: "These are ruins. What happened?"

"Everything will be all right," Window said. He bent closer, and as he did so he sensed Ma-ah within Proteus quite clearly. "Both of you relax a minute," he said. "Get your separate thoughts straight. Don't worry."

Proteus took a deep breath, his-her eyes riveted on Window's face.

"What year is it?" Window asked.

"October, 2254," Proteus said.

"You're the boy from my dream," Ma-ah cried, through Proteus's lips. "Where are you? I can't see you."

"Window, what's going on?" Proteus asked.

"It's Sumpter," Ma-ah cried; then, forlornly: "You look like him but you're a wrong version—" The voice sounded panicky.

Quickly Window said, "Listen. Everything will be all right. You can get back where you belong. You're in the wrong place. Now wait and listen."

His voice, so like Sumpter's, held Ma-ah's attention. She tried to organize her thoughts and perceptions as best she could.

"Proteus, you be quiet for a moment, too, so I can help," Window said. "I'm named Window because I can see things happen in other times or places. But Proteus, you must be like a psychological window. Or looked at from the other way, Ma-ah is. Proteus, this time be quiet, and let Ma-ah speak if I ask any questions. Will you try it?"

Proteus nodded numbly.

"Ma-ah, somehow you got into another reality," Window said. "I'm very curious about your own environment, but I'm also concerned about my friend here, and this is a trickly situation. I want you to think hard about where you belong. Picture it vividly, and you'll return safely. Just follow my suggestions. Picture where you want to go."

"I feel whooshy. . . ." Proteus cried. "Oh—it's gone, or she's gone."

"Are you all right?"

"I guess so. Was it really someone?"

"We'll talk about that later. You're sure you feel all right now?"

"Just a little shaky—"

"So am I," Window said. "To all intents and purposes you seemed to be two different people, and the girl gave some pretty evocative answers—or you did, speaking for her."

"She lives here, in the past—as this place was," Proteus said, awed.

"Or maybe she's . . . a personification," Window said.

"No, that's the logical answer, but not the real answer. Still, there must be a connection. No wonder Story felt she was a threat."

"In a funny way I could almost follow her," Proteus said. "At least I feel that I could, but I'm too frightened to right now, I guess. But I have the impression that she's on a couch, opening her eyes."

The room was there. Ma-ah looked about. She was in her body. Her relief was making her shake. Her real, lovely, physical body! Laughing and crying, she hugged herself. A few minutes later she fell into an exhausted sleep.

Chapter Twenty-four

Discussions Between Lives
In Which Lydia Doesn't
Believe She's Dead
but Cromwell Knows

Lydia and Lawrence drove along. Contentedly Lydia polished her sunglasses, put them back on, and lit a cigarette.

"You've got to believe me," Lawrence said desperately. "I tried to tell you on the picnic. We're both dead. This whole thing—the road, landscape, the trailer—it's all a hallucination. In, well, greater terms, it doesn't exist. It just isn't real."

Lydia petted Greenacre. "And Greenacre. He's dead too, I suppose?" She delighted in baiting him.

"No, Greenacre, the real cat, isn't dead. Or, I don't know. He may have died. I just don't know enough to state the mortal status of that particular cat."

"Well, I'm glad to hear you admit that. What is this, anyhow, a new philosophy that you've picked up somewhere? It certainly took, I'll say that. I've never heard of anything so—"

"Lydia, you've got to believe me," Lawrence said.

"If the trailer's a hallucination, how come you aren't taking your eyes off the road?"

"Habit. Just habit," he said.

"All right, for the sake of argument I'll go along. But if it isn't real and you know it, then you wouldn't believe in it and it would all go away. Isn't that how hallucinations work?"

"I *don't* believe in it."

"Hush. Don't you yell at me, Larry. I've never heard you argue like this or raise your voice before in your life, much less over an esoteric point of philosophy."

"But *you* believe it," he cried. "And as long as you do, it'll all keep happening. Besides, that old man, Oversoul Seven, is maintaining it for you too—"

"Why, how nice of him!"

Lawrence shut his mouth and went on driving. After a while he said, "You know how young you've grown. Look in the mirror. You look thirty. That should convince you, if nothing else."

"There, that's something else. What makes you think I'd be alive and getting younger if I were dead? If I were dead, I'd be a corpse, and I wouldn't be getting anything. I wouldn't dream, either, if that's what you're going to say next."

"No, you aren't dreaming—"

"Of course I'm not."

He groaned.

"I just don't understand what's happening at all," Lydia said. "I admit it. And how come you still look near sixty?"

"So you'd recognize me."

"Honestly, Larry. That's plain silly. You aren't sick, are you?"

"If not, I don't know why not. Lydia, I'm not sick. I'm dead. I've never met anyone so stubborn in my life."

"Honestly, I'm getting fed up, Lawrence. I just don't understand you at all. If we're dead, prove it."

"All right, I will," he said. He thought about being young, tried hard to remember what he'd looked like. Beside him, Lydia shouted with astonishment.

"You did it, just like I did! You look fantastic. Oh,

Larry, what on Earth have we hit upon? If scientists find out, we'll be famous."

Lydia's tone caught him off guard, then he realized that her consciousness wasn't quite . . . together yet. She wasn't functioning with her complete reasoning faculties. He suspected she wasn't because she was afraid that she'd discover the truth. And the truth was against her belief in the nature of reality. This was all quite new to Lawrence, too. He tried to figure it out.

"What will we have for lunch?" she said.

"Anything we want will be in the refrigerator, I suppose," he said dryly.

"Well, if that's how hallucinations work, then I'm all for them," Lydia said. "Oh, Larry, I don't mean to hurt your feelings. But driving along with a man who's convinced he's dead is something new. You've had some weird ideas in the past, but—"

"We're *alive,* but dead."

"Well, that's a much nicer concept, I'll say that. . . ." She paused and stroked the cat. "Greenacre, you certainly purr loud enough for any two cats, dead or alive—"

Lawrence said, "Do you know what it's like, driving through a hallucinatory landscape, trying to convince your mistress that she's dead?"

"Larry, you have to admit that that sounds pretty wild. It would make a great short story, though. . . . You *are* joking, aren't you?"

"Lydia, what do you think would happen if you, well, went back to that old folks' home? Tell the truth," Lawrence said.

"That was a dreadful nightmare. What an awful thing to suggest."

But Lawrence remembered how things worked, or seemed to work. If thinking about being young made you young, then thinking about. . . . He concentrated on Lydia as the old woman in the home, and what it must have meant to her. He tried to think about what it must have been like—

They were walking down the corridor.

"Lawrence!" Lydia grabbed his hand. "What's happening?"

He looked around them. Well, at least he'd gotten rid of the trailer. Maybe memories from the old people's home would snap Lydia out of it, and make her face the truth,

221

he thought. He said, "This is the home you were in, as an old woman. Don't be frightened. It's all over now."

"I'm not frightened. I'm mad. What happened to the trailer?" She broke off. "Why, I know those nurses. That's Mrs. Only talking to Sweet Young Thing."

"See, it'll all come back to you," he said.

"Well, suppose I don't want it to?" Lydia said defiantly. "I'm young now and I'm going to stay young."

"You can. You are."

"Don't take that tone with me, Larry, and in public. What *are* you up to?" She paused. "Oh, I just remembered something else. An old man. His name is Cromwell. I think I'll just look in on him. Don't go so fast. Should I speak to the nurses, I wonder? They'll never recognize me, of course. I'm so young."

Lawrence just shook his head. It was useless, he thought, to say anything. The two women stood there talking, taking no notice as Lydia and Lawrence passed by. "Why, they didn't even nod," Lydia said. "You'd think they didn't see us at all."

"They didn't," Lawrence said. "Darling, we're ghosts."

Lydia stared at him. His age had stabilized so that he looked about twenty-eight. She felt so exuberant herself and for him, and here he was talking all that nonsense. She said, "Here I am, trying to figure out what's happening, and all you do is spout this idiocy about our being dead. Now either stop it or don't come in with me. You'll just upset Cromwell. When I saw him last, he was confused enough."

"I'll be quiet," Lawrence said.

"Well, that's better." Lydia grinned and went waltzing into the common room.

She gasped. Toothless Cromwell looked simply awful. "Oh, Larry," she said, involuntarily. Lawrence said nothing. He just tightened his grip on her arm. Patients sat in wheelchairs all around the walls of the room. Some, like Cromwell, were tied into their chairs. Cromwell's face was sunken. He'd kicked off his shoes and socks, and he no longer had any teeth at all. The TV was on: a ball game, poorly focused.

The announcer called the plays of the game. An old woman snored loudly. She was sitting up quite neatly in her wheelchair, and held a melting chocolate cookie.

222

"That old woman looks vaguely familiar," Lydia said. "I've had this dream before."

"Have you?" Lawrence almost smiled. He might be able to convince her of the truth now. She might believe it, if only to get out of this place.

"What's that noise?" Lydia asked. "You can't hear yourself think."

He listened. "Drums, singing, a terrible band. . . ."

"Oh," she said. "The Mission Society's Sunday services! I never went to *that*, thank you, mad or no—"

"When didn't you go?" Lawrence asked.

"Well, on Sundays when they had it—"

"That's not what I meant and you know it."

"Oh, hush. Who knows what you mean." Lydia stopped. A young man sat on the windowsill, reading. He had red hair and wore a green fedora, which was silly but nice, she thought. She poked Lawrence. "I wonder who he is. He doesn't act like a visitor, and he certainly can't be an attendant."

At the same time a young woman appeared. She looked agitated, almost angry, and before Lawrence or Lydia could say or do anything, she strode to the door and out into the hall. They followed her. The off-key band was louder now, its "music" obviously coming from an open room at the end of the hall. The young woman stood in the doorway, looking in. Almost insolently. Then she cried angrily: "Lousy racket. For God's sake, can't you just quit and go home? These poor old people—you'd drive them mad if they weren't already—" The music went on. "Idiots!" the woman shouted, coming back. "Isn't that the end?" she said to Lydia. "Who are you, anyhow? You don't belong here."

"I'm Lydia—"

"Lydia! What on Earth are you doing back here?"

"Well, I don't know, really. I don't recall meeting you before."

"Didn't Tweety reach you?"

"Tweety?"

The young woman turned to Lawrence. "Listen, she isn't supposed to be here. And I don't know what you're doing here, either."

"It's a bit difficult to explain," Lawrence said.

"Cromwell," the woman shouted. "You better come over here."

223

Lydia turned toward Cromwell's body, which just sat there. The young man looked up from his book. "What's the matter? I'm reading." He came over, tipping his green fedora when he saw Lydia.

"This is your old friend, Lydia, believe it or not," the woman said. "At least I think it is. And she doesn't have the slightest idea what's going on. Figure that one out."

Cromwell smiled with brilliant recognition. "Of course! I was so busy I didn't pay any attention; I just knew some people had come in; our kind, I mean." He looked at Lydia. "But you turned into your younger self once when you were out of body with me. I'm sorry I didn't recognize you."

"But I—" Lydia began.

He interrupted her, smiling. "Fantastic to see you again. Is this gentleman a friend of yours? We're the only ones left of—hah—the old crew!"

"The old crew?" Lydia asked.

"She doesn't know," Lawrence said significantly. "She won't believe me."

"Oh, she doesn't know?" The young man grinned. "So you don't want to remember, huh?" he said to Lydia with a laugh.

"Remember what?" Lydia said sharply. "Are you Cromwell's grandson or something? It's not very nice of you to carry on so, when he's in such terrible condition."

"It certainly isn't," he said gleefully. "He can't even spit through his teeth any more."

Lydia was shocked. And suddenly she felt very tired.

"How long are you going to avoid facing it?" the young man said. "Watch."

He grinned at her and walked over to old man Cromwell's body—and disappeared into it. Cromwell opened his eyes.

That's all that was necessary. Lydia ran over to the window, crying. And in her mind's eye she saw herself and Cromwell, two senile old people flying over the grounds, looking down at the strollers below, and the benches. And it all came back.

"What a nasty trick," she gasped, when she could talk. "I'd have faced it myself. It's just so unbelievable—"

"You're so hardheaded," Lawrence said.

Cromwell, the young one, sauntered across the room.

"At least you're safely dead," he said. "We're studying and learning, but we still have the death bit to go through—"

"And all those idiots out there, shouting about heaven and eternal bliss," the young woman said. "Incidentally, Lydia, do you remember me now? I'm Mariah—over there—the old lady with the cookie."

"Oh," Lydia cried. "My body, then, where is it? It must be buried."

"No. Cremated," Lawrence said. "Mine too. We decided on that ahead of time."

"Usually you have to wait till you're really fed up with your body," Mariah said. "I mean, it just gets so it doesn't work right. See my body over there? It still likes to eat. I mean, it still wants to . . . and up to a certain point, a body has its rights."

"Mine fights back," Cromwell said. He stood there looking very elegant and dapper, staring at it. "I tried to bow out twice, but it just mobilized itself and pulled through. So you have to give it credit, in a way. I'll just have to ride it out; and while it lasted, it was a great body."

"But I just went all at once," Lawrence said. "I thought everyone did. No, of course, Lydia didn't even know when she died. I *knew*. I felt a twinge of regret, I suppose, when I left my body on the park bench—with Lydia's help. I know I didn't want to get old in it, or I didn't want it to get old. But now I wonder: there was still a lot of vitality in it. I'd made up my mind, though, half without knowing. That must have made the difference."

"Die and learn," Mariah said, grinning. "But seriously, Lydia, Tweety's been looking for you."

Cromwell interrupted, "I tried to help you when you died, Lydia, but you wouldn't let me—"

"That's all right," Lydia said. "But who is Tweety?"

"I don't know," Mariah said. "Maybe she has something to do with . . . well, the classes we attend. We pretty much understand what's going on around here, and we help the other people as they begin to operate independently of their bodies, like Cromwell tried to help you. Now we're pretty certain that the classes are hallucinatory in some way, but real in another way. The things we learn are certainly real enough. We think that perhaps the room, the teachers, and so forth are just images or projections for our benefit, so we'll understand—"

"But the fact is, we're deciding if we want to be born

225

again, and if so, under what circumstances," Cromwell said. "And we're learning that we can't intellectualize everything."

"You certainly sound more educated than you did," Lydia said. "You used to say 'ain't' all the time."

"You were a bit of a snob, in your way," Cromwell said.

Lydia sighed. "I suppose I was."

"Well, you'd better find Tweety. She was around when you were here before. Once I tried to tell you," Mariah said.

"I *do* recall a voice once. . . ." Lydia stopped, then said, "But Cromwell, if you want to . . . die, why won't your body let you?"

"Oh, it would if I really pushed it. But the cells are still alive, and parts of it work great. And to tell the truth, I think my body's relieved and at peace with me out of it, and not bugging it all the time. As long as I'm busy and happy, I suppose I shouldn't begrudge it that."

"And bodies change, too," Mariah said. "Thank heavens. The cells and the awareness in them; bodies want their own fulfillment. Strange, even with mine, eating those lousy chocolate cookies all the time. I've felt it, yearning to return to the Earth again, unorganized for a change, free to be anything. I mean, just scatter. . . . And it's amazing, the vitality of bodies. The ones we have now are great, of course; they don't *age*—but they also make you appreciate your physical bodies even *more,* with all the stresses they go through."

"I think I'm going to cry," Lydia said. "I don't even know where mine is."

Lawrence grinned. "Roger has the ashes in a mayonnaise jar. I don't know how he worked that."

"Larry, that's awful. Before I do anything else I'm going to unplug that jar and let the ashes out, scatter them someplace where they can be free. Oh, I never even liked mayonnaise." Suddenly she broke off. "Why, if I'm alive though I died, then *I must have a soul.* I always thought that that was just a big bunch of nonsense—"

"Listen to that racket," Mariah cried.

The Sunday services were winding up. Just as Lydia finished speaking, and Mariah interrupted, the band broke into a resounding off-key rendition of "Nearer My God To Thee."

Lydia glowered and said, "That's what I mean. That . . . stuff!"

But in the meantime, just as Lydia said, ". . . I must have a soul," Oversoul Seven appeared. Now Lydia turned and saw him. In his eyes she saw all of her memories from the day of her birth as Lydia. She knew who she was, and who Seven was. She saw the love and order that had always been beneath her days. And the hospital disappeared, and Lawrence, and Mariah, and Cromwell.

Chapter Twenty-five

In Which
Lydia Meets Tweety,
Discusses the Meaning of Life
with Oversoul Seven
and Stakes
Out Her Future Parents

Tenderly, actually with crafty tenderness, Josef eyed Bianka while she lay next to him with her back turned. A while ago her body had just been a buxom, tasty one (mmmmm, he grinned). Somewhere along the line it had become *her* body, a natural, joyous expression of her . . . Biankaness, so that sometimes he actually got embarrassed (him!) when he touched her.

She was asleep. He'd just wakened from one of his old-man dreams, another vivid one in which a crowd of people were *inside* his courtyard painting. Now he ran his fingers down Bianka's smooth naked back. How alive the flesh was, the veins like buried rivers—ah, the body like a landscape—a *fleshscape*. He could try a painting from that angle.

"Mmmmm," Bianka said.

"You'd better get back to your own room," he said. "After all, the wedding's today. At least we won't have to sneak around any more."

"Mmmmm." She wiggled with sleepy seductiveness, not at all worried. In fact, she wanted to laugh out loud, but she didn't dare. "No more worries after today," she said. "Can't you just imagine Jonathan's face if he caught us, even now?"

"Ugh. Come, come, get up then. Hurry, into your own room."

She stood up slowly, stretching, arching her body in the particular way that always excited him. "I suppose I should. Yes, I'll hurry."

God, she was magnificent. His flesh warmed. His penis started a delicious ache. Yet to be caught, to antagonize the family at the last minute, after all their tortured sneaking about— "Ahh, they'd let you sleep late the day of your wedding, wouldn't they? They wouldn't call you yet?"

She turned. "Oh, no, I'd better go. There's my hair to do and I have to help Mama. There's extra butter to churn, though maybe I'll get out of that. Besides, if Jonathan caught us now—"

He groaned happily, grabbed her arm, and pulled her back down on the bed, while she looked tempted and willing, and confused and partially unwilling all at once.

She closed her eyes, groaning herself. She loved him and she loved the game. Oh, Josef! Again she wanted to laugh because the whole family knew what was going on. How did he possibly think that they could hide all that—her careful tiptoeing through the hallway from her room to his —his sly, barefooted rush to his door, ear glued to the wood, afraid someone was spying? "What should we do?" he'd say. "I'll hide under the bed," she'd say—

All *that*, to add spice to it; to give him his excitement. And after the wedding, sometime when it all seemed quite usual, she'd think of something else. An imaginary lover? No, he'd be likely to kill anyone he suspected. Her thoughts stopped. She let herself go in great emotional rhythms that were all bound up with their flesh—his and hers.

"Ah!" he shouted, plummeting through her. Though the delicious tunnel of her was mortal, ended finally with a bone, still he felt as if he went traveling through and be-

229

yond flesh; his seed impatiently shooting into places he could not imagine, yet carrying him too. He felt this. No thoughts were involved, only a luxurious joyous, tormenting acceptance and acquiescence. Here, now, you could push, shove, thrust, yell, laugh, shout—

"Oh! Oh!" Bianka cried, dizzy with him.

Her cry brought him back. He was finished, triumphant, yet scared. Awed, as he always was. You could get lost in that tunnel. You *did* get lost in it. Ahh, who cared?

And so the seed was planted; and an opening was made in the tunnel that leads to other realities.

In one of these, Oversoul Seven was talking to Lydia. "Do you feel better about things now?" he asked.

"You'll have to forgive me for staring," she said. "But I've never read any etiquette rules for talking to your own soul, and it's a bit disconcerting. And what am I supposed to call you? Besides, I didn't know that souls looked like people."

"I'm a people soul," Seven said. "What did you want me to look like?"

"You're laughing at me and that's not fair."

"I'm *your* soul," Seven said, reasonably. "And *you* have a very funny sense of humor. Actually, I just form myself into an image so you can relate to me, or so we can relate to each other. You'd find talking to someone you couldn't see much more disconcerting, with your background. I could look like a ghost, but I prefer not to. That's too conventional."

"And this place?" Lydia asked. "It's so beautiful. The trees and hillside. I can feel the grass under my feet. Is all this real?"

"You need a location. You'd get upset if you thought you weren't anywhere," Seven said. "You always need a *where* to put yourself in, at least at your present stage of development." He coughed, remembering to cover his mouth because Lydia was still concerned about manners. "I seem to be in an in-between stage myself, so I can sympathize," he said.

"And this conversation?" Lydia stood up, musing, very aware of her body, the lithe form, of herself moving (yet, in what terms?). "I need the words, too. Is that what you're going to tell me next?" she asked.

He grinned.

"And I suppose if I believed in heaven—"

"Then you'd experience it for a while," Seven said, "Until you got bored or finally listened. It can get quite complicated."

"Can? It is now," she said, still musing. "How strange. Oh God— Anna and Roger down there, still caught in all of that, and I can't tell them. But of course it's not *down* there, is it?"

"No, it's right here," Seven said. "A different kind of focus."

"I don't have to be born again, do I?" she asked.

"Well, you have to do something," Seven answered. "And you need a framework right now or else—well, you have to learn to use your consciousness within a framework or you can get very confused."

"And God?" Lydia asked.

"Who?" Seven said.

"Are you a soul or aren't you?" Lydia demanded.

"I thought you didn't believe in God," Seven answered. "But you're a soul; *my* soul from what you tell me, and what I feel. You're supposed to believe in God or who else will? What's the use of souls and all this if God is dead?"

Seven didn't want to laugh and hurt Lydia's feelings. In fact, he didn't know how to handle the situation at all. "I'll ask Cyprus," he said.

"Who's that?"

"Don't get me off the track," Seven said. "If you aren't really dead, how could God be dead? I didn't say that there *wasn't* one, and I have my own ideas of Who It Is, or What It Is. See, when I use your terms, I get all mixed up."

"Well, for heaven's sake, use your own terms then," she said impatiently.

Seven sighed. "In many ways I'm still an Earth-bound soul, or you wouldn't have already decided to be born again."

"I've decided no such thing," Lydia retorted.

"Yes you have."

"Well, not that *I* know of," she said. "I've always suspected it—this proves it—there's no free will."

Seven closed his saintly-type eyes and mentally called for Cyprus. She appeared looking feminine and lovely, but with the clearest, most brilliant intelligent eyes that Seven

231

personally had ever seen. He smiled gratefully; a touch for Lydia who trusted the intellect so, he supposed.

"Would you please explain free will to Lydia?" he asked. "She's worse than Josef—argumentative, that is."

"Like someone else I know," Cyprus said, but so pleasantly and with such sympathy that Seven couldn't take offense, much as he wanted to.

"Who are you?" Lydia asked, liking her at once.

"A friend."

Lydia and Cyprus looked for all the world like two young woman friends, walking arm in arm, which was precisely what they did. Seven felt left out, or he would have, but part of him understood what Cyprus had in mind.

"This reminds me of my college days when I was trying to learn so many things at once," Lydia said to Cyprus. And Seven smiled—why hadn't he thought of that?

"Look over there," Cyprus directed. They stood on the rim of a hill. Cyprus pointed to the edge. Beneath, through clouds, a scene appeared. A lovely woman—no, wait, a child—first young, then old. "Oh God," Lydia cried, out loud. "Do I remember that? Or hasn't it happened yet? That's the seventeenth century, isn't it? And that girl—"

As Lydia spoke, the girl detached herself from the scene and walked up a shining ladder to the hill's brim. A bit too much, Seven thought, but Lydia seemed entranced. Then he took a better look.

"It's my independent study—Tweety," Seven cried.

"You're not *that* independent," Cyprus said.

Lydia sat down with surprise. "Why, that knocks the breath right out of me," she said, and Seven laughed. "Why, I remember now," Lydia said. "I remember making up my mind, quite on my own, to be born again. Only when did I decide?"

"In the dream state," Tweety said. "And in that old people's home. But you forgot, and I was afraid that you might not remember," she added forlornly. "My real name is Daga. I adopted this form so you could see what you'll look like—"

"Daga, I told you it was just a matter of time," Seven said.

"Of *what?*" Cyprus asked.

"Well, there's no need for me to have this image now," Daga said, "You won't be using it for a while—"

"In those terms," Seven said quickly; and Daga disappeared.

Lydia scowled. "I still don't understand clearly."

"You decided to be born again, as you remember now," Cyprus said. "Tweety, or rather, Daga adapted the image for you so you could see how you'll look. Seven always calls Daga 'Tweety.' It was a nickname of sorts. You liked that, too, and decided to use the name as well. Seven was giving you a good deal of help on his own. It was in the nature of a surprise for me, so I could see that he was acting independently." She added, looking nowhere in particular, "He wanted to keep one step ahead of me, in other words."

Seven lowered his eyes.

"But you're quite free to recall all the things that you've forgotten, Lydia," Cyprus said. "I'll give you a clue. Remember the young artist you met the night you died, at the poetry reading?"

"Of course! Now I remember. He'll be my father! I'm so . . . verbal, but I'd like to deal with experience in terms of color and emotional richness for a change, yet still continue to be connected with the arts somehow. And for once, I'd like emotional parents. I've been quite intellectual in many ways, which is good; and I've enjoyed it. But often I'd get so involved in ideas that I had trouble really feeling. And I do have strong abilities I haven't begun to develop along those lines—"

"Josef is emotional. I'll say that," Seven said.

"I'd met him in my dreams often before that too—I just remembered. When we're . . . alive? Is that the term? . . . Then we don't recall what we do when we're asleep—"

Seven beamed. "You're doing very well."

"Why, I was drawn to him at once," Lydia said. "And he and Bianka need someone to give them . . . intellectual balance, too. And, oh, yes, I remember something else. I'll be the model for many of his paintings." She turned to Cyprus. "But how can I be reborn in the seventeenth century if I died in the twentieth? Funny—I was always attracted to seventeenth-century literature too. That must be because I knew I'd be born there."

"Seven will explain," Cyprus said, with a smile. "But you see, there is free will. We just knew what you'd decided, while you'd purposely forgotten."

And Cyprus disappeared.

233

"Tweety. Tweety Landsdatter," Lydia said, musing. "That will be my name. Tweety, daughter of Bianka and Josef."

Josef squirmed. "I feel funny," he grumbled. "Like there's someone else in the room."

"You're just nervous after all the festivities," Bianka said. "You're embarrassed to be alone with your virgin bride." She giggled.

"I ought to—" he said, laughing, but he was exhausted. "My God, there's a ghost or something in here!" he thundered.

"Go to sleep!" she cried.

Lydia grinned, staring at the boots thrown on the floor, the pile of clothes beside the bed, the smell of sweat and love. How odd, she thought. She trailed about the room, smoking an hallucinatory cigarette, looking about twenty-five. But in other terms they were all of the same age—ageless. God! How intertwined their lives would become.

The Final Chapter

The End of This Particular Examination— Seven "Graduates" He Learns Something About Himself and Discovers Who Wrote This Book

Seven grimaced and began the final portion of his examination. It was entitled "Comprehension." "Lydia comprehends a lot," he said to Cyprus. "Proteus is learning, and so is Ma-ah. Josef certainly has made great strides. I mean, he's really painting, and he relates to people better than he ever did before. But will he have a time with Lydia—I mean, Tweety! She'll teach him a thing or two, and it serves him right."

"That's not a very nice attitude," Cyprus said. "I imagine Tweety can learn quite a bit from him, too, and from Bianka."

"But I'm worried about several things," Seven admitted. "Ma-ah doesn't know her origin, and" (he looked down) "I seem to have forgotten it myself. Proteus doesn't understand how the Tellers' dig went undiscovered all those centuries, much less why the Floaters haven't found it now—"

"Yes?" Cyprus said.

"Well, I don't understand how I knew enough to lead Ma-ah and Rampa to the Speakers to begin with—"

"Keep going," Cyprus said.

"I can't. Something else is wrong," Seven said moodily. "This whole scene I've chosen, the classroom and benches: it was fun in the beginning, but it doesn't fit now. I don't even like the wastepaper basket any more. Worse, I've been so busy that I suspect I've missed several important issues. And so far, you aren't helping me one bit."

Impatiently Seven waved his hand, and the entire scene vanished. Now he and Cyprus stood, invisibly, in Ma-ah's 35,000 B.C. courtyard. "I have the feeling that there's something here that I still don't understand," Seven said.

"You just made up for several points by making this move," Cyprus said. "Very astute."

"I did? Mmmm," Seven said. "That reminds me of something else. Do you mind if I bring my analogy back?"

"Not at all," Cyprus answered. "That's a very good idea, only don't let it run away with you this time."

Seven grinned sheepishly. Once more in the skyscape, the glittering letters appeared.

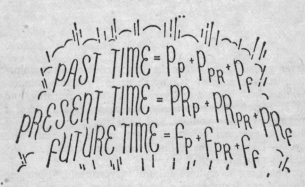

$$\text{PAST TIME} = P_P + P_{PR} + P_F$$
$$\text{PRESENT TIME} = PR_P + PR_{PR} + PR_F$$
$$\text{FUTURE TIME} = F_P + F_{PR} + F_F$$

"Do you remember what the letters mean?" Seven asked.

"Indeed I do," Cyprus said quickly. "And I certainly hope you do, too."

236

"There's just one problem," Seven said. "But wait." And above the letters, Seven projected his three boxes, representing the three kinds of time with their three subdivisions.

"Now just give me a moment," Seven said.

"A *what?*" Cyprus said, with mock shock.

"Well, in my present state of development it takes time to understand the nature of time."

"In your *what* state of development? Don't you *see*, Seven?"

Her words rang through Seven's mind, and in some indescribable way his mind expanded. Barrier after barrier previously invisible and unfelt dropped away, until Seven's comprehension itself encompassed everything he saw or knew or perceived. His consciousness circled the analogy in the sky—and he went *through* it, finding that all these times were different appearances of one inexpressible experience in which all Happening Out of Itself kept newly, freshly Happening.

All of his Boxes
Merged.
They Changed into
Circles
in Which Other Circles
(And "Times")
Were Constantly Happening.

And the Circles
Changed into Shapes
Of Sound
On the Other Side
Of Silence,
Until the Very Breath
Of
Nothingness
Danced in Time-Drops
And Light-Drops
And Finally
Thing-drops,
And out of the
Thing-drops
His Boxes Emerged—
And out of the Boxes
Came
Lydia's Time
And Josef's
And Ma-ah's and Proteus's
And the Tiles
In the Courtyard.

And Seven shouted: "Oh, I've got it! The Speakers'
ruins were never discovered before Window's time because—" He was so excited that he projected his words
outward so that the letters seemed to come out like minutes one at a time from his open boxes.

"The Speakers' ruins
Didn't appear until the twenty-
    third century
Because
They weren't there *earlier*—

Because
They were fresh action
Happening in . . . the future of
 Past Time
and only *then*
Emerging in the past of Present
 Time—

They were brand-new ruins!"

"Will you elaborate?" Cyprus asked, smiling.

"Of course. Oh, gladly," Seven said. "The nineteenth- or twentieth-century ruins are *underneath* the new 35,000 B.C. ones because those appeared "later" from the future of Past Time, where there's always fresh action and new things happening. That's why Window couldn't figure it out. It's a complete dilemma in the framework of time as he understands it—"

Cyprus said, very softly: "Seven, remember you create your own reality. We all do."

"I know. You keep telling me," Seven said, somewhat impatiently. "What does that have to do with this?"

"It has to do with other questions you haven't answered yet, and it all fits together. And it's a clue."

"Oh, well, then. Let me see—"

"You Make Your Own Reality," Cyprus said again, in the weirdest fashion, and suddenly the words rang in Seven's own mind, from within *his* own consciousness, not from outside it. And with that, Cyprus disappeared.

Yet in a microsecond that could also have been a century, Seven experienced a richness of being beyond any he had ever imagined, in which he was himself, or rather itself.

And he and Cyprus were both participants in a multiplicity of selves; multiple existences rippling inward and outward like constellations. Each self was unique. Seven knew who he was, yet in experiencing Cyprus he knew he was glimpsing only a portion of his own reality. His consciousness reeled. He couldn't grasp it all. Somewhere within him, Cyprus laughed with the most delightful brilliant understanding. And images appeared, sometimes inside him and sometimes outside him until he could no longer keep track.

And Seven's Consciousness
Parted Four Times.

In one he was Proteus, in the courtyard of the Dig of
the Tellers. Window was beside him. And though Seven
was Proteus, Proteus was himself and inviolate, and Seven
from far above saw the entire scene. Proteus's face was
grave, yet full of excitement, and Window was looking at
him with the eye of a father such as no boy ever had.

"I know I'm on to something important," Proteus said.
"From now on, I'm a Teller, too. This dig has secrets that
no one's discovered, and I'm going to learn what they are.
Sometimes, like now, I feel so close to knowing. I'm going
to work with these sound-embossed tablets until I know
them backwards. I think that the sounds themselves are
far more important than we realize."

Proteus looked up. He could feel himself teeter on the
edge of some new comprehension that was still beyond
his reach. It was twilight. As Window stood there, his skin
seemed to absorb the blue of early evening so that to
Proteus he looked blue-green, almost fluid, joining the sky
and the ground, growing into the sky like a figure-shaped
tree for him, Proteus, to climb. What a weird idea, Proteus
thought.

For a moment he almost got dizzy, watching, because he
did "see through" Window, as he explained it to himself
later. Then Window seemed so physical Proteus's stomach
lurched, and he thought: We grow up, reach up through
blood and flesh as trees grow up or emerge from the flesh
of the Earth.

So in leaving Earth, man had left the growing medium
of himself, and Proteus knew in that moment that he must
help man return to the Earth again, even if it meant returning sometime himself to the floating city. Admitting
Earth, man could travel and live wherever he chose. Deny-
ing it, he denied the heritage that gave him such yearn-
ings.

And experiencing Proteus's thoughts, Seven knew that
he would descend again and again into flesh, for there was
no descent or ascent, only being in its many forms. Proteus
and Window vanished, and where they had been, Ma-ah
stood with Sumpter.

240

"I don't know where I came from, that's what it amounts to," Ma-ah said. "I have no memory of parents; just finding myself, with Rampa, in the outside world a long time ago. How we got here I don't know. I suppose we were born into it."

"In certain terms, none of us know," Sumpter said.

"But I want to know. I insist on it," Ma-ah cried defiantly. (And Seven laughed.)

"And if I have a child, I won't know where it came from, not really."

(And Seven laughed louder). Dear, dear Ma-ah, he thought.

"I thought I heard the old man," Ma-ah said.

"It's all right," Seven said to her, knowing that he was also reassuring a part of himself.

But Ma-ah said, *"What's* all right?" just as Seven had so often questioned Cyprus. "And how did you direct me here, with Rampa?" she asked.

Before Seven could say "I don't remember," he was suddenly back, lost in Ma-ah again, struggling to walk beside Rampa, while the body signaled its great alarm. And a whispered voice that was his own and also Cyprus's broke through only for a moment, telling him where to go and how to get there. Only then, he hadn't been consciously aware of the voice, lost as he was in Ma-ah's dilemma. But how did he, or Cyprus, know?

With the question came a new onslaught of images. Again he could only capture a few of them.

Cyprus: Free of being male or female, containing both, writing the first Sumari records of the Speakers; "writing" them in sound before the birth of words in terms of time —but in a reality *still happening*—

Images he could not decipher—

Sounds that operated directly on *matter.* . . . Of course! A force field, protecting the land of the Speakers, called into activation by . . . Sumpter, who was Window—but as Window he'd forgotten what he knew, and it would be Proteus who would help him remember—

And Josef—

Seven saw him swearing and painting, roaring, despairing—heard him yell at the baby, Tweety, who screamed back at him just as lustily. Seven fell into Josef briefly, looked out through the warm brown eyes, felt the intimacy of the buzzing flesh, looked at Bianka who in this

241

now was full of a form into which Tweety had not yet entered.

"We'll be left all of this," Josef said with joyful craftiness. "The house, the land—"

"And you'll grow fat and prosperous, I suppose, and give up painting," Bianka said, grinning.

"No, no, never!" Josef thundered. But Seven as Josef felt the divisions, the conflicts, saw— But then Josef as Josef vanished, replaced by Josef the Speaker, painstakingly etching in stone the Sumari pictures that would be found by Ma-ah and Proteus in their times.

And Lydia—

Was Story!—and he, Seven, had forgotten who he was and what he knew. Forgotten, so that his parts could grow and learn on their own. Yet all the while unknowingly he nourished them as *he* was—

Nourished by Cyprus, who had learned to remember, to teach with a light hand, and to learn, gracefully. And the sounds of the Speakers were an important key that Cyprus would help him decipher.

Seven's consciousness flew together, and then parted seven times in which he glimpsed Ma-ah, Josef, Lydia, Proteus; and, with surprise and wonder—Story, who would develop quite on her own as Tweety would and Lydia had; and Sumpter, who was Window—each a part, yet whole, knowing and unknowing—

And Cyprus's consciousness parted—into such myriad shining realities of being that Seven could no longer follow, and he yelled out, "Cyprus!"

She sat beside him by the tiles, changing form so swiftly that he said, "Now stop that. I've learned so much that I'm dizzy. I don't suppose you could have just told me?"

"Oh Seven, *told* you?"

"Forget I said it," he replied hastily.

"Well, this examination is over," she said. "I thought you'd like to know." Cyprus paused, looking nowhere in particular, and added: "You passed, you know."

"I'm too confused to think," he said. "And what about Ma-ah's origin? I didn't answer that question yet."

"That's for next time," she said. "Anyway, some questions can't be answered in the context of the question itself. You have to find a new context. Of course, the question itself is deeply symbolic—"

But Seven said, *"Next* time?"

242

"In your terms of experience," Cyprus said gently. "Of course, in other terms—"

"Never mind," he said. "And if I'm correct, then you're to me as I'm to Ma-ah and Josef and—"

"Precisely," she said.

"So, what did you do for this examination?" Seven asked. "I did all the work."

Cyprus smiled. "I wrote this book," she said.

"But Cyprus—you aren't physical," Seven cried.

And Cyprus sighed. "Seven, you still have a lot to learn."

Epilogue to This Book and Prologue to The Further Education of Oversoul Seven

Cyprus said: "This is how the next book will begin:

> Lydia was
> Called Tweety
> Because
> Biankà said
> She was
> Skinny and
> Tiny
> As a new-
> Born bird.

"Wait a second," Seven said. "I think your tenses are wrong. Even though Lydia died in the twentieth century and is reborn in the seventeenth, shouldn't you say, 'Lydia *will be called* Tweety,' because she hasn't experienced that life yet? Or is 'Lydia *was called* Tweety' correct, because people think that the seventeenth century happened first? Or—"

They both burst out laughing.

Cyprus said, "You'll just have to wait and see. That is, though all time is simultaneous, I'll have to wait until writing the book catches up with my experience."

Appendix

For those readers who may be interested, the
following information is provided:

Although all the Speakers in Ma-ah's time were Sumari,
the term refers to a type of consciousness, generally speaking—a grouping together of consciousness with certain
characteristics. The Sumari are initiators, highly creative,
playful, given to originating systems of reality and then
going on. As a friend of Seven's once said: "They don't stay
around to mow the grass, though." A Sumari is a Sumari,
in flesh or out of it.

Seven and Cyprus are both Sumari, as are all the main
characters in this book.

Careful attention should be given to Sumpter's explanation of the use of words in Chapter 12. The Sumari lan-

guage is not a language in the ordinary sense. Its importance lies in its *sounds,* not in its written patterns. The sounds do things. The meaning is apart from the power of the sounds, and rides on it as fish swim in water.

The meanings rise out of the sounds, then; and the sounds are channels through which the meanings come. The sounds can seem to have different meanings at different times, and yet always be expressing aspects of the same reality. Sometimes many words can come from one sound, sometimes only one will emerge. This is apparent when you study the same song in Sumari and in its translation as written by Lydia. The following examples will make this clear:

FIRST SONG FOR BEGINNERS

(Sumari, as learned by Ma-ah.)	(from *Songs of the Sumari* by Lydia)
Angella pur tito	This is one side of truth.
Angella to panito.	This is the left side of anger.
Angella pe toto panto	
B o a eto	The stars are singing.
Rameta.	Listen.
Ando andolato	From east and west
Me do repen rabelli	Messages come richly. Like
Me no latillo	leaves falling
Angelo le peju lacol	You cannot hold them.
Mendo. Rendo be woopta	Secrets beneath hearing ride on the wind.
Has a vendelli	This is forever rising out of the silence.
Indo lato	Rejoice
Angell ella	In knowing unknowing.
Suri la mari	
So la pinto	Beneath the starlight
Contella.	The Earth stirs and opens.
	The Earth stirs and opens
Indo rito	To our touch
Angella gondula	Unfolding.
Pito. miro.	
Angella peto torello	The moonlight cries out

248

Soli in do.

Angella pindo
Pindu and tito
Pungula vito
Deto.

Ando capeto
Angella peto
Ingol. angol.
El lo go.

When it touches
The forest floor.
The forest flowers are filled
    with
The light born of darkness.
This is the beginning

Ending and center
Rushing ever
Outward.

From the lighted heavens
The gods come and wander
Inside and outside
Over and under.

Their footsteps are starlight,
Their voices are echoing
Beyond the edges of silence
Never sunken in yesterday
Or tomorrow.

ANIMAL DREAM SONG

(Sumari as learned by *Ma-ah*
in the Land of the Speak-
ers.)

(from *Songs of the Sumari* by
Lydia)

Frea tumba, tul j leta
Greenaje odaro
Deleta umbarge
Sel var denoto
De na evisa
To marro insida
De ne r o.

Gramaje netaro
Denita visa
Flo marro ontoa
Deneta demari.
O ne demari.
On a es par.

See us, see us,
In your adjacent world.
We are your dreams living
In fur and blood.
We are the animals
Blessed and holy,
Savage and bony,
Thrust out by you
Into the world.

We sing your praises.
It is good common sense,
For we know that we come
From the ribs of your slum-
    ber,

Ma ne o de vista
De magna on to o
Grem age an to a tum
De es splen ato
Gre ne a torum
In e a go.
Silva vista ne ta
Gre en ad e bus
Tumba.

Born, torn, and rent
From desires
Glowing and raging.

O nea umba
O framage tu a
Oh le e on to
A de um timbi.
Gravi timbo taru
Sev r ant a to bum
Grim age endeo
De midge a a tu um
Mari on umber
Grey e a on obus.

In the midnight of your
  senses
We rise up all splendid.
Perfect and agile
We leap out into the forests
We race across the landscapes
In moonlight and shadow.
We are your dreams escaping
The dream cage forever.
The door is wide open.

We dream our dreams. Re-
  member,
Entreaty and warning.
Our vowels are dancing
With splendor and longing.
Under tomorrow
We live by your spell.
But our dreams rise up
Even as yours, and confront
  us.
The animals' animals
Must be nourished and
  tended.
The dreams' dreams are not
  orphans
To be cast into darkness.

We congregate before you
For your attention.
We are the blood and hide
Of your dreams prancing
In midday.
We plunge through forests

And hillsides,
Carved out of your unknow-
ing.
Know us who wander
Beneath the moon of your
brain.

FRAGMENT FROM A
SUMARI SONG OF ORIGINS

(Deciphered by Window
in the land of the Tellers
from stone tablets)

O shel u a stare
Le munde tu am
Del an o resplendi
Tel mal del o
Fram mondi.
De na resplendi
O terum nesta
Far bundu. Tarra
Ne o responde
La dum. La day dum
Framba.

Out of the knowing
Darkness of unknowing
We lifted ourselves, rising
On the webs of our thoughts.
We dangled above the warm
Nest of nothing,
Climbing the images
That rose from our yearning,
Grasping the syllables
That circled
Our muteness like stars.

(This song was not among those "written" by Lydia in
the twentieth century. The rest of the song is in the records
of the Speakers in Ma-ah's "time.")

Window is still translating portions of Sumari songs,
fragments of what seem to be mathematical documents,
and other records. One such document in particular seems
to be leading toward an explanation of the connection between sound and matter, suggesting a relationship between
numerical values, atoms, and syllables. This same connection is also hinted at in several Sumari songs. This "mathematical" statement has only been deciphered in fragmentary
form thus far, and Window is certain that other portions of
it are still to be discovered. A part of it is included here
because of its implications in terms of the Speakers' method
of erecting buildings through the use of sound.

The first section, devoted to quite a different matter,
seems directed to the general student. It is a preamble to

251

the body of the material, and shows the basic ideas upon which the Speakers built their civilization. For that reason, it is also being included here. The following is Window's translation:

(from *The Sacred Script of Covenant*)

Honor your body, which is your representative in this universe. Its magnificence is no accident. It is the framework through which your works must come; through which the spirit and the spirit within the spirit speaks. The flesh and the spirit are two phases of your actuality in space and time. Who ignores one, falls apart in shambles. So it is written.

The marriage of soul and flesh is an ancient contract, to be honored.

Let no soul in flesh ignore its Earthly counterpart, or be unkind to its mate in time.

The mind cannot dance above the flesh, or on the flesh. It cannot deny the flesh or it turns into a demon demanding domination. Then the voice of the flesh cries out with yearning through all of its parts; the ancient contract undone. And both soul and flesh go begging, each alone and without partner.

Who feeds the body with love, neither starving it nor stuffing it, feeds the soul. Who denies the body denies the soul. Who betrays it betrays the soul. The body is the body of the soul, the corporal image of knowledge. As men and women are married to each other, so is each self wedded to its body.

Those who do not love the body or trust it do not love or trust the soul. The multitudinous voices of the gods speak through the body parts. Even the golden molecules are not mute. Who muzzles the body or leashes it muzzles and leashes the soul. The private body is the dwelling place of the private guise of God. Do it honor. Let no man set himself up above the body, calling it soiled, for to him the splendor of the self is hidden. Let no one drive the body like a horse in captivity, to be ridden, or he will be trampled.

252

The body is the soul in Earth-garments. It is the face of the soul turned toward the seasons, the image of the soul reflected in Earth waters. The body is the soul turned outward. Soul and body are merged in the land of the seasons. Such is the ancient contract by which the Earth was formed.

The knowledge of the soul is written in the body. Body and soul are the inner and outer of the self. The spirit from which the soul springs forms both—soul and body. In Earth time, the soul and body learn together. The genes are the alphabets by which the soul speaks the body—which is the soul's utterance in flesh.

So let the soul freely speak itself in flesh.

The body is also eternal. The soul takes it out of space-time. The body is the soul's expression, and its expression is not finite. The spirit has many souls, and each has a body. The body is in and out of time, even as the soul is. Let the soul rush freely throughout the body, and breathe life into all of its parts. The first birth was a gift, freely given. Now you must acquiesce and give your blessing to the life within you. Trust the spontaneity and health of the body, which is the spontaneity and health of the soul. For each morning you spring anew, alive and fresh, out of chaos. . . .

(Another fragment, deciphered by Window, is from the same document, from a verse portion connecting the above with the later material on atoms, sound, and numerical values.)

> The universe is the body of the
> god's soul,
> The flesh of his utterance.
> In the beginning man was given
> two homelands,
> His body and his planet.
>
> The calculations are written
> everywhere,
> Inscribed in each object.

The body is a language
Of atoms instead of words.
The body is the most ancient of
   alphabets,
And atoms spoke before the
   Earth knew sound. . . .

(The following fragments are from the main body of the statement. Other portions, still being deciphered, seem to point toward a multidimensional mathematical system.)

Speaking the body . . . so the body is built also on sound principles, sound becoming matter in your terms at certain pitches.

In reality, numbers are magnified in all directions. They represent points of emerging energy, as it intrudes into the third dimension. . . .

Integers represent pivot points or centers of radiating activity, out of which energy emerges, in terms of light and sound. These qualities—light and sound, for example—exist on both plus and minus sides of all equations and on all sides of magnification.

Much of the document will be beyond the interest of the general reader. As it continues, however, it suggests an inner property or value that exists within all physical matter. Since the Speakers seem to have utilized such knowledge, and the Tellers are trying to decipher it, the following three paragraphs are included merely as an example of how the subject is handled:

These hidden values [of numbers] only emerge under certain conditions, though they are always acting and must be considered as a part of the integers' characteristics. These hidden or invisible values are often responsible for instabilities that seem to arise without reason to undermine an equation's effectiveness. They are also responsible for phenomena that seem to defy equation.

The whole is more than the sum of its parts because of these hidden values. They exist on the minus side

254

on all sides of magnification. They affect the plus reactions or the behavior of integers on the plus side, and under certain conditions can sap their energy. Usually they magnify all existing properties, however, and leap over the plus border into regions in which the integers' characteristics are vastly changed—in comparison to their behavior in a three-dimensional system. These invisible values root the integers firmly in dynamics superseding your space-time continuum.

Some integers are more susceptible than others to their own inner nature. They lean toward their invisible values. These integers are those from whom surprises can be expected, though they are less stable in a numerical relationship. They are explosive in nature, easily combined, rather than binding. Such integers can experience a temporary cave-in, a momentary physical collapse, in which a hole is created through which all values fly (black hole). Here, the invisible values rise paramount, affecting the behavior of other numerical values, connected with the integer. . . .

This small sample of the document shows its complex nature. As Window, with Proteus's help, tries to decipher the rest of it, the Tellers hope to discover the secrets of the Speakers' civilization.

This same idea appears also in the following Sumari song that was found among Lydia's papers after her death. From a scribbled note in the margin, it's apparent that Lydia had no idea what the poem meant, and did not include it in her published version of Songs of the Sumari.

SONG OF THE CHOOSING

Before the Earth light was born
We wandered
Scattering alphabets into silence
And out again, splashing
Silence into vowels
Until silence spoke
With the voice
Of a million worlds.

255

The tongue of the universe
Chose silence
And silence chose sound,
And the Earth sprang forth,
An utterance
Congealed into form.

The atoms are syllables,
Forever unspoken, yet speaking.
The silence is sound
Forever circling and gathering.
The rock is mute
To listening ears,
But the deaf eyes of watching
    clouds
Hear piles of vowels
Continually dancing.

The time of choosing
Opens the rift
In the rock,
And the hidden voices
Of Earth
Rise up.

The following is a partial copy of the simple alphabet or "cordella"—the symbols etched into the cliff walls in the time of the Speakers and rediscovered at the time of the Tellers. Fingering the outlines of these symbols gave forth the appropriate sound values. These were discovered in the order given here. Others exist in different groupings; some still unknown to Window's people.

Another partially deciphered Sumari script suggests that the word *cordella* rather than *alphabet* is used to break up usual conceptions connected with the word *alphabet*, while conveying an idea of symbols closely related, upon which alphabets are based. Seen in this way, there would be cordellas beneath the sensations of hearing, smelling, seeing, and so forth. The fragment further implies that the skin has its own alphabet.

Since the Tellers have translated so few of the Speakers' manuscripts and records, only hints of their significance can be given here. The process of translation and discovery continues, of course, and publication of further songs and records will take place as the work continues.

Because the Sumari philosophy includes such a rich mixture of theory and practical understanding, the appendix will close with a translation of one of the first songs learned by Ma-ah in her early instruction as a student. The advice is pertinent in any "time."

THE GODS' GIFTS

Those who are given gifts by the
gods must use them.
Polish your gifts in the morning,
Shine them with yearning,
Pluck them from the trembling
tree of creation.
Tenderly tuck them in the basket of your loving endeavor.
Use them or they will turn from
fruits into stones that are
heavy.

The fruits of the gods are juicy
and nutritious.

257

Ignore them and they turn into
teeth that bite you.
The gods' gifts are worth more
than night or morning.
Ignore them and night and
morning pass away.
The pit of your knowing is buried in the gods' fruits within
your being,
Spit out the pit and you are lost.

The god's gifts are the yellow
piths that glue together
The fruity fibers of your knowing.
Use them or your parts fall
away.

Used, the gods' gifts are abun-
dant and increasing.
They grow as they are con-
sumed.
Shake the branches of creation,
And the gods' gifts fall into your
lap, resplendent.
Turn your back and the tree
withers
And the wind carries the seed
away.

Use the gods' gifts, then, with
great abandon.
They are your nourishment.
They are the fruits that bloom
in dreams' darkness.
They are the light that falls out
of chaos.
They are the fruit of the tree
that is unknown
But always present.

They are the fruits growing ever
on the branches of unknowing

Made visible.
They are sweeter than the evidence of love in the body.
Let no man stand with his back turned as the fruits fall,
But gather them.
They are your abundance and sustenance.